HUGO HAMILTON is the author of a bestselling memoir, *The Speckled People*, the story of his German-Irish childhood in Dublin, where he was prohibited by his revolutionary father from speaking English. He has written nine novels, two memoirs, a collection of short stories and three stage plays. His work has won international awards, including the French Prix Femina étranger, the Italian premio Giuseppe Berto and the DAAD scholarship in Berlin. Hamilton is a member of Aosdána and lives in Dublin.

ALSO BY HUGO HAMILTON

Surrogate City
The Last Shot
The Love Test
Dublin Where the Palm Trees Grow
Headbanger
Sad Bastard
The Speckled People
The Sailor in the Wardrobe
Disguise
Hand in the Fire
Every Single Minute

PLAYS
The Speckled People (adaptation)
The Mariner
Every Single Minute (adaptation)

DUBLIN
PALMS

HUGO HAMILTON

4th ESTATE • *London*

4th Estate
An imprint of HarperCollins*Publishers*
1 London Bridge Street
London SE1 9GF

www.4thEstate.co.uk

First published in Great Britain in 2019 by 4th Estate
This 4th Estate paperback edition published in 2020

1

A catalogue record for this book is
available from the British Library

ISBN 978-0-00-812813-5

This novel is entirely a work of fiction. The names, characters and
incidents portrayed in it are the work of the author's imagination.
Any resemblance to actual persons, living or dead, events or
localities is entirely coincidental.

Printed and bound in Great Britain by
CPI Group (UK) Ltd, Croydon

MIX
Paper from
responsible sources
FSC™ C007454

This book is produced from independently certified FSC™ paper
to ensure responsible forest management.

For more information visit: www.harpercollins.co.uk/green

1

The city is full of lovers. In the park, on the grass, two of them have a small radio playing. They are singing along to the radio. Loud and exaggerated. Miming the images in the song like synchronised swimmers. They make the vaulting shape of a bridge. Their hands flutter over troubled waters. They lay their heads down to rest on folded elbows. She gives a dirty laugh and kisses the side of his face. He raises his fist in the air with a hoarse growl.

It's summer. I have my lunch in the park with the lovers – two slices of brown bread, a piece of Cheddar, a pat of butter from the corner shop. I lie back on the grass and listen to the soft voices around me. The sound of traffic has an interior quality, a large room with lawns and trees, enclosed by a square of terraced buildings.

I work in one of those buildings, in the basement. My day is spent underground. From my desk, I see the feet of pedestrians passing by through a small window above my head. The neon lights are left on all day, even when the sun is shining outside in the street. I am a young man with a full beard and curls in my hair, open expression, quick to smile. I am content in the basement, only that I have contracted

1

some strange, unidentified condition. A virus, a fungus, some parasite must have entered my veins. My face is drawn. My skin is translucent. My teeth feel like glass. I am overwhelmed by fatigue and sleep at my desk. I wake up with underground eyes.

The organisation I work for has been set up to preserve a minority language. Normally referred to as the native language. Some people call it the dead language. It is not spoken on the street, only written in the shadow script above the street names. My work is carried out entirely in this ghost language – Gaelic, Irish.

I run the vinyl record department.

We have a unique collection of native singers. It is my job to collect them from the train station. I bring them for something to eat in a hotel where people from the country gather and recognise each other, a drink before going to the recording studios. They are self-conscious when the red light comes on, the shallow acoustics, the mute face of the recording engineer behind glass staring as if they come from another continent. They get startled by the sound of their own voices played back around the sound-panelled walls. One of them tried out the headphones and said it turned him into a different man, his voice was never the same again.

Some of them go missing. I had to search the entire city for a man who disappeared with a nurse not even half his age, when I found him she was putting on her blue trainee uniform and he stood naked in front of me only for his tweed cap and his fists up. Some of them need to be held by the hand while they sing. Some are equally good at American country music, they will start with a nasal hum at the back of the throat and deviate into the Wichita Lineman. Some of them refuse to travel, we go to record them in their own kitchens. I once had to deliver payment to a singer who would not accept a cheque and insisted on being paid in person. In a village in Connemara where the ghost language is still widely spoken, I met him in a bar with cash. He wouldn't touch the money, his hands were enormous, a pint of Guinness was no more than a thimble in his fingers, it took three days until he was fully paid.

Our most popular album was recorded live in a Dublin theatre where the audience can be heard yelping with excitement in the background. There is a sense that our moment has come, our music is raw, straight from the earth. It gives me the feeling of being carried back in time. We belong to a country with less roads, less lawnmowers, a place with more wild bees nesting in the grass banks.

One day I arrived at work to find everyone standing in the hallway crying. The commander of the organisation lay at the foot of the stairs, his face gone cold. His naked head was resting on the first step. His right arm was laid out as though he had been giving a speech when he fell. His shoes were off, his socks were yellow, a diagonal design along the side, as though he played golf. Which he never did, nothing further from his mind. The socks merely brought home how normal and integrated we could be while being so devoted to the restoration of a great treasure from the past.

We spoke in low voices, praising his wisdom, his vision, his words had the power to infuse us with emotion. When the ambulance arrived, he opened his eyes. He waved the paramedics away and tried to stand up, resuming his speech where he left off. Entirely in character with the language we worked so hard at reviving, the commander was brought back to life by the sound of a teacup and carried up the stairs to his office. The floor was strewn with newspaper cuttings, some empty bottles, the desk lamp was still on, covered with a garment that was beginning to burn. His secretary appeared and helped to lay him out, she rolled her cardigan up into a cushion. We arranged his tie over his eyes to shield him from daylight.

It's a happy place to work. Being part of this marginal community in the heart of the city gives me a sense of place. Something glorious about a culture under threat. Hearing the endangered language around me brings back a recurring memory of going out to the islands. Leaning against the rusted white frame of the ferry boat with the engine throbbing in my shoulder. Quiet places with sunlight coming through stone walls, patches of green and blue, gannets diving, waves bashing into the cliffs. Everything in my work is devoted to a silence in the landscape, to what is receding, what is being kept alive.

When it's time to go home, I tidy my desk and switch off the lights. The remaining daylight seeps in through the high window across the ghost faces along the walls. The basement returns to its forgotten peace. On the way out, the receptionist smiles. She is the niece of an author who wrote a novel in the native language about dead people arguing in a graveyard. I can no longer hide the fact that I am partly dead myself. Half alive. Perhaps undead. As dead as a dead language refusing to die.

I make my way across to the German library. It is situated on the other side of the square in a building that is identical in every way to the one where I work in the basement, same façade, same ratio of windows overlooking the park of lovers, same door, only painted red.

As soon as I step inside I have the illusion of being at home, seeing German newspapers and magazines displayed on tables in the front room. Going up the stairs to the library on the first floor is like going to my bedroom as a child, finding the latest acquisitions propped up in a row on the marble mantelpiece as though it's my birthday. They have the heating full on. I spend an hour there with my jacket off, a stack of books beside me, until the librarian politely tells me it's time to go.

The books I borrow give me a fictional character. I see myself being invented in everything I read. I am a boy unable to grow up. I spend weeks in a sanatorium. I take on the anxieties of a goalkeeper. I read about a journalist going undercover, doing dirty and dangerous jobs, washing out metal tanks with acid to demonstrate what it was like to be a migrant worker in Germany. I read the story of a writer who buys himself a new suit for a prize-winning ceremony – after accepting the literary award he brings the suit back to the tailor because it no longer fits him. And the story of the adult child who escapes from a cellar and stumbles onto the streets of Nuremberg without language, gradually claiming back the power of speech.

I grew up in a language nightmare. Between German, Irish and English. I could never be sure what country I was in. My mother was German, my father was Irish. She came to Ireland to learn English but ended up teaching my father German. He refused to speak English, she never learned Irish. At home, we spoke her language, we went to school in the ghost language, my father was a revolutionary who prohibited us from speaking English. It had the effect of turning all language into a fight, a fortress, a place of hiding. It felt like emigrating every time I went out the front door. On the street, I had to look over my shoulder to see what words I could be at home in.

The native language is referred to as – the tongue, our mouth, tongue and country, our famine mouth, the place we come from and the people gone away and the story that cannot be told in any other language.

German is the language of looking back and digging deep and starting again, the language of people who love Ireland more than their own country and sit for hours staring at the full moon over the Atlantic.

English is the language of the street, the language of rule, victory, valour, the language of rock and roll and Shakespeare and James Joyce, the language of freedom and fucking off and never looking back.

This war of languages has left me with a deep silence. I doubt the ground I walk on. I make my way around the city as though I have only recently arrived. Still arriving. Never arriving. My viewpoint is unstable, seen from multiple places at once. Everything is in contradiction, the words are full of blasphemy, I hear the grinding of translation in my head.

Does it have to do with the maritime pressure? The humidity, the cold breeze under my shirt, the empty streets with the veil of rain under the lights? Does it have something to do with shifting from the cold basement of one building to the overheated first floor of another and straight into a noisy ground-floor bar around the corner? The creaking floorboards underneath the carpet. The sound of bottles and fizz, people laughing. Something about switching between these different levels that makes it impossible for me to belong fully to either of them? The basement part of me has nothing to do with the library part of me. The bar part of me laughs at the basement part. The library part is slow to rub shoulders with the others.

Each part of me has its own silence, like maps overlapping. A different history, a different now, a different here. Different ways of being at home. Each country has its own denial and guilt and not being accepted. I remain loyal to each part of myself and true to none.

On the way home, I have the feeling that I am not fully consenting to the place where I live. The streets are refusing to dry. There is a sticky glaze on the pavement, like walking on a strip of adhesive paper. I am in a place that does not correspond to where I stand. My body has become detached from my thoughts, my feet in Ireland, my head in Germany, my voice left behind in a landscape of shadows in the west.

Back home, Helen smiles with her head tilted to one side as though everything is up close and simultaneously far away. I bring the children to bed. I make up a story for them about a wedding in the lighthouse. The bride wore a necklace of strawberries. I gather up their toys and put the books back in the bookcase, they love nothing better than piling them up in towers to sit on.

The light is left on in the hall. Helen is getting into bed. Her freckled shoulders. Her vertebrae. In the bathroom, the toothbrush falls out of my hand into the sink. I turn away and hold my face. Leaning slowly forward, I go down onto my knees and place my forehead on the floor.

Silence is not emptiness. It's not the absence of matter. It is a solid state, full of love and language and things collected from childhood. A frozen river of emotion. My condition, though it remains undiagnosed until later, must have something to do with this silence.

It breaks out in my teeth. It begins in the front teeth and gradually spreads across the back teeth, the severity of it leaves me unable to say a word. There is no medical explanation. I have been to the dentist a couple of times, but he can find nothing wrong. He took X-rays, tapped each tooth, froze them one by one, he went as far as refilling some of the old cavities, what more can he do?

It goes away. It comes back. There is no pattern. It flares up at random when I am happy and untroubled, in the park with the lovers, at my desk in the basement, back home with everything calm, the children asleep. I curl up on the bathroom floor like a poisoned snail. My eyes fog over. My mouth is full of glass. I lie with my ear against the wood and the shining white toilet bowl rising like the bow of a ship above me. A hissing dribble of toothpaste emerging from the corner of my mouth.

Helen's voice comes in around the tiled walls, her hand is pulling at my arm. I shake my head like a horse and get up on my feet.

You have got to stop working in the basement, she says. It makes you sick. She says she will start up a business, a drama school, a theatre, she will open a café, I need to get out of that basement.

We were in Berlin together. The city where I went to escape from my silence. Where I sang in bars at night, songs in the shadow language that nobody understood. I can reconstruct the configuration of streets, the faces in the bakery, the order of train stations. The announcements in my mother's language, as though everyone in Berlin was related to me, a city of cousins. I can hear the train doors closing, crawling through dimly lit stations with border guards and dogs on the platforms, emerging from underground over abandoned city land, the ruins, the sand, a tree growing up through the tracks.

I stood on the platform waiting for her. I was wearing a white shirt that was too big for me. It was passed on to me, along with a second-hand great coat, by the caretaker in the apartment block where I lived. He was a big man. The shirt was so wide and loose fitting, it billowed in the breeze coming along the tracks and gave me the feeling I had stepped into the life of a much larger being. The excitement

I experienced at that moment was not my size. My body mass could not hold that amount of joy. The words I had were too small to contain the magnitude of what was happening to me. I was entering an oversized future, with desires and feelings of luck that were far beyond my capacity to understand. My arms, my chest, my open neck, I was in danger of floating away inside a flapping white tent.

Helen arrived with a big belly. She carried a portable radio. Her shoes were painted over with oval handwriting. We made slow progress through the streets, reduced to the speed of an oncoming baby. We sat in the park while she ate a tub of quark, her belly was full of quark.

I brought her to a bar, she looked underage, just out of school. The barman had a knitting needle through his nose. A man with a female voice came in with a Great Dane and bent over for a joke to let the dog sniff his backside. A woman in a sleeveless leather jacket and gashes along her bare arms spoke in a slow voice to Helen, asking her what it was like to be pregnant, how can you sleep?

The city was warm. We spent the summer in a long pause, not doing very much, going to galleries, sitting in cafés, as if we were living inside a photograph waiting to move forward. Every night I stood up in bars wearing my white shirt, singing songs in a lost language. Every morning I got out the almond oil to rub across Helen's belly with the windows open and the tree at the centre of the courtyard swaying. Her navel was a pre-historic spiral at the top of a shining dome. We were constantly hungry. She needed tons of cheese and apples and smoked mackerel. The future was

Item(s) checked out to
D4000000547966

Every single minute / Hugo Hamilton.
Date Due **5 Feb 2022**

Dublin palms / Hugo Hamilton
Date Due **5 Feb 2022**

To renew your items
Online at librariesireland.com Ph: (01) 462 0073
Mon-Thurs 9.45am-9pm Fri/Sat 9.45am-4.30pm

Paperless overdues coming soon!

From December 1st we will no longer post overdue
notices. Please sign up to receive email notices via
your online library account

expanding inside her, it seemed she could hold it back and stop the world and never have to give birth. Our lives remained in that place of refuge before coming into being. We were in a time before knowledge. The moment before memory. All we could think of was now.

We walked through the streets at night when it was cooler. We passed by posters showing the faces of wanted German terrorists. A woman leaning out the window watched us from above in silence. The street lighting was dim. The buildings were decayed, gaps where houses went missing, the war was not far behind.

We found the viewing platform and I helped Helen up the wooden stairs. We looked across the wall at the open death zone. A stretch of empty ground lit up, guards in a watchtower, houses on the far side like canyons left in darkness. The platform had been erected in a time of handkerchiefs, for people waving to their relatives on the far side, holding up their children, calling out their names. When the people on the other side were prohibited from waving back, the platform no longer had any function other than for visitors coming to have a look over the edge of the world.

Leaning on the rail, looking at the frontier before us, I understood the shock in my mother's eyes when she read about the Berlin Wall being built. The newspapers sent over from Germany by her sisters only confirmed how far away Ireland was, how much apart she was from her family. I grew up with that distance. The wall became part of me. Describing it was like describing myself. A human division which had spread into every corner of the world, into every family, every heart. The wall had yet to come down. The barriers had yet to be opened, people streaming across, their jubilant faces, smiling and crying, crowds on top of the wall hacking. None of this had happened yet, all that freedom was still impossible to imagine, like the sound of a new born baby.

We stared across the Berlin Wall, a kiss, a smile, the dirt of border lighting in Helen's face as she turned to me and said – let's go back.

Everybody in Dublin is back from somewhere. The pubs are full of returning. They talk about their encounters, drug voyages, bus journeys on death roads. They laugh at mortality. They laugh at life. They laugh at the strangeness of things, the invention of difference, the great mind-altering misunderstanding of the world.

They stand at the bar in Kehoe's pub full of books to be written. Stories of heroic distance, cities and characters I could never dream of. One of them was robbed on a train while sleeping in the luggage rack. One of them took a piece of tubing into his nostril, his life came and went, he woke up a week later in the same place, same voices quietly talking around him, same dog lying on the ground in a curl. One of them was left between two countries, rejected at the border to Iraq, refused re-entry to Afghanistan. One of them refused to pay the price of a bottle of whiskey for a bottle of Coke and nearly died drinking the water in a river. Another one was nearly killed in a German car plant, a millisecond away from being pressed into the shape of a car door, his elbow brushed the safety button.

They have come back amazed at what women can do, what men can do, what food can do to you. An actor Helen knew from the theatre in Dublin got shot in New York by his lover, he came back in a wheelchair. A neighbour of mine got lost in Goa and never made it back to his family. A woman Helen knew at school returned from Brazil, her husband ran away with another man, the same in reverse for a man I knew from Galway, his wife went off with his sister.

One of them brought back a story from Morocco. He was in a town called Fez, a narrow street no wider than a hallway. There were three young women wearing head-scarves in front of him when a donkey came rushing by with panniers full of olives and boy rider whacking a stick. The donkey was farting on the way through. The girls, the young women in their hijabs, turned around, unable to help themselves. Their hands were up to their mouths, they were in tears holding on to each other, choking, doubled over in the street.

We are back from Berlin with our story.

What have I got to tell? A Nativity scene, with the Berlin Wall in the background. I became an overnight father, we returned to Dublin, Helen breastfed Rosie in the snug, a glass of Guinness for the baby. We got a place to stay, I took up a job in the native basement, we now have a second girl, Essie, our immaculate family.

Back where?

It makes no sense.

Back to where we first met? Back to the first words she spoke to me. Back to where Helen worked in a small theatre, back to the places I brought her on the Aran Islands, she didn't speak the ghost language, she was a visitor, I had to translate my songs for her.

Back home? Back to my country? Back to where I am from – where I am only half from, where I have tried to be from, where I have never been from?

Back to where she is not from either?

Helen grew up in England. Her family lived in Birmingham before they double emigrated to Canada and left her behind. She was sent to boarding school in Dublin, still a child. They went to live in a town with a salt mine, by one of the Great Lakes in Ontario. Helen found herself emigrating in reverse, going back to Ireland, a country she didn't know.

She is a piece of Irish soil in her mother's shoes.

On Sunday night, she's on the phone to Canada. She sits by the payphone in the hallway with her back to the wall and her knees up, playing with the cable. I stand in the bedroom listening to her, the children asleep, I have their shoes in my hands, pinched up off the floor. I hear her paraphrasing her life. She describes the ground-floor flat where we live, sectioned off in the hall with two separate entrances. She says it's fully furnished, fitted with a pastel-green carpet, nice neighbours upstairs, not far from the sea.

I can hear the questions her mother is asking in Canada by answers Helen gives in Ireland. Everything is enhanced in her voice. Our lives are magnified out of proportion by distance. She converts everything around me into a fabrication. She puts the world into my mouth.

The school, the streets, the people upstairs are very funny, the Alsatian next door is enormous, the shopkeeper is always giving her the wrong change. The furniture auctions next door, the swivel-mirror she bought, the auctioneer took her name, a sticker attached – Helen Boyce.

Our surroundings are enlarged to fit the wider spaces of Ontario. Things that remain locally reduced in my head are brought to life with big-sky clarity by Helen's enthusiasm over the phone. For over an hour, everything is released from the prejudice of reality, all previously undiscovered. Nothing is valid, nothing is true until it is spoken.

It makes me feel at home, listening to Helen describe nearby things in such a faraway tone. That same excitement with which my mother spoke to her sisters on the phone in Germany. I grew up in this removed story, never quite matching the place where we lived. I once asked my mother where she felt at home and she said it was where the postman delivered her letters. It was the letters coming from Germany that brought her home. Helen is the same, sending back the news, rerouting our lives to a place on the far side of the world.

I hear her telling her mother in Canada that we are settled down now. She says I have a good job in the music business. I am responsible for signing up new talent. She says she has a part time position teaching drama at her former boarding school. She has begun to teach yoga classes, we keep the front room clear of furniture. She says my brother is a good carpenter, my sister Gabriela gave us a porcelain teapot. I have a little brother who works in a bicycle shop nearby. My sisters sometimes come to look after the children.

We are living on the main street. On the bus route, same side as the veterinary surgery and a grocery shop, further down a pub on the corner. The house next door has been turned into a guest house. A white, double-fronted building with a terracotta path running up the middle and patches of lawn on either side, each with a cluster of palm trees at the centre. The palm trees give the street a holiday atmosphere. They are not real palms. A non-native variety pretending to be palm trees. They manage to grow well in the mild climate, up to the height of the first-floor windows. There must be something in the soil they like. They have straight leaves that get a bit ragged, with split ends. At night you hear them rattling in the wind.

The people upstairs are laughing again. They make me conscious of my life downstairs. I pull the curtains. I put the books back. I check to make sure the girls are asleep. I lay out their clothes for school in the morning. It all seems to give the people upstairs more to laugh at. They laugh until it comes to the point where I can't help laughing myself. And as soon as I laugh, they go silent. I find myself laughing alone. I hear them putting on music. They always play the same track, which becomes a problem after a while only because I like the song myself. Whenever I want to play it, they get there ahead of me. The song I love becomes my enemy.

I hear Helen's footsteps on the tiled kitchen floor. I can see the shape of her body in the sound of her shoes. Her straight back, her arms have no weight in them, she has long hair, apple breasts. I hear the silence as she moves to the carpet for a moment and returns to the tiles.

At night, the dreamy passengers on the upper deck of the bus can see right into the house as they pass by. They catch sight of us for a fraction of a second, we sleep on the floor in the empty front room, the mattress pulled in from the bed, with the fire on and the curtains left open. The passengers see nothing, only two people with yellow bodies staring at the ceiling, remembering things.

She talks about growing up in Birmingham. The garden around her house with the monkey-puzzle tree, her family packing up and leaving for Canada. The farewell party was held in Dublin, the landing of her grandmother's flat was filled with suitcases. Her aunts and uncles came back from England and France to say goodbye. Everybody laughing and talking about Donegal and Limerick and Carrick-on-Shannon, then everybody in tears when one of the uncles sang her mother's favourite song, how the days grow short, no time for wasting time, who knows when they would be in the same room again.

Normally it is the child who leaves the mother behind, but Helen got switched around. She found herself watching life in reverse, seeing her family off at the airport in Dublin, standing with her grandmother at the bottom of the escalator waving and her mother unable to turn around to look back. The streets were wet with recent rain, the lights reflected on the surface. Men with collars up going across the bridge, the river not moving much, only the neon glass of whiskey filling up and going dry again. Two buses back to the empty flat, staring out the window all the way. Her grandmother lit a fire and drank some brandy. They sat face to face in the bath, their eyes red, their legs dovetailed, two girls, twice removed. The pipes were creaking, a finger drawn through the steam on the tiles, flakes peeling off the ceiling. The soap was oval shaped, it smelled like smoked mackerel and cough mixture.

The term for emigration in the native language is the same as tears. An emigrant is a person who walks across the world in tears. Going in tears. Tearful traveller.

Some weeks later Helen was called out of boarding school when her grandmother was taken to hospital. Her uncles came back once more, they brought three bottles of brandy, one to be confiscated by the nurses, one to be drunk on the spot, the other to be hidden for later. When everyone was gone again, her grandmother tapped on the bed and told Helen to get in. That's how they fell asleep. Her grandmother died during the night beside her, the hospital was quiet, only a thin extract of light left on in the corridor and the nurses whispering.

★

Long after the buses stop running, she sits up and talks with her back turned to the fire, her spine melting like a wax plait. Her eyes are full of departure. All that travelling in tears. All the packing. All that leaving and arriving and leaving and re-arriving and leaving all over again.

She tells me how strange it was to visit her family in Canada for the first time. In the summer, when school was finished, she found herself going home to a place she had never been to before. Her father picked her up from the airport in Toronto. In the crowd of faces waiting behind the glass, he looked so international. The distance made her shy in his company, like being in a doctor's surgery, he spoke in a series of directions, driving out of the car park on to the main highway. His freckled hands on the steering wheel as they passed beneath a huge billboard of a woman in a swimsuit holding a cocktail with a pink umbrella, the seams where sections of the poster were joined together crossed her legs, it took a full minute to go by. At a service station he bought some root beer, a medicinal taste that never occurred to her before.

People speak in big voices, she says, it's all straight roads, endless skies, no fences, her eyes were too big, too open for the brightness of the sun. The shadow cast by a tree was a deep pool on the lawn.

The strangest thing of all was seeing her family waiting on the porch, as if they were practising being at home. Everything was the same as before in Birmingham, the furniture replicated in the same order, only the view outside the windows had changed. Her mother's welcome was exaggerated, warmer, more pressing, a hurried photograph taken of them all together in the living room, the family complete again. She sat duplicated beside her mother on the chaise longue, their hands clasped, their knees aligned, her brothers and sisters standing along the back in a series of family variations.

Her mother is full of shrug. She shrugs off what she left behind by turning her head aside in a mock-expression of disdain, closing her eyes and placing her chin on her shoulder. She laughs and repeats a family phrase brought to Canada all the way from Limerick – when I think of who I am.

They never say the word emigration.

The town is situated on a bluff, overlooking Lake Huron. Designed in the shape of a large wheel. It's like a clock, Helen says, with streets radiating out from the courthouse at the centre. She laughs and tells me her family live inside a clock, facing the sky. It is reputed to be the prettiest town in Canada. You can see the sun going down twice. Once at shore level and then again if you run fast enough up the wooden steps to the lighthouse, you see the same red sunset repeated, she says, the clock waits, you get a second chance.

She speaks like a postcard. Her voice is full of streets I don't know. The town is her invention, even the name sounds made up – Goderich.

I'll bring you there, she says.

It has the biggest salt mine in the world. Sifto Salt – the true salt. Our salt on every table, she says. Our salt going all over Canada in winter to clear the ice off the roads. Carried on big salt ships across the Great Lakes to Michigan. The mining company has erected a shrine at the edge of the town, a glass pyramid with a faceless salt figure inside. It's the height of a young woman, she says.

The Salt Madonna, they call it.

Her family home looks right over the mine. You see the lights at night, she says, like a carnival down there. You hear the salt loading arm swinging across in your sleep, voices shouting, trucks reversing, trains like owls coming to take the salt boulders away. And sometimes, she says, the blasting underground will send tremors up through the floor into your bed like an electric current. It's a city underground, a thousand feet down, going out for miles underneath the lake. Giant trucks, two-way traffic running through halls with white cathedral ceilings, bright with arc lights shining. The air is so dry you can't even sneeze. Your lungs crack as you breathe. The giant equipment used for extraction is left buried down there in empty salt chambers when it stops functioning, no rust, nothing ages. Her father gave her a stick of salt from the mine, she keeps it in a small case along with her letters.

The sky was beginning to clear up. I got the children ready to go out. I buttoned up their chequered lumber jackets, sent over from Canada, one blue, one orange. They both had colds, red cheeks, Essie coughed like the bark of a seal. We slipped out past the front room with the yoga session in progress, ten women in a circle with their eyes closed, breathing and humming. Helen is an actor, good at playing the part of an instructor.

We turned left, past the guest house with the palm trees, past the veterinary surgery, the grocery shop, we crossed the road by the eucalyptus trees. Along the seafront, we met the veterinary surgeon coming back with his children. His name is Mark, I know him from school, a bit older, he married a French woman, his children call him Papa. My children call me by my first name. I don't encourage them to say – Dad. Other children at school think I am their older brother.

The sea was calm. Some cargo ships in the bay waiting to be loaded. Close to the horizon, there was a bright section of water where the sun shone through the clouds. For me, there is an abnormal emphasis on those fragments of light, on the mood of the coastline, on the rocks moving under-water. The seafront is full of sand and sex and shivering and wet bathing costumes pooled on the ground. Everything is familiar, the granite pier, the lighthouse.

You can be bullied by things you love.

I am a quiet father. Given to brief outbursts of emotion, followed by long spells of expanding silence. My anger is mostly self-directed. I remain in my own thoughts, detached as a book. I have my hands in my pockets, paying no atten-tion while Rosie and Essie are climbing on a wall with a ten-foot drop on the far side. I get them down and look at the rocks below, the full terror of being a father. The fear of my own childhood?

There are things I should be telling them. Warnings, bits of stories to make them safe. Everything my mother described to me in her language, I now find myself converting into the language of the street for my own children. They are my audience. I speak with that same breathless enthusiasm in which my mother described the sea and the salt air, the tide like the hand of a thief slipping through the rocks. I pass on the tragedy in her voice when she spoke about the men who died in a lifeboat going out to rescue people from a sinking ship one night, drowning in sight of their own families on shore. I tell them about the cruel sea captain who once visited the harbour and whose ship was later taken over by mutiny. The black canvas fisherman's hut. The white house that looks like a ship run aground on the most dangerous rocks in the world.

My words come to an abrupt stop. Everything has now been said. Those few bits of information I placed into their minds have left me drained, I feel the cold around the shoulders, I want to sleep.

The bandstand at the park was designed in a time when the country was still part of Britain. I watch Rosie and Essie running around the circular bench around the bandstand. It causes me to remember my own father, the unavoidable memory of his silence, the day he gave me and my brother plastic cameras that squirted water when you took a picture. We ran along the same bench and my father didn't say a word. He was not the type to speak to people in the park. He spoke the ghost language, he spoke my mother's language, he never spoke his own mother's language. He turned his back on his people, the place where he grew up in West Cork. His soft Cork accent went missing in German, it left him open to misunderstanding.

A woman sitting on the bench close by wanted to know if I was the father of the two girls.

Are they your kids?

I smiled.

She was concerned about the way I was staring at them. People might get the wrong idea.

I know your family, she said. Your mother is German.

That's the thing about returning home, it's the furthest you have ever been away. The hotels along the seafront, the blue benches, the baths where I used to go swimming, the things you love turn against you, they feel snubbed and they will snub you back. You have become a spectator. The granite is not credible. The grass is implausibly green. The sea is raised up to eye level in a broad blue line, you feel cheated by what you know, you remain a stranger.

My mother was waiting for us with an apple cake. The smell of baking came rushing through the hall, like entering another country. The house was unchanged, my father was dead, but his voice was still present on the stairs, his anger, his love, his music reaching up to the roof. A man had come to take away his beekeeping equipment, his mask, his gloves, the smoker with the green bellows. The buzzing of bees remained in the rooms. The picture of my grandfather, the sailor in the British Navy, was hanging in the hallway, rescued from the wardrobe where my father had banished him.

My mother spoke to Rosie and Essie in German, they smiled and didn't understand. They responded in English. They played outside language, they dressed her up like a child in scarves and jewellery. She held their faces in her hands – who washed your eyes?

The youngest in my family are still living at home – Greta, Lotte, Emil. Greta is working as a nurse. She takes Rosie and Essie into the kitchen to bake biscuits, I sit in the living room with my mother. I want to know more about the town where she grew up. We go over everything – her father's business in ruins, her father dying when she was a child, her mother dying not long after, the house on the market square left empty.

My mother and her sisters went to live with their uncle. He was the Lord Mayor, hounded out of office for refusing to vote for the Nazis. Standing in the polling station holding up a rigged ballot paper, demanding true democracy. His friend, the journalist, was taken away to Dachau, back a year later no more than a shadow of himself. There was trouble on the square when somebody daubed slogans on the walls against Hitler. People suspected of putting up the anti-Hitler words were dragged out of their houses and forced to clean them up. Her uncle told her not to acquiesce, not to join up, not to be torn along, not to give the Nazis anything but her best silence.

My mother got work in the town registry office. A decrepit place, she said. Her supervisor was a man with gastric problems that required the windows to be left open, he was constantly eating boiled eggs brought into the office by his wife, the same boiled egg every morning at the same time. Her job was in registration, keeping the records on births, deaths, marriages. Where people came from, who they belonged to, surnames and dates going back centuries, many of them descendants of refugees from another time, like her own family who had fled pogroms in the low lands. She found herself constantly running up and down the stairs with the human ledger. People coming in a panic to check their ancestry.

There is a man in the town who falls in love with two sisters, she told me. The sisters live in a house on the market square, he is studying to become a lawyer, he calls to the door to collect them both and they go cycling in the country. The three of them cycling through the flat landscape. The wind in the fields is like a comb through green hair. They come to a lake and go swimming, their bodies turn gold, they spend time lying on the grass together. He watches them getting dressed, he admires them both equally, their feet, he wants to understand the mechanism in their ankles, how does all that work?

He cannot make up his mind which of them he should marry and says – if only I could marry you both.

The sisters smile their best. They all cycle back to the town and go to the cinema together. On the market square, there is more trouble, a crowd has gathered to say the cinema cannot be used by people who are Jewish. They leave. He walks them back to their house, he carries on alone through

26

the church grounds, past the house with the fountain in the basement where Thomas à Kempis lived. On his way home, one of the sisters he is in love with comes running after him, she kisses him wildly on the street, she pulls him into a run, out along the streets through the town gates to the windmill, they disappear inside, their faces in the dark.

They hear glass breaking.

The town is full of unrest. The fire brigade is on the way to make sure the fire does not spread. There is smoke all over the market square when they get back. The following day, the student lawyer meets both sisters together and takes them to a café in Krefeld. Goods have been thrown out of the shops into the street. In the café, people make grunting noises, tapping on their cups with their spoons until a Jewish family with three children at one of the tables is forced to leave. He takes the two sisters out, leaving the cakes half finished behind them, he holds them by the hand, one on either side. They go to the opera and afterwards they sit over a drink in the foyer. He tells them that he has made up his mind, it's only right for him to marry the older sister, the younger sister who brought him to the windmill bursts into tears and runs away into the street.

The windmill in my mother's town has been disused for many years. It is situated right outside the medieval stronghold and the fortress wall. When my mother was born, the town was occupied by French and Belgian troops stationed in the fortress. Then it was taken over by the Nazis. Then it was taken over by the American forces stationed there after the war.

The student lawyer continues meeting the younger of the sisters at the windmill every night. He loves her, but the protocol of families forces him to marry the older sister first, the younger sister cannot jump the queue. The preparations go ahead, permissions in place, his happiness is in the windmill but his future calls, he cannot delay, the war is coming. The younger sister is left behind in grief at the windmill, watching him walk away, back to the town through the entrance gate with the dawn arriving onto the cobbled streets and the roof of the church a bright pink. Glass crunching underfoot.

In the morning, the younger sister goes to the registry office, calling up documents which have nothing to do with her but with the student lawyer she loves and cannot have. She sits in the office, reading the dates, his entry into life, his mother, his father, his family going back in time. From the documents, the people of the town appear to be scattering, the arrow of time in reverse, uncoupling, unmarrying, dead people coming back to life, children disappearing, families thinning out to the point of arrival, when they first merged into the town.

Tears enter the records. A jealous smudge of vandalism. The letter J is found attached to the family name. The wedding never goes ahead, the names are never joined. The law student disappears. Two sisters left broken hearted, the windmill never moved.

*

The garden at home had become terribly overgrown since my father died. My mother asked me to do something about it, make a start, at least. She loved the sound of the soil being turned. I brought out a chair, she sat sheltered from the breeze, by the greenhouse.

What I liked about digging was that it had no meaning. I was happy doing something with no great purpose. It was like reverting to childhood, taking over what my father used to do. It was good to have Rosie and Essie there with me. They had their own patch of ground each to work on. They gave me the feeling that I could pass everything on to them, no need for me to achieve anything more.

My life is limited to the vision of a father. My ideas are all designed around them. I love placing things into their minds and watching them bounce back in their crooked words. My success comes through them, I am at their disposal, I love hearing them laugh, my despair returns every time they fight. When Rosie is angry she shouts the word – anything. When Essie is angry she shouts the word – blood.

It was not long before the spade clacked against a solid object. The sound of metal travelled up through the wood into my hands like a tuning fork. It took a while to dig up. It turned out to be an old pair of shears. They were rusted solid. The blades were fused together and could not be prised apart. The wooden handles had completely rotted off, leaving only two core metal prongs. The prongs had been moulded with a twist in the metal, presumably to prevent the handles from slipping. A flat metal cap had been welded on to the top of each prong.

The girls came over to see what I found. With the wooden handles gone, it looked like a set of antlers. My mother laughed. Antlers, she agreed. She called me a poacher. What I'd recovered was a piece of gardening equipment belonging to my father. The fact that the handles had completely rotted away seemed to date them back to when he first bought the house. The garden was a wilderness when my mother arrived from Germany. My father was too embarrassed to take it on. He felt the eyes of the neighbours looking at him through the windows. She didn't care who was watching and went out to dig the garden herself, while he looked on from the window along with the other neighbours. It was only when he saw her digging the weeds unbothered by the audience that he changed his mind. She freed him from the fear of being judged. He no longer cared about being seen and took over the work himself, growing vegetables in neat rows, a section for flowers, new fruit trees, a patch of lawn and a place to sit in the sun.

His garden fire is what I remember most, the smoke drifting over the boundary walls, sending a message across the world, the neighbours could hardly see a thing, they had to close their windows, it drifted through the house, it was in all the rooms, in our clothes, in our beds, it went out onto the street, the big cigar cloud of his gathered weeds smoking through the afternoon, into the night, still smouldering in the morning.

Helen arrived as soon as her yoga class was finished. My sisters ran to open the front door and let her in. She was like a visitor from another world. They examined every inch, the black beret, her long dark copper hair, the black corduroy jeans, her light green jumper finished off square across the front. Her freckled shoulder came leaping out as she leaned forward to put down her bag on the floor in the hallway. In the kitchen, she spoke in German, remembering words she had learned in Berlin, testing them out on my mother with a contorted twist in her voice. My mother laughed and treated her like a child, slapping her on the thigh – you are a mouse.

It's a time of revolution. Every act contains some degree of rebellion and disobedience. There is a feeling that things are changing, civil rights, women's rights. The art scene is full of naked bodies. Things have become less sacred, less respected. Irrelevant things are being brought centre stage, a strange truth is discovered inside objects which have previously been merely functional.

We hear about a German artist who is using butter and felt in his work. He makes a legend of his own life story, he wears a hat to cover up the head injuries he suffered when he was shot down as a pilot in the war. He puts on spontaneous happenings, in New York he sat in a room with a coyote, in Berlin he took up a brush and began to sweep the street with an audience around him – sweeping out, he called it.

New ways of protesting. New ways of challenging the past. In Berlin, I had been to a play where the actors did nothing but offend the audience. Everyone was being shaken awake. There was respect for madness.

The bar where I used to sing in Berlin was full of people with new ideas. One night, a man came in carrying a sports bag with him. He didn't order a drink. He slapped the bag down on the ground and fell on his knees. He opened the bag and took out a large raw bone. The meat had been stripped from it, straight from a butcher shop, a dog would love it. There were some red bits of flesh attached, the knuckle of a joint, like a gleaming white door handle.

Right in the middle of one of my songs, the man held the butcher's bone up in the air like a warning. The bar had a cobbled floor and a green wrought-iron fence around the stage, the ceiling was a backlit panel of stained glass. It was located right under the railway bridge, near the main station. Trains could be heard rumbling overhead.

Everybody stood back.

I stopped singing. The man with the bone was in his thirties, long hair down to his shoulders. He wore clothes that attracted no attention, a pair of worn jeans, the collar of his shirt had rounded ends. His boots had the laces undone.

Kneeling on the cobbled floor, he held the raw bone in his hand and let out a roar. Without saying a word, he began gnawing at it, ripping off bits of pink flesh, snarling as he ran his teeth up and down along the white bone. His jaw was unshaven, there was a rage in his eyes, staring ahead into a distant place. The bar was silent, no drinks were being served, even the trains seemed to have stopped running.

Nobody knew what to say. We were given no clear signal whether it might be reality or invention. Hard to know if the man was performing or whether he was truly hungry and couldn't wait to eat. Was he angry, was he out of his mind, was he doing it to scare the customers, growling like an animal as he licked and tore at the remaining meat? No indication that he cared if people were watching, he seemed unaware of his audience looking on with astonishment, amusement, pity, mistrust, afraid to laugh. The space around him was clear. He might as well have been kneeling in the middle of a steppe alone, a man in war, a man holding on to his life, a man who had come across this treasured section of bone, glancing anxiously over his shoulders to make sure nobody was going to take it off him.

Each country has its own way of breaking the silence. An artist arrived in Dublin one day carrying a huge wooden crucifix. On Good Friday, he was seen walking down the main shopping street with the cross on his shoulder. People might have mistaken it for a re-enactment of Calvary, but it was more of an art installation, a happening, he was questioning the power of the church. He leaned the man-size crucifix up against the wall of Kehoe's pub and went inside for a drink. His art had no fear. He sat at the bar staring at his pint as though he was looking at the Atlantic.

All that revolution unleashes a provocative force inside me. I don't need much encouragement. I am still trying to escape the grip of my father's rule. I am full of rebellion. I believe in nothing. I have no collective instinct. I find it hard to belong to any group, I follow no team, I even have trouble shaking my head at rock concerts.

I stage my own private happenings. I get into a senseless confrontation in court one day over a parking fine. The fine had been issued on a quiet road with no parking signs. It was my right to park there. I had a perfectly good argument for saying the law was unjust. But it never even came to the point where I could present my case because I refused to swear an oath on the Bible. I told the court I did not believe in God, the judge roared at me – who made Dublin Bay?

It was too much of a crusade.

What is the point in trying to make a point? The first thing I need to change is myself, my silence, my inability to articulate or even work out what I want to say. My vocabulary is inadequate. Fighting the system, going against the establishment, breaking the hold of authority, none of those terms work for me. I speak in crowded sentences. A rush of misplaced words that don't belong to me. I express confused emotions in public that are more suitable for letters. What I say is never memorable, just clumsy and exposed.

I have no gift for concealment. I do my best to speak with guile, but it sounds contrived, like borrowing a scarf without permission.

Better to keep listening.

I am struck by a book I borrowed from the Germany library in which the main character decides to create something that will never be recognised. It describes the furious love of a man who devotes his entire life and fortune to the task of building a monument for his sister in the middle of a forest. His decision to place the structure out of sight is central to his achievement. He builds his cone-shaped construction in a silent place where it will never be seen by anyone, not even by his sister, the person for whom it has been created. It becomes a monument to what is unsaid and unseen.

What a wonderful idea, I thought. A man compelled to squander his living energy on something that makes no sense, erecting an utterly useless edifice in a remote place, for what? For the sake of nothing? For love?

Do something useless today.

Helen has been encouraging me to write. All those silences can be put together into a book, she says. Things I have been collecting since I was a child. The absurd language wars, the mismatching countries, I have a needless need to put things in writing.

I brought the rusted shears found in my mother's garden with me when we were leaving. At home, I propped them up on the mantelpiece in the empty front room and stepped back to admire the shape. Something about the fact that they could no longer be used as garden shears appealed to me. I began writing down what they looked like. Metal antlers. The skull of an impala. The eyes are missing. The skin has been torn off. What remain are the bones of a face. The rest of the carcass has been severed, possibly dragged up into a tree by a leopard.

Why was I grasping at these comparisons? Going for the refuge of a story? What things look like instead of what they were, the suggestions they flung out rather than the material facts? Was I protecting myself from the real world? Was I describing myself? Does everything turn into a self-portrait?

I went back to the object in front of me. Rusted garden shears. Beyond use. Nothing more than a piece of unearthed metal with no significance attached. I mistrusted even that bare description. The words were full of opinion, imposing a function on the object, it was being looked at, being conquered, given value. I tore up the few sentences I had rolled together and went back to the physical artefact itself. I stopped trying to explain where they came from or who they might have belonged to. I saw them only as the senseless shape they had become. I tied a thin piece of invisible wire to the metal prongs. I drove a nail into the wall and hung them up.

The morning is spent in the basement conducting a stock inventory. Many of the album stacks in the storeroom have been untouched since the last count. I have introduced a stock control system adopted from a publishing house where I worked for a while in Berlin. Each item in the catalogue has a card attached to the stack with the number of copies left in stock. A person filling an order, often myself, will cross out the number and enter the new figure with the amount of sales deducted. If stocks run below a critical figure, the card is brought to the attention of the person in charge, myself in this case, so the item can be re-ordered in time to meet demand. The idea is to avoid the awkward situation of running short of either one of the components, the disk or the album sleeve, one without the other is worthless.

The system is more suited to firms with a greater turnover. At the native basement, some of items in the catalogue sell only a couple of copies a year, some cannot even be given away, ever more precious for being so rare. The stock can be counted with good accuracy in a couple of hours, so there is no need for an early warning system. If a record shop in Saint Paul, Minnesota, for example, orders unusually high volumes of a native singer whose family and friends have gone to live in that part of the world, there is no problem rush-ordering copies. There might be a delay while the latest Madonna album takes precedence at the pressing plant, it can all be explained in a letter, the music on our list is timeless.

The card system is soon abandoned, mostly by myself. We go back to counting by fingers. Numerals are safe provided they are written down. Spoken in Irish, they can be tricky. They seem more scientifically accurate in English, everyone on the street can understand them. The same goes for phone numbers and appointments, less room for error.

I have entered the results of the count into a report sheet. I have the sales figures in one column. A separate column for wastage, returns, warped pressings, damaged or discoloured album sleeves. There is a further column for stock given away as official gifts. Complimentary albums are frequently rushed by courier to key personalities in the community – government ministers, priests, bishops, school principals, theatre managers, men and women in positions of influence.

Once I was finished, I compiled the various figures into an annual audit and sent it upstairs to the commander. He sent me back a note to let me know that he was impressed with the figures. The organisation had been ingeniously established by him as a charity, sustained by a giant lottery held each month in the shadow language. There was no need for the figures to balance out in any commercial sense, no requirement on any of the artists in our catalogue to make a profit. Decisions were based entirely on cultural reasoning, on keeping things alive that would otherwise die without trace. Our loss-making was repaid in a surplus of heritage. One of the latest recordings was made with a solo dulcimer player, his sales remained at zero, but the number of copies given away as promotional material was higher than average.

The commander spoke to me at length about expanding the catalogue, he wanted me to recruit new bands, younger singers, more women. We signed up a singer with red hair from the west of Ireland who had a fantastic voice, she was well known for singing in English, she carried the shadow language in her pronunciation.

Gradually, with the kind of work I do, recruiting the best of Irish talent, the urge to sing begins to disappear in myself. It doesn't feel right. I still have the rage and the sadness in my repertoire, all the songs I used to sing in bars in Berlin, but I don't believe I can be genuine without being fully native. Being an outsider makes me inauthentic, half Irish and half German, half man half horse, some say. I don't get away with singing back home in my own country, only in Germany where people thought I was as genuine as butter.

The Irish for singing is the same as speaking.

One of the band members I toured with in Germany came back to Ireland with a similar problem, not being able to speak. He found it hard to adjust to being among his own people again. In a Galway bar one night, he sang a song about emigration they said he had no right to sing. No matter how good his voice was, no matter how long he had been away from home or how much he missed the land-scape of Mayo where he grew up, they accused him of appropriating grief that was not his own.

He might have been a bit like me, a daily migrant, going out the door to a country he was not sure he belonged to any more, he had to check to see who was listening. People treating him like a non-national. He sang from the heart that night in Galway, but he was forced to stop when some-body roared across the bar at him – go back to where you came from.

He grew up in a big house near Westport, there was a triple stained-glass window above the stairs, a view from the windows onto a lake and rolling lands, only himself and his mother and all those empty rooms. He was the last descend-ant of the Fitzgerald line, directly related to the famous fighting Fitzgerald, a historical figure who was given a ring by Marie Antoinette in Paris before she was beheaded, then he ended his life in a similar way, hanged in Castlebar for imprisoning his father in a cage with a circus bear. The ring was kept in a tobacco tin, the gem was on a swivel with the stamp of the French court underneath. His people were kind during the Famine. The house was later given over to the state to be turned into a museum of country life.

He plays the guitar left-handed. He has blond hair, a blue freckle on one cheek. He sits sideways at the table with his legs crossed while eating. He barks when the music is good. I saw him once kicking over a chair with excitement while he was listening to a band playing the Céili at Claremorris. I saw him yelping and slapping his hands on the dashboard for Voodoo Chile as we drove into the Brenner Pass.

There is nothing I want to do more than sing, but the catalogue of speaking songs no longer works for me. I am no match for those great singers. I try new ways of calling out my frozen mind, I pick up the guitar, I learn some contemporary songs, but my voice is easily dismantled. I settle back into my long listening.

The veterinary practice was closed. We heard the news that morning. The boy was found lifeless on the floor of the surgery. A note on the door mentioned the word bereavement.

I knocked. It took a while before Mark, the vet, came out. He didn't take me inside. We stood on the pavement. He didn't want me to see exactly where it happened, the empty space on the floor where he picked the boy up and ran out the door into the street late in the afternoon, racing to the hospital, hoping he was still alive. I was not brought in to meet the boy's mother in her grief.

I'm sorry. That's all I could manage to say.

Ah listen, he said.

We stood in silence. His eyes were flooded, nothing more he could say either. Two fathers trading encouragement, full of words we could not say, looking at the ground. The eucalyptus trees on the corner across the road smelled like a hospital. The shopkeeper in the adjoining premises was looking out the window at us. We had no conversation. For the sake of talking, it occurred to me to mention a book of short stories he had recommended the last time we met, but I kept it to myself. There was a story in it about a couple renting a house in a remote place where they love each other with great intensity until the owner suddenly wants the place back for himself, their love comes to an end.

I stared away towards pub on the corner. He stood kicking the wall with the tip of his boot.

Jesus Christ, he said.

We heard the breeze rattle the eucalyptus trees across the street. The leaves were sickle shaped, green leather knives. The smell of sap was suffocating, a toxic preparation for parvovirus in dogs. Hardly any cars went by, no buses, I would have noticed. It was hard for him to face going back inside. As though he wanted to stay out there on the street with me, that might be the best way of remembering when things were safe, I was a person who brought him back to a time before the tragedy.

I stood there without saying anything more. Like a child trying to hide something, refusing to say there was a bottle of blue liquid I thought was a drink of lemonade.

He put his hand on my shoulder.

Look after those girls, he said. Then he slapped me on the back of the head and went inside.

The white coffin went to the church, people were standing in the street, I didn't hear what they were saying, I didn't talk to anyone. He stood with his sister's arm around his shoulder at the graveside, a small group of mourners, his wife held his hand for the last prayers. The loss of their son took the streets from under their feet. He gave up the veterinary practice, she went back to live in France, he worked for a while in the North, in Coleraine. I ran into him from time to time when he was back, at the fish shop, at the fruit and vegetable shop, sometimes down at the harbour, we always stood for a while and he told me the news, we never talked about the dead boy or his family breaking up. His shoulders were hunched, he moved with delay, there was a cut made in his voice. Maybe it was a form of surrender in his eyes, half turning away and coming back to face you once more, it was good to hear him laugh again. You met him in the pub on the corner full of rugby fans and pictures of James Joyce. You saw his bike outside with a basket full of books.

★

I have a friend who went to Australia.

He has a gift for talking. His memory has legal accuracy, he studied law. He is tall, he speaks in a stride, it was hard to keep up. He was run off his feet revealing things he had heard about people, things about ourselves that we had forgotten, you felt good because your life mattered to him. He could remember Helen and myself in Berlin, the time I sang my sad songs in the street for passing pedestrians until a woman from the offices above came down and paid me to go away. He could remember Helen on the U–Bahn, a man staring at her love belly, the three of us walking arm in arm across Hermannplatz, she was carried along, not touching the street.

He got talking to people easily, people who normally avoided each other were glad to be in the same place together when he was around. He gave me the feeling of being in motion, being alive, being lucky, it was our responsibility to celebrate. His information had no false avenues. His grasp of human emotions was generous, you could trust him with your thoughts. I allowed him to put words in my mouth. I spoke so little. He did most of the talking for me.

If I could write the way he speaks, I thought, I would be at home anywhere in the world.

We stood at the bar in Kehoe's pub. I was happy listening to the scattered voices. The twirl of a coin on the counter, a beer mat flipping upwards and being snapped between thumb and finger. Everything was worth remembering, the worn rung on the bar stool, the spill of beer, the discontented faces of barmen on the wrong side of life. Things you overheard – No, fuck off, I owe you a pint. Snatches of nonsensical conversation that didn't join up – the permafrost, my twist, Galileo, you're due a refund. I loved that disjointed prose of the city, the abstract way in which something serious could be said in one part of the pub and people burst out laughing in another corner.

In a flood of enthusiasm, I told my friend I was trying to write. The manner of the announcement made it look as though I had no other choice, each one of us was trapped inside a book, the only way out was to write it down. At one point, thinking that I had the speed of his voice in mine, I pulled out a couple of pages from my bag for him to look at.

It was a section in which I described my silence. Waking up at night, wandering around the house where I grew up while everyone else was asleep. I became an intruder in my own home. Avoiding the creaks on the stairs. Not switching on the light. Looking around at the objects belonging to my family, the photographs on the mantelpiece, the town where my mother came from. In darkness, it felt as though I had walked into a strange house where I didn't belong, the people who lived there had nothing to do with me. When the light started coming up at dawn, I caught sight of myself in a mirror. A strange figure I could not recognise, standing alone among the furniture and family possessions I knew so well. The reflection was not mine, it belonged to someone else, from nowhere.

He read it quickly. He said it was a bit raw, a bit honest. I saw no difference between his honesty and my honesty, only that everything he revealed had time to evaporate overnight. His stories were full of travel. The names of cities and rivers in faraway places.

He told me that he was leaving. We met and got drunk together. I missed him. His departure left me short. It removed the map. I no longer had any connection to the talking grid. He carried crucial information away to Australia with him in his shirt pocket. Doesn't every emigrant do that? I thought to myself. Each person leaving takes away some essential knowledge that cannot be replaced by those left behind.

A photograph sent from Fremantle shows him wearing a bright blue shirt with floating vintage cars and palm trees. By the angle of his shoulders, he must be standing in the kitchen, opening a bottle of wine. Everything I attempt to say from that point on is directed like a shout across the world to a distant reader, waiting for the echo to come back.

Another episode with my teeth. Brought on this time by an attempt to write in German. My mother's tongue gave me no protection. It was like pointing at myself. I became the accused. I took on the banality of somebody waiting to be caught and brought back to face trial. Normal words like bread and butter were extremely childish and at the same time loaded with pre-existing meaning. Milk was no longer milk. I could not use the word ground, nothing to do with land, territory, domain, home, belonging.

Writing is no place to hide.

It may have been the mashed potato, it scalded my front teeth. I knew what was coming and didn't want my children to see me flinching. I got up from the table and left the house. Helen asked me where I was going but I had no idea. I walked as far as the lighthouse, it felt as though I was biting granite, my teeth scraping at the pier wall. Then I walked in a great hurry back to my mother, asking her if she had ever seen Hitler.

Once, she said.

Where?

Düsseldorf, she said.

She was in a department store looking at fabrics, feeling for quality, when everybody suddenly rushed out the door onto the street. He's here, somebody shouted. The wind sucked them out, shop assistants included, leaving the till behind unguarded. She was the only person left inside. The crowd was lined up along the street, people on their toes, straining to see over shoulders, leaning in the direction where the cavalcade was expected to appear. The buildings were decorated with swastikas, everybody waving flags.

My mother used the expression – torn along.

It was her way of describing that moment on the street, what her uncle the Lord Mayor had warned her about, how everyone was being swept along by a euphoric feeling, by a longing inside each breast for a strong leader after so much disaster. She said the people had an appetite for lies and false facts. It helped them to hide what they didn't want to know about themselves. They stood waving with great happiness in their hearts, they had been promised holidays in the mountains, family trips on a cruise liner, their country was winning again, they were expecting heaven on earth.

Inside the abandoned department store, my mother said she felt unsafe. She was afraid they would accuse her of stealing. She went outside and saw a small woman who had just left the shop with a broad new hat. The cavalcade passed by with Hitler in the back of an open-topped car. A small man with a modern moustache. It was known that he had a warm smile and his eyes had the ability to look inside each person.

The moment was brief, my mother said. She stood at the back of the crowd. She hardly knew it was Hitler, only that the woman in front, wearing the wide-rimmed hat, not paid for, the label was still attached, turned around with great excitement in her voice and said – did you see him?

After the cavalcade passed by, everyone went about their business. The woman with the new hat walked away down the street. Another woman crossed the street wearing a new tweed coat, the gifts of Hitler. My mother was working in Düsseldorf by then, in an employment office, she had some money, she went back into the department store to buy gifts for her sisters, the two eldest ones were already married, things they needed. She said it was a time of high fashion. A time you could not easily trust men. Most of them were in the Nazi party. Her boss was a senior Nazi member, he was married, always asking her to go for a drink.

A lot of the women in Düsseldorf looked elegant and provocative, she said. The style was to show how perfectly rounded your backside could be. They wore tight dresses that turned the bottom into a walking globe, spherical cushions in bright colours and stripes. She laughed and sang the line of a pop song from the time, about a woman walking down the street with her round bottom swinging and all the monkey men turning around to look at her.

Walking back home, the granite bite in my mouth slowly began to let go. Nothing, to my mind, can be as intoxicating as the grip of denial being released. The enormous energy that goes into refusing the past comes flooding back in a wave of peace once I face up to it. It is not possible to choose my history. I cannot favour one part over another.

They were all asleep when I got back. I made sure the children were covered. Helen woke up, there was a sleep cloud of warm air around her neck. I whispered to let her know I was going to stay up and listen to some music. I had borrowed a set of headphones from work. I put on one of the albums from the basement catalogue. The accordion player from Galway with a cigarette in his mouth gone to America, a jig called the Rambling Pitchfork. Three, four times in a row I played it.

The Rambling Pitchfork.

The country is full of black flags. We see them hanging from the windows, attached to lamp posts, on the goalposts in sporting fields. Black flags tied to the gates of a car park, on the back of a delivery truck, on bridges over the dual carriageway. Some of the flags are tattered, made of material that doesn't last. Some of them no more than black refuse bags, stuck to the branch of a tree in the wind.

The black flags make it impossible to ignore what is going on in the north of Ireland. They are there to remind everyone of people on hunger strike. Hunger has a deep meaning in our country. In some places, the flags are accompanied by the faces and the names of the men on their fast along with the name of the camp in which they have been imprisoned. They look thin and gaunt, their hair long, their eyes sunken, one of them had been elected to parliament in London while in prison, his face bore a smile from an earlier time.

There was a letter published in the paper, sent by the mother of one of the hunger strikers to the prime minister in London. It was requesting a meeting to explain why her son was refusing food and water. It described what it was like for a mother to see her child slowly dying. The prime minster was a mother herself, she wore a blue scarf around her neck, but her response to the mother of the hunger striker was unequivocal, she saw no need for compassion, a crime was a crime. The men on hunger strike could not be regarded as political prisoners. They were asking for too much, a letter a week, one visit a week, the right not to wear prison clothing.

On Saturday morning, I drove into the city. I circled around the square to show Rosie and Essie the basement where I worked. I pointed out the park where I had my lunch every day, the corner shop that sold two slices of brown bread and cheese, the German library with the red door. The building beside the German library used to belong to the British Embassy, but it was burned down after a massacre in which civilians were shot dead by British soldiers on the streets of Derry, now it was a solicitor's office. We parked by the National Gallery, they giggled at the painting of nude women in the countryside. Afterwards, we went to the café with stained glass, we had our own sandwiches. We bought two cherry buns, gone pink inside, but we had to leave them behind unfinished because Rosie got sick.

We should have brought the bowl, Helen said.

We had a stainless-steel bowl at home which was used whenever they were sick. It was also used for baking and washing lettuce and other things like soaking beans and chick peas. From time to time, Rosie and Essie wanted it for playing with water, a doll's bath, teddies dripping and shrunken. It was a bowl that could be used for many things in the family, though we generally called it the sick bowl. It was dented in a couple of places and had the sound of a bell.

Get the sick bowl.

I grew up alert. Listening like a soldier in perpetual war. When I heard the voice of a child, I woke up running, a hundred doors opening, my bare feet along the green carpet, bursting into the bedroom holding the bowl in one hand, Rosie too weak to stand, waking up from a sick dream. Her forehead wet. Her face white. My other hand keeping back her hair, rubbing her tummy – you're OK, it's all out now, all gone. Helen coming with a warm facecloth, then everything was fine again, they eventually went to sleep again as if nothing had happened.

Next day, the sick bowl was back in the kitchen. The sound of water rinsing it clean was a swirling echo of sickness. The bowl was like a steel stomach throwing up a dizzy gush of bubbled hot water. Dried and stainless again. The warped faces of children laughing, reflected from inside the bowl, used briefly to send messages to other civilisations in a distant universe. Then the bowl was ready to be used once more to make a chocolate sponge. Everything looping in a cycle of cakes and steeping lentils and nauseous bell sounds.

Was it some illness I brought with me from the house where I grew up? The country my mother came from, the country my father invented in his head. Something in my overlapping history that I am passing on to my children?

My memory is full of sickness. My father bursting into the room with the sick bowl. Bursting in with medicine. Bursting in with a hot poultice. Bursting in to accuse me of speaking the language of the street inside my head. Bursting in to let me know that innocent people had been shot down on the streets of Derry. Bursting in to tell me the British Embassy was on fire. Bursting in the following day with his beekeeping gear over his head, climbing out the window of my bedroom onto the flat roof wearing big gloves and the smoke of burning sackcloth coming from the nozzle of his bee calmer. Bursting in that same night again with his fists in my sleep after I climbed back in late through the window past the beehives, my mother begging him to stop, the whole family awake on the landing and my brother appearing at the door like a boy adult with one single word – peace. My father finally brought to his senses, his fists turned back into hands, my mother led him away and my eyes got used to the light on.

My father bursting in to apologise with a book, with a box of oil paints, with a small fact about helium he thought I might be interested in and might get us talking. The reconciliation music coming from the front room, Tristan and Isolde, their love death rising and rising up the stairs.

And my little sister, Lotte.

My mother has asked Helen to teach Lotte how to read and write in English. They are doing Tolstoy, a page a day. Lotte fell behind as a child because of her asthma, the language of the street was forbidden in our house, she missed a lot of classes at school. Helen is a good teacher, she waits for Lotte to catch her breath after each sentence.

I remember lying awake hearing Lotte trying to breathe, unable to say a word. Her hair was soaked with sweat, my mother wiped her forehead. The doctor came late one night. We heard his deep voice in the hall, he gave Lotte a Valium injection. She fell asleep and I thought she would never breathe again. Next time the doctor was called, he said it was all in her mind, nothing more than a psychological impediment preventing her from breathing normally like every other child on the street. I heard my father coming up the stairs, bursting into Lotte's room. He slapped her and told her to go to sleep – you're making this up. My mother tried to calm him, but he continued shouting, commanding Lotte to start breathing properly. She was quiet after that.

But worse again the next day. My father prayed and got his brother the Jesuit to make the sign of the cross over her. He ordered the latest medical journals. Cortisone was known to restrict bone growth in a child. He gave Lotte a glass of liquid yeast instead. He gave her goat's milk. The cat disappeared. He put on Bach. He read about bronchodilator medication, he discovered an inhaler called Ventolin.

If only it was possible to understand his vision, the mixed family enterprise he created. If only it had not been so obscured by his rage, his love, the silence he cast over the family with his crusade. I thought of him reading to improve his German. The care my mother took to correct his grammar. The risk they entered into. The adventure in their eyes when they started this strange family out of place. The house was full of love and misunderstanding. She encouraged him to do things he would never have taken on in his own language, this beekeeping enterprise he got himself into.

I think of the bees arriving for the first time. Like visitors, given refuge in our home. A swarm delivered in May from West Cork. A dome-shaped straw skep with bees talking inside, buzzing with ideas. My mother welcomes them with an embroidered tablecloth, a blue bowl of star and moon shaped biscuits, her voice high with excitement. Her language is a running diary, observing my father, the strangeness of a man in his own country. He wears a protective cage over his head, stepping like an astronaut onto the flat roof while we watch from the window above. Seven faces leaning out to see him punching the humming skep with his fist. It rolls away like an empty hat. He stands back with his big gloves held up in the air. A white sheet spread out, a colony of bees dropped out before nightfall, walking up the beach to a new hive waiting.

We drove out across the mountains until we saw no more black flags. We came through a bog with yellow signs showing a black car veering over the edge. Another sign with a black hump, warning about the uneven surface. The car we had was beige, maybe mustard brown. It had a boxy shape, a biscuit tin with no seat belts in the back, the gear lever was up high by the steering wheel. A slide window, so you could leave your elbow out. The girls were screeching in the back, lifted off their seats with every bump in the road. Helen had her bare feet on the dashboard, I was distracted by her knees.

Hard to say if I was driving away from something or driving towards something. My decisions were random, based on forces in my childhood I could not explain. Behaving at the mercy of feelings that never matched the time we were in. I was creating my own mixed family enterprise, doing my best to be unlike the family I came from.

It was late in the afternoon, we got fish and chips. I had a bottle of wine, some shallow styrofoam containers from a Chinese restaurant for wine glasses.

I drove the car into a field. The weeds squeaked along the paintwork, slapping under the wheel arches. The silence when I turned off the engine was enormous, nothing but ourselves and the sound of wrapping paper and the smell of salt and vinegar. The country was depopulated. Only us, sitting with the doors open, facing the sunset. It was warm. The breeze was like a hairdryer coming through, it blew a paper napkin up against the windscreen.

We waited for the sun to leave, the children went to sleep. In the middle of Ireland, we sat watching the field going dark. The wind came up. A few drops of rain at first, then louder, bouncing on the roof of the car. Helen said it was as heavy as the rain in Canada. She told me how she was once caught in a thunderstorm and could not find her way home. The streets all looked the same, the rain bounced a foot off the ground, it created a halo around the world, her hair down on her skull, blinded by the weight of water in her eyes.

She sat in the car staring into the field of rain as though she was back in Canada, with Lake Huron in front of her. A solid black plate lit up in a flash of lightning, the salt mine, the two bright lines of the railway tracks, her family home in view for a brief unreachable instant.

Give my love to the lake, she said. Give my love to the night-heron. Give my love to the boardwalk and the big empty salt rooms underneath the lake.

I started up the engine, we had to go before the mud kept us there for the night. I was the expert at getting home, driving like a lover, like a father, picking the children up in my arms from the back seat when we got home, one after the other in sleep level six, carrying them inside. Helen opened the doors, taking their shoes off, shielding their eyes from the light. I placed them without interruption into their beds like time travellers, straight from the field of fish and chips to the next morning with the light coming through the curtains. Nothing but the crown of a thistle caught in the bumper for proof.

There was a trick I taught them on that trip. They climbed up on the stump of a tree and jumped into my arms. The leap of trust, we called it. I was the catcher, standing ready. They had to take it in turns and wait for me to shout – jump. Essie was fearless, she threw herself backwards off the bonnet of the car.

It gave us a false sense of security. As though nothing could ever happen to us. Our lives were accidental, full of love and luck and family chaos, rescued by our children.

We collected them from their art class. We did some shopping on the way home. I parked the car across the road from the house. Helen went around to get the groceries, a bag in her arms with the stalk of a pineapple growing out of her shoulder. I went to get the children out and saw Rosie standing in the middle of the road.

I didn't have time to ask how she got there.

The sound of tyres was so loud it silenced the entire street, there was blue smoke rising, it smelled like Halloween fires burning. Rosie closed her eyes, her body shivered, her hands held up to stop the car. It came to a stop inches away from her. The driver sat motionless with his grip on the steering wheel, unable to get out, staring ahead at the child in the street. Helen looked at me, the bag with the pineapple fell out of her arms. It was that soundless space in between us that frightened me more than anything, the dry mouth words we could not say to each other, the leap of trust, where was the catcher? She ran without looking and picked Rosie up off the street. She continued running until she got inside the house. I grabbed Essie by the hand. The traffic was held up, the whole street waiting until we had the door closed behind us.

Helen stood screaming in the front room.

I took the children into the kitchen and started making pancakes.

Her scream continued for a long time. It went back to the time when she was a child only five years of age herself. In Birmingham. The house on the corner with the buses going by and passengers looking in the windows. Her father at work, her mother in the kitchen with earrings on peeling potatoes. Helen standing on the street, the side gate had been left open, her younger sister was getting into the back of a car. The driver was holding a bag of sweets. Her other sister, no more than three, was climbing in to join her. It was a Wolseley with leather seats, their legs were dangling. And the housekeeper from Ennis running out when she heard the scream, making up for everything she had lost in her own life, the baby she had to leave behind in Ireland. She was shouting Holy Jesus. Mary mother. Reaching into the back of the car to clutch the two girls by the arms at the last minute before the car took off around the corner with the rear door swinging. The howling of tyres creeping like a wounded animal along the wall.

The side gate was locked again.

Her mother's face was at the kitchen window like a photograph gone black and white. To make them forget, the housekeeper put them all three into the bath and taught them a song about James Connolly, a working-class hero. Nobody called the police, it would have been shameful to have them come around to the house, people asking if it had to do with being Irish. Nothing happened, everyone was safe. He was caught some ten years later, an engineer, the Cannock Chase man. Only some of the bodies were found. He never admitted anything apart from the fact that he loved cars, somebody bought his Wolseley at auction to be burned in a public ceremony with a crowd of people standing by to watch.

Was that the reason?

The reason for going to Canada. The reason they could never speak of and for which they made up so many other happy reasons to go and live in a quiet place with a salt mine.

Rosie and Essie ate the pancakes with yoghurt. Essie caught me sprinkling invisible sugar with my hand. Rosie spilled yoghurt on herself, on me, it was on the carpet, a pink footprint. I brought them to bed and read the book about the boy in the bakery at night getting milk to go into the cake for the morning. We sat up in bed for a long time, all four of us. Helen was clutching them, one on each side, rocking back and forth until they were asleep.

It never occurred to me to get the groceries fallen on the ground in the street until a neighbour came to the door and handed them in to me without a word.

After midnight, Helen got up and went out to the public phone by the front door to make a call. There was no answer. She walked up and down the corridor, then she tried again.

In the house overlooking the salt mine, the phone rings around the hallway, into the kitchen, into the blue room with all the furniture brought over from Birmingham. It rings out onto the porch, as far as the white picket fence. Her mother has just left the house, on her way to the court-house square to meet her friend. She puts on her sunglasses getting into the car. The lake has no meaning for her, the sunlight is full of scorn, the glare of things she wants to forget.

The day is hot, the cicadas are deafening. There is a child cycling along the sidewalk, in and out of brightness under the trees, making a soft tapping sound along the concrete slabs. The neighbours are gradually moving a little further along their lives each time the child comes back around – a man gardening, a woman on the porch with ice cubes ring-ing, blue shouts coming from a swimming pool.

The town is calm and polite. They drive slowly, they speak with caution, they call her by her first name, she gets invited to parties where people eat with their hands and it's all paper plates and paper cups of wine and women standing around in shorts. A town where she first turned up in swel-tering Donegal tweed and sang a song that brought the house down. The town by the lake where students drive themselves to school. Where the hairdresser has a swimming pool. Where the judge will be seen having coffee with the local electrician, there is no difference between people only what you have.

Helen's mother has attached herself to this Canadian town like a story made up out of nothing. She has turned her back on Birmingham. The city in which her children almost disappeared. The city of fog. Fog loitering in the streets. The sound of coughing and cars starting at night. The headlights of a bus pointing through a dense grey curtain, the doorbell ringing and the fog slowly coming up the stairs.

The world is full of things that have not happened.

Helen gave up trying to phone her mother and came back in. We sat on the floor in the front room. The curtains were left open. Her face was gold. Her eyes were green. Her hair was copper with the light coming in off the street.

Was it wrong to feel lucky?

We ate some of the leftover pancakes. We drank two bottles of Guinness each. We made love. The dog next door was barking. The people upstairs were laughing. The buses stopped running. I got up to check on the children. I stood watching them for a while with the light from the hallway across their faces. The force of them asleep was greater than all their time awake.

My silence has become unbearable. There is a forest growing inside. Trees springing up in the kitchen, trees in the hallway, around the bed, roots running under the green carpet into the front room. The curtains have a pattern of falling leaves, the entire back wall of the house looks like open country with nothing but silence.

My mother tells me that she was in hospital once. It was in Düsseldorf, she says, during the war. She started bleeding, maybe this is difficult for her to explain. She doesn't tell me what exactly happened, only that she could not stop bleeding and was taken to hospital.

In the room next door to her, she says, there was a man who kept screaming at night. He was a soldier, he had been stationed in the east. He was brought back injured, but the doctors could find nothing wrong with him, no medical explanation for his pain. He experienced terrible stomach cramps which made him vomit, he could not eat a thing. He crawled along the floor, he lay curled up in the corridor, the nurses had to lift him up and carry him back to his room. They said it might have been shell shock. He was more frightened than wounded, he couldn't sleep, his arms and legs were shaking.

One night, he started talking, other patients in rooms off the same corridor could hear him speaking in a raised voice to one of the nurses, she was holding his hand. He had been commanded to a place on the outskirts of a small town. It was on the edge of a forest. Soldiers in his regiment had been given the job of clearing the town, separating women from their children. The women were rounded up into a small group of about thirty or forty. They kept looking back at the children from whom they had been separated, but the soldiers continued to push them towards a ravine. One of the children broke free and ran after the group of mothers but was held back. The child fell.

There was a soldier filming all of this with a moving camera, the man said.

The story went around the ward in a shocked whisper. The man was given an injection to calm him down. He continued speaking a while longer, then he was quiet. He was said to be delusional. Before the night was out, he was gone, his bed was vacant. The nurse said he had been discharged. There was no more talking, no more whispering, the story disappeared. My mother brought it to Ireland with her.

The dental practice is across the street from the former veterinary surgery. The waiting room is still in use as a dining room, a table and chairs for eight people, magazines like place mats. In the corner, there is a cabinet full of crockery, a porcelain teapot. Above the fireplace, a large picture of a turf boat with dark brown sails.

The surgery is in the living room, to the front, facing onto the main street. The dentist speaks to me at first in the native language, then he switches back to English. He's from the North, from Derry. He smiles and flicks his head to one side as he speaks. He whispers to himself while he examines the X-ray, my ghost mouth.

He wants to know what is causing the trouble. I tell him I have no idea. The slightest thing can set it off, the air, the ground, the street, the sound of my own feet in my mouth. He asks me if I have been clenching my teeth, grinding in my sleep. He gives me a gum shield. I sleep like a boxer for a couple of weeks, but it makes no difference. Back in the chair again. He begins to single out one of the upper molars on the left. He undertakes the required root-canal treatment. It involves many repeat visits, lots of drilling, I take several days off work, I go back some weeks later and he puts in the crown.

The buses stop right outside the surgery. Passengers upstairs get a good look at me lying back with my mouth wide open and the light shining across my face. The sight must fill them with horror. The dentist reaching into my mouth with his fingers. My hands gripping the armrests.

I hear the dental assistant speaking to him softly in the background, handing over instruments I don't want to see. Everything feels so enlarged. His rubber gloves make a squeaking sound against my teeth. He asks me questions he can only answer himself, all I can do is consent with a crow sound at the back of my throat.

When he's finished, he removes the rubber gloves and says I should have no more trouble. He flicks his head to the side and apologises for not fixing the problem sooner. He refuses to take any money. I try to pay him, but he tells me to go. He smiles and says the tooth is dead, it's beyond pain – come back to me if you feel anything.

2

Their school is on a street leading to the harbour. A terraced white building where the mariners used to gather for prayers with their families before they set sail. I wait outside in the car an hour early, falling asleep. In a dream, I trip over a tower of books and wake up with a snarl, not refreshed but confused, mothers and fathers standing by the gate talking in quiet voices, arranging play dates.

They came running out, handing me their drawings. Rosie had done a man inside a space capsule. Big dish ears. He was wearing a red shirt, the sky around him was full of onion rings. That was the song they wanted to hear again and again, about the man who gets lost in space and continues travelling far above the world in a tin can. As soon as we got home it was engines on, lift-off, we had chairs called Venus and Jupiter. I tried explaining infinity to them. The man in the spacecraft keeps going away for ever and ever.

Essie said – but he will come back.

Everyone was talking about the solar system, the Voyager space mission heading into the unknown, the drug allegories, there was a plaque erected on a wall nearby for somebody who died in a road accident – gone with Nash to the dark side of the moon.

While Helen was teaching her class, I sat in the back room playing the astronaut, they had me sitting in the armchair with the sick bowl across my chest, making swirling sounds. The launch buttons were carefully arranged along my knees. The aerial on the portable radio fully extended. They held a pink hand mirror up to show me how crooked my nose was. A battery-operated toy kept repeating the same phrase over and over in a voice that I found disturbing, I vowed to make it disappear overnight. A malevolent gift, given to them by one of Helen's aunts, the aunt with the bunch of keys.

Here I was, floating above the world, two children and a talking toy.

As soon as the yoga classes were finished, I disappeared into the empty front room with a small foldable school desk Helen got for next to nothing from the furniture auctioneer next door. The room was heavy with perfume. I had a portable typewriter that belonged to my father. Essie left me a plastic zebra for company. There I sat for two hours alone, doing nothing, staring at all the things I could not describe.

Every sentence tied me down. Words often came to me first in my mother's language. I was faced with a choice of three versions of the same object, like a street trick where the correct word was hidden under one of three matchbox hats, lifting the wrong one, the meaning had already moved.

I formed a sentence in German, then I veered down into the native basement and came up at street level with the verb in English, a rough stone with no value. My descriptions kept alluding to something larger which was not contained in the words. If I mentioned a crowd, I was equating it with a crowded train station during the war, if I mentioned a space left vacant in a bar, it was a place where you could settle down for the rest of your life and never move again. Everything was loaded with distress and joy, full of misunderstanding.

I stood up to look out the window. There was salt on the glass. The houses on the far side were turned a dull yellow by the street lighting. My face was a yellow death mask in the window. A bus went by from left to right with a single passenger upstairs. An estate-agent sign was budging a little in the wind, sale agreed. The long straight leaves of the palm trees outside the guest house next door began rattling. The street lights gave them an orange sheen, like artificial leaves, strips of plastic cut in slices from a large sheet. The clacking made them seem lifeless, as if they understood no seasons, as if they felt nothing.

I had the need to keep moving. I walked out the door. My yellow face turned left past the palm trees. The beat of my feet gave me a feeling of urgency and purpose. Some instinct made me always turn down towards the sea, as if the truth could only be found by facing the water, something in the large space in front of me that opened a large space inside me. The silent bay at night brought an understanding of my own silence.

Somewhere around the derelict public baths, with the boarded-up windows and the roof caved in, the pool silted up with sand and rocks thrown in by the winter tides, there was a heron calmly standing in the water and it came to me that there is no single story. There is nothing but restless fragmentation. My skin inside is black and white, ragged and incoherent as the palm trees. It is in this disorder that I will discover everything.

Every morning, I buy the newspaper from the vendor outside the train station. I take the same train to work, I get off at the same station, I turn the same corner and walk along the square with the park of lovers at the centre. The continuity is inescapable. I am following in my father's foot-steps. To the onlooker, I must appear like an updated version of my father without the limp, the same forehead, the same smile, the anxiety in the eyes. The same unfinished life going on into infinity. I give myself the illusion that things are changing, my music is different, the grip of the Church might soon fade away, there is a freedom coming. I get my sandwich from the corner shop, I lie in the park at lunch-time dreaming, watching the clouds, the ground underneath me begins to slide. By the end of the day, I cannot help stepping back into my father's shoes again, going to the German library, retracing the same route by the park back to the station, the same train home.

In the German library, they have a cataloguing system whereby you can see the names of previous readers marked on a sheet at the back of the book along with the return date. Many of the books on history I borrow have already been taken out by my father while he was alive. His name is there like a forerunner. His hands turn the pages for me. In one of the books I found his posthumous train ticket, punched five days a week. It gives me the confidence of a man whose mistakes have already been made in advance.

Does your memory ever grow up? Or will it always stand still at the age of happening?

Over and over, I go back to remembering my father with the bees. His death keeps turning up at the most unpredictable moments, forcing itself on me with a surge of fear. Even when I am surrounded by other people, standing in a bar, at a party with music playing, I become exposed without warning to the sight of my father fighting off bees. Swinging his arms around his head, his face mask dislodged, bees getting inside, the anger, the mutiny. Bees jumping up from the open hive like a black cat. They have turned on him, they are in his mouth, in his ears. The house is full of humming, the children have locked themselves into the bathroom. My father's hands, my father's face, flinching with each sting, his pain, his limp from birth, his childhood calling for help.

On the stairs, my mother's voice calls up to the roof – God in heaven. In her language the bees have gone out of their minds, they are wild with rage. She is prevented from going near him by the bees all around the house, on the stairs, in every room. Bees buzzing up and down the windows. Bees lodged in the curtains, under the beds, crawling in dying circles on the wooden floor. My father falling backwards, holding his chest. She finally pulls him out into the street, the hall door is left open. She waves her arms, but nobody takes them in the car with the war of bees all around them.

Followed by the day of the funeral, my mother lost, far away from home in the wrong country. She is surrounded by people outside the church that she hardly knows, in the confusion of grief she has trouble remembering their names, even the butcher seems out of place. The shame of death. The ridicule of life. How alone you are in a foreign place when the coffin goes into the ground. How empty the words can be in the language of the street.

The silence left behind by my father is a choir of voices unheard.

After I have my sandwich in the park, I walk through the streets and come across a hardware shop where they are selling some second-hand carving tools. Chisels with curved blades in various diameters. I buy three of them. I get advice on how to maintain the tools with linseed oil. In addition, I buy a rounded wooden mallet, like a shiny ostrich egg with a handle. I also need some fine sandpaper, and French polish.

Why am I buying these items? I have no idea, only that I am copying my father, the need to do something useless. As they wrap up the tools for me, I think of my father when he was alive, he must have done the exact same thing at lunch-time. Perhaps he even came to the same hardware store, with the same expression of eagerness, the same questions, the same smile.

With these tools in my bag, I walk back to the basement. Along the way, I come to a joinery. There is no office, I walk right into the workshop. The saws are going, wood-turning machines spinning, they are producing legs for chairs and tables. There is a sweet smell of wood all around that reminds me of my father. It's hard to see, cloudy light, everything is covered in a layer of sawdust. Cobwebs around the light fixtures, heavy and drooping like netting bags. I speak to one of the men, he takes his protective mask down and reveals a clean patch of his face, his lips are blood red, his eyelashes gone white. It's hard to hear him with the noise of the machines. He points to a pile of cut-off wood, tells me to help myself, he doesn't want any money. I pick out a couple of small pieces of mahogany, a section of walnut, and a piece of white basswood.

Back home, I start working on the basswood. It's the softest of them all. The chisel makes it feel more like wax. I decide to carve a mouth. I go into the bathroom and look at myself in the mirror. With a pencil, I draw the outlines of an open mouth onto the wood. The mouth holds the silent pose of a word, a song suspended. I get to work, hammering and chiselling on the kitchen table with a sheet of newspaper underneath. A section from under the nose down to the chin. The lips are parted, the front teeth showing, the interior hollowed out. It takes me a couple of weeks to get it right.

My silent mouth goes on display. It sits on the mantelpiece speaking for me. Calling out the latest news. Everything in the newspapers, opinions heard on the radio, images on

TV faithfully spoken back as though saying the worst will protect you from the worst. It has become a household witness to everything that is happening around the world. My wooden voice repeating new words for atrocity and shame and senseless loss of life in the North. It becomes hopelessly enraged, getting in on every dispute, every injustice, people imprisoned for crimes they did not commit. It speaks in prophecies, in warnings, in exultant waves of bad news. Helen says it's hard to live with. The children don't want to hear all this.

A wooden mouth, stalled in belated protest. Making up for student revolts I never took part in. Anti-Vietnam War demonstrations I was too late for, civil rights marches, sit-downs, house occupations I missed out on. A mouth full of wayward rebellion, all those door slamming wars with my father, followed by hours of unending silence.

Helen threw a party. Her family rule was not to dwell on misery. Her second family rule was not to be mean with drink. Make people sit down. Make them feel welcome. Ask a lot of questions. As a child in Birmingham, she could remember finding a man's shoe half burned in the fire, the leftover crisps, the bitter taste of gin. She remembered the singing, the sound of her mother laughing on the stairs, the perfume and the soft touch of her face coming to tuck them in late.

She went around making sure everyone got introduced to each other. Some of them were utterly incompatible. She put the most demented stoner in conversation with a sailing fanatic. She had a native singer talking to a woman who despised everything to do with her own country. A friend back from California in tattered tennis shoes was trying to explain the meaning of a song to a woman who seemed too laid-back to care, he told her it was inspired by a German philosopher who said we were all thrown into this world – oh, that's terrible news, she said. Most of them were leaning against the wall, one armchair shared between three, a few straight-backed chairs. Right in the middle, there was a couple sitting on the floor like a street protest.

I stood around like a guest in my own house, listening, overhearing things, saying as little as possible. I was unable to get drunk. I spent the evening memorising things, stealing what other people said, my mind was full of theft.

Somebody picked up the carved wooden mouth from the mantelpiece and started examining it, running a finger across the lips. It got passed around, they checked the back of the carving as though they were expecting to see the larynx. They held it up to their own mouths, they used it to tell each other to – fuck off. Somebody sang out the words of a song – the heat pipes just coughed. One of the women laughed and leaned forward with a retching sound as though it was going to puke. When she discovered it was hand-carved, she quickly gave it away like a piece of voodoo.

They managed to get the mouth talking.

I was unable to prevent the wood carving from revealing things about myself, speaking openly in a wave of personal facts. There was a mixture of surprise and fascination in their eyes as the talking mouth started telling them about a time in Germany when I was hitchhiking from Frankfurt to Berlin. I stood on the autobahn and a car pulled up. I thought I was lucky. A man got out. Did he show me a badge? I could not remember, all I saw was the gun. The faces of terrorists were posted up in all the service stations. I must have looked like one of those wanted people. I had a wanted face. A wanted beard. Wanted clothes. He ordered me to open the mandolin case. He told me to take the mandolin out and place it on the ground. He told me to step over the crash barrier and walk through a small stand of trees with my hands up. He was right behind me. He motioned me forward, down a steep slope, into open ground, well out of sight of the passing traffic overhead. He told me to take my coat off. It lay pooled on the grass. He looked at my passport. He looked at me. He refused to believe I could be Irish and speak fluent German. Waving the gun, he told me to take off my shoes. My shirt. My trousers. It was cold. I didn't know what he wanted from me. After some time, he turned and walked away. I watched him climb the slope to the motorway and disappear. I stood in the field in my underpants without moving. I waited for him to come back, but he didn't.

My mouth was too honest. It spoke like somebody in the witness box. Answering questions without much tactical intuition. Under cross-examination, it revealed that I worked in the native basement, that my father was from Cork, that I had a German mother. Helen was afraid they would be able to extract all kinds of personal information that she wanted to keep private. She went over and politely asked for it back. She placed it on the bookcase where she could keep an eye on it. She didn't want somebody walking away with my mouth.

Helen's friend Martina was there, wearing a long colourful dress and cowboy boots. She lifted the arms of her brown suede jacket and let the tasselled fringes underneath rise like the wings of a bird of prey, swooping down to pick up her drink. Her wrist jangled with handmade jewellery. She allowed her long hair to fall across her face and shook her head like a rocker. Free dancing, she laughed, in her Kerry accent. She had once been to a famous concert in the Isle of Wight.

Martina and Helen had gone to the same boarding school, they regularly escaped out the window and changed their clothes in a telephone box and went drinking in the city together, sitting with their legs crossed. Both had revolution and misconduct in their bones, different ways of applying it in life.

I overheard Helen talking about Canada, telling Martina and others in a group by the fireplace how couples drove along the gravel roads of Ontario with a crate of beer in the back seat and all the wheels off the ground. A couple were recently found dead in each other's arms, a single car collision, they had driven into a tall beech tree on the way out to the peach orchards. I heard Martina saying it was easier to get airborne in a parked car on Ventry beach.

At one point, the couple on the floor got up and Helen caught them going into the bedroom where the children were asleep. My mouth was numb. I heard Helen shouting, flinging their shoes out into the street after them, the dog next door was barking continuously.

I got talking to a journalist.

He asked me if I played chess.

Long ago, I said. My father taught me.

My wooden mouth began telling the journalist that my father could not bear to be beaten. He turned the chessboard upside down in anger one day when he realised I was winning. The same thing happened to a chess champion in a Russian novel, his father flipped the board up in a rage, mirror families in Ireland and Russia.

You must be good, the journalist said.

Not at all, I said.

He invited me to come around one evening for a game. His house was on the same street, a redbrick terrace beyond the furniture auctions.

He kept staring at Helen.

She was wearing a powder blue, crêpe-de-Chine skirt she had got in London while she studied drama. The fabric was thin as a glove, slightly burred to the touch, it gave her just enough freedom of movement.

Helen found herself agreeing to a bet. She stood with her spine straight, she had her mother's shrug – what do you take me for?

Martina clapped her hands – I dare you.

To demonstrate how unchanged and fit her body was with all the yoga, Helen took up the challenge of getting into the baby high chair. The high chair no longer had any function other than to act as a drinks counter, the children had grown out of it, it was not accepted back into the cycle of furniture auctions next door and there was nobody with a baby to pass it on to. Martina said it was not humanly possible for a mother to fit into a high chair that two of her children passed through and that still had dark remnants of their mashed potato stuck in the grooves.

Look, Martina said – black as a bog.

Helen lifted her powder-blue skirt above her knees a fraction and began to climb up on the table. From there, one foot after the other, she stepped into the high chair, rocking like a canoe, held by the hand for support on each side.

The journalist was getting ready to catch her.

Martina said – go on, girl.

One of the other women said it was unwise, the man in tennis shoes said nobody in California would try it, I didn't say a thing, I watched and admired her.

It took Helen a while to slip each leg into place, it was a puzzle of bones and knees. There was a vertical bar at the centre intended to prevent the child from slipping out, one leg on either side. It's like fitting into a wooden corset, Helen said – they'll have to cut me free. Followed by some jokes going around the room about corsets and Helen mentioning the fact that she once had a job in the corsetry department at Harrods in London, where it was not only women who bought them.

Slowly, she managed to sink down into position. Her black velvet shoes were still on. She had one leg on each side of the dividing safety bar. Everybody was applauding.

The crêpe-de-Chine skirt was halfway up her thighs, a brief view of white. In one hand, she held a beaker of wine, in the other she had a handmade wooden rattle. The rattle was constructed as two halves of a hollow egg with a kernel inside. A wooden shell clacking freely up and down a stick with rounded stoppers at each end that babies had been putting into their mouths for years, it came from Germany, pre-war, before Hitler.

On Sunday night, while I sit at the foldable desk in the empty front room, I hear Helen in the hallway on the phone. She is telling her mother in Canada that we met some very nice new people, a journalist and his wife, John and Audrey – he edits the education supplement, sometimes the health supplement, she is from England, a schoolteacher now a full-time mother, thinking of changing her career. They are both extremely interesting, Helen says, nothing they don't already know. They live in a terraced house to themselves, one daughter, a dog, lots of paintings and ornaments. She says I go there to play chess with John, he usually wins, though not always. Audrey calls around during the day, you can have a nice chat with her about growing up in England.

There is no other news.

The shopkeeper tried to short-change her again but she's up to him. The yoga classes are going well, but the front room is too small for that many people, nobody knows where to put their legs any more. Helen is thinking about hiring a separate venue. Her picture was in one of the

Sunday papers, she has posted it over to Canada rolled up in a baton.

Our car windows got smashed one night, right outside on the street while we were asleep, we heard nothing.

I hear her saying that my mother is ill, she has been diagnosed with cancer. Both of my mother's older sisters – Marianne in Salzburg and Elfriede in Russelsheim – have already died from cancer. My mother says it's her turn now, everybody in a row. There was talk of surgery, but she doesn't want any of that, my sister Greta is looking after her.

And the children?

New words. Essie was heard saying – I hate consequences. Rosie keeps using the word – sundown, we have got to get home before sundown. They drew human faces on the potatoes, we couldn't peel them.

Listening to Helen speaking on the phone to Canada comes close to writing a novel. It has that first-hand honesty I want, nothing invented, just the latest news. If I can write the way she speaks, I will be happy, all I need is to faithfully put down every word. Now and then, I have the urge to hand her a note with a missing detail, such as the zoo, don't forget the zoo. Tell your mother about the lion we saw asleep, he opened one eye, then he opened both eyes, then he raised his head a tiny bit, then he went back to sleep. Later we heard him roar behind us and we ran away, Helen told me to stop scaring them. And the conversation we had on the way home in the car about the most dangerous animal in the world – hyenas or leopards?

Or humans?

The latest news from Canada. They have begun building the new public swimming pool in the town and found some human remains. The town council discussed removing the remains to another location but there were so many it was eventually decided to leave them in their original resting place and cover them over with the new pool. The whole town is built on bones. Helen's family home is situated on ancient burial grounds, to catch the spidery lightning storms over the lake.

Helen repeats enough of what her mother says, I can work it out and imagine the rest.

Her mother was invited to dinner by the judge across the street, his house is enormous, ten rooms and a tiny picture window in a Rapunzel tower under the roof, a crescent-shaped driveway with an oval lawn in front. The spare ribs were a bit awkward. There was a bowl of water on the table for people to dip their fingers into, it had a greasy surface sheen. The judge was interested in everything to do with Ireland, he wanted to know about horse racing and river fishing, and a castle where he once stayed in Connemara.

I place them in a dining room interconnected with the sitting room. The judge at the top of the table with Nessa on one side and Helen's mother on the other, two best friends, his favourite people. The entire gathering eating spare ribs and the dog sniffing underneath, a cool nose like a wet finger pointing. The judge throwing something across the room behind him like a bad thought, some judgment in the past that sat badly on his conscience. The dog scampering with the sound of beads across the wide maple floor-boards and sliding to a stop below the window overlooking the lake, the bone held upright between his paws, chewing sideways. Helen's mother not eating very much, just a bit of dignified coleslaw she could manage with a fork, persuaded at the end of the evening to sing a song – The Kerry Dancing.

I have a longing to live in Canada.

Brought on by what is happening in the north of Ireland. The news is full of new words being invented to express outrage and incomprehension. The tattered black flags are still hanging around the country. Shrines with photographs of dead hunger strikers. The inflammation is spreading. The hot breath of freedom. Songs about rivers running free, people singing in fighter voices, strumming the guitar like a weapon. And the drumming.

I want to take my family away to a landscape where you can begin again without memory. Only the memory of the people who were there before us. Cities where everything I grew up with will be out of range, where I can forget where I come from. No borders inside my head.

My mother sat up waiting for me. She put down the book she was reading and looked up when I asked her if it was possible that as a child I had seen houses on fire.

Houses on fire? By night? While we were crossing the street. I must have been around six years old. I have a perfect memory of flames coming out the windows and the sky glowing orange, smoke like a big grey coat with long arms coming down the street. I remember holding my mother's hand, my brother Gerd on the other side with a rucksack on his back, my father ahead of us with my sister Gabriela, limping as he carried the suitcase, he stopped to switch hands. We were coming from the train station, I saw it with my own eyes, a terrace of houses in flames, five or six storeys high. The smell of burning interiors, horsehair sofas, wooden toys, paintwork bubbling. There was a hum coming from the fire engines, the ladders extended, a crowd of people watching, some in their nightclothes with blankets around their shoulders. My mother was pulling my hand and telling me not to look, maybe that's why I remember it so well.

Was it possible I never saw this fire?

Had I received the memory from her? Had she passed on the duty of remembering to me? Her fear of flames. Her inability to feel settled. Her readiness to leave at any moment. Her language of alarm, her looking back, her mistrust of glass.

Going up the stairs, I linked her arm. There was no hurry. She rested on the first-floor landing to catch her breath. On the second landing, she stopped again.

She began to tell me about the time she was bleeding, during the war, when she was haemorrhaging and was taken to hospital, then she stopped as though it was too difficult to talk about.

What is it?

Another time, she said.

Greta came up to help her into bed.

They talked about the butcher, Mister Dunne, he was in hospital. My mother had suggested getting a card to wish him a speedy recovery, Greta said it didn't look good, he had cancer. There was a handwritten sign in the window of the butcher shop, apologising for the inconvenience, due to illness the premises would remain closed until further notice. The wooden block was washed off, the knives were stored in neat rows and the knife holder worn by the butcher like a holster at the side of his blue apron was put away behind the counter. The S-shaped hooks were hanging along the steel bars, only three or four bits of plastic parsley and two plastic red tomatoes remained in the display cabinet, a blue light was left on.

Greta showed me the card with all the signatures she had gathered. She had gone around to the fish shop, the barber, the pub on the corner, the flower shop, they all wrote greetings calling him Napper. We never knew that was his name. To us he had always been the butcher, Mister Dunne. We didn't think it was right to start calling him Napper after all this time, that would be like pretending we knew him better than we did, more as friends than as customers. We didn't know how he got the nickname, did he like being called Napper?

Would he feel insulted if we called him Napper?

Nor did we know until then, only because Greta had a conversation with him while he was signing the card with flour on his hands, that the baker's name was Jim and that he played golf, his wife Marie who served behind the counter couldn't bear going to Spain, she didn't play golf, she said it was like Spain without golf beside the ovens all day. The baker said Napper was a great butcher, one of the best.

Nor did we know, that the barber who cut my father's hair until he found a barber in the city who could speak the native language, the same barber who cut my hair and my brother's hair and once said we looked like two plucked chickens, was a night fisher. He told Greta that when he finished for the day he would drive down the coast to one of the long beaches in Wexford where nobody went and sit on a fold-out chair with the waves at his feet and a light at the top of the rod. Sometimes he cooked the fish, plaice or black sole, there and then, with a beer, a couple of them went down together, he told her, they called themselves the night herons.

Nor did we know, that when the man in the fish shop started his business, my mother saw him selling fish from a pram on the street when she first arrived, he was told by the priest to go in and out of the church through the penny door at the side, the main door was for rich people. Look at him now, my mother said, they must be begging him to come in the front door, one of his sons is a psychiatrist in London, another son has taken over the business, wearing a boater and a white apron.

What else did we not know?

We were latecomers to our surroundings.

The information Greta gathered on her card-signing tour of the shops was known to everyone ahead of us. We had been so caught up with houses on fire and the Berlin Wall and Nazi trials and cities left in ruins. Even the bakery in the

84

Rhineland town where my mother came from was destroyed by a surplus bomb dropped on the way back from a night raid on Cologne. These things were irrelevant where we lived, nobody knew any of the people killed lining up for bread.

I stood in the hallway and heard them talking upstairs. A game they played every night. My mother sat down on the bed and Greta pushed her over so that she fell backwards and began laughing like a young girl. Her quiet, inward laugh. She got herself up and Greta pushed her back down a second time until they were both laughing. Then Greta pushed her down one more time and she went to sleep.

Helen was asleep by the time I got back, a bare knee left outside the covers. I took out the sick bowl and began making oatmeal cookies for the following week. The recipe was taken from a Mennonite cookbook that came from Canada, some of the pages were stuck together with ancient pastry. Enough to last until Wednesday. Laid out on racks to cool, ready to be placed into tins in the morning. The smell of night baking brought a warm shock of happiness, it drifted up the hallway into the bedroom, into the empty front room, past the public telephone by the door, all the way upstairs.

The windows of the recording studios are boarded up. You ring the bell, it takes a while before somebody answers. The narrow hallway has a series of framed photographs of legendary singers, many of them signed with thick markers, a country star from the Midlands with a white smile. You go in through a heavy door insulating the studio from all external sound of traffic. Another double glass door into the recording booth.

The silence is pure. More than silence. A place demanding to be filled with sound. The dull black padding along the walls is like the inside of a coffin. A cough stops dead around you. A spoken word dies in your mouth. Every tiny noise is sucked away, all that remains is clear ambient sound. The engineer breaks in over the speakers like a voice from another galaxy, it's hard to see his face behind the dark glass screen.

The place is dusty, splashes of coffee on the carpet. Empty cartons of juice stuffed behind a radiator. The remains of an Indian takeaway left on top of a speaker unit, things that have no bearing on the sound. The recording engineer is dressed for the beach in shorts and sandals, his shirt open to the waist, he speaks to me as though I have come to record a rock band – groovy.

I am there with a native singer from Cork who has put music to a poem in the shadow language about two swans on a winter lake. The backing track is made up of remote guitar strumming and traditional uilleann pipes. Drones and chanters recreating a humming in the reeds around the lake. There is love between the swans, their white necks reaching, lightly touching down on the frozen water.

The singer has a moustache. To me, he looks Turkish, like the shadow men I worked with in Berlin, it gives him a broad smile. He can switch easily between singing in Irish and singing the blues. While the song is being recorded, he wears the headphones half on his head, one over his right ear, the other on his forehead.

After the recording session, I briefly slipped into the German library. Going home I fell asleep on the train and woke up at each station as though I was being assaulted, the flounder book leaped out of my hands.

Audrey was there when I got home.

She had time to hang around, allowing slow afternoons to slip into early evenings with a gin and tonic. She had joined several yoga courses, beginners and advanced. I was used to women in leggings coming through the house, slipping through the kitchen to the bathroom at the back. The outlines of Audrey's salmon-pink leggings were more intimidating in a confined space. She kept looking to see if I was looking.

Her husband John came to join us after work. Four of us having a bottle of wine. Audrey sat in a cross-legged position on the floor, with her back to the bookcase. John sat in the armchair with his legs stretched out, wearing a tweed jacket. Helen spoke about expanding her yoga courses, she was intending to get a brochure printed and John offered to take the promotional photos, no charge. He was a good photographer, he had shown me his darkroom, mostly it was Audrey in a swimsuit with their daughter Lucinda, on a beach in the west.

We got talking about London.

They had both lived there for a while. John spoke about parties he had been to, he mentioned several poets and rock stars, famous artists. Audrey said she would love to be painted nude. John said he was at a party where a well-known beat poet turned up and took off his clothes, the only person sitting naked on the sofa, in winter.

We were impressed.

Helen talked about how she had lived in a tiny bedsit in Kensington where you could reach everything from your bed. She had once gone to visit the house where the American poet Sylvia Plath killed herself in a rage of self-doubt. There was a plaque on the wall, she said, to let people know that Yeats had once lived there, nothing about Sylvia Plath. There was a telephone box nearby, but it was hard to be sure it was the one the poet used to make the final call to her husband.

She spoke about sitting in a café with her coat open, her black beret across the back of her head, some drops of rain like beads attached. She stared out the fogged-up window at the people of London with their umbrellas. In a copy-book full of notes on her drama course, monologues and reported speech, she began reconstructing what Sylvia Plath might have put into her missing diary, the last one, the one that was burned – my love was a bite, you will dig up my bones and sell them off for souvenirs.

Audrey and John were both older than us, over thirty, full of knowledge. Audrey spoke with expertise about Sylvia Plath and her English husband, the poet Ted Hughes. She said Plath was jealous of her husband's fame as a poet long before he left her for another woman. She drove him to it, she was obsessed, it was artistic jealousy.

Had she stayed alive, John said, she would have become a great novelist.

My wooden mouth began to speak up. Why did Sylvia Plath hate her German father? Was she not allowed to love him? Afraid to be associated with him, his beekeeping knowledge, calling him Daddy in a cynical voice, placing him on trial for grotesque Nazi crimes he could never have committed because he had already gone to live in the USA. Was this her way of fitting in with the world gathering of poets? Disowning her own father? Disowning his history? Disowning herself? Did this love/hatred for her own father ultimately keep her locked out?

The conversation turned back to jealousy. John said it was a primitive emotion – shows lack of courage.

Foolish instinct, Audrey agreed.

John said – good to remain open-minded. Why break your own heart?

Audrey boasted quite openly that her marriage to John was based on a pact of non-jealousy. They allowed each other maximum freedom, she said. It was important to be receptive to new ideas. Free love. Their relationship was unrestricted. John listened with his legs apart while Audrey told us how he had gone ahead one evening, kissing another woman in the back of a taxi. Coming home from a party, he began snogging the woman while she was right there on the other side of him. She had nothing against it, only that the woman's husband was a pure horror. It was not a fair exchange.

My God, she said, his stomach was practically fermenting every time he opened his mouth.

They smiled at each other.

We said nothing. Our lives seemed so ordinary. Their lives seemed so cool, so confident, more like writers' lives, full of inspiration and reckless ways of doing things for the sake of adventure.

A week later, when the recording sessions came to an end, I brought the singer and the backing musicians to the pub on the corner. The money to pay for drinks in the native language was called welcoming. Drinking was done in little drops.

They talked mostly about music. They said there was nothing like a traditional music session in full swing, it was an animal running, a buffalo, a stampede. The music was so vibrant it left you standing, it rocked you on your feet, it lifted you up by the armpits and held you dangling in the air, all you could do was yelp.

They said there was a subtle hierarchy in the music. It broke out in a high-speed duel, then it calmed down again like a slow bicycle race, the last player to reach home was the best. All musicians admired each other and feared each other and stole from each other. They had a way of elevating and diminishing each other with humorous understatement. A nod was the safest way of showing appreciation. Praise was a delicate thing, it could easily be overdone, a word too much could turn it into a snub. They got into a debate about who was the best flute player in the country. They drew up a shortlist of celebrated names, minutely comparing the way each player performed a reel called the Bucks of Oranmore. They mentioned a flute player from Mayo and finally agreed that he was the most outstanding of them all. One of them over-agreed and went a bit further. Not only was the Mayo man the best in the country, he was also bald – he's the best of the bald flute players.

We laughed.

They spoke about a well-known uilleann piper with a lung condition. The piper suffered from what was called chronic pulmonary obstruction. He was separated from his wife in London and had come back to live in a caravan outside Dublin. She sent his X-ray after him. A friend met him in a pub to pass on the bad news, handing him a large envelope with the name of the London hospital, do not bend. The piper ignored the message from his former wife. He put the envelope containing the X-ray aside on the bar counter. He was thin as a lead pencil. He had a soft nasal voice, a vast musical memory. His favourite drink was milk and whiskey. It was only much later in the evening that he finally took out the X-ray to have a look. He held it up to the smoky light above the bar and examined the ominous shadows like an accusation that followed him home. He paused for a moment and said – Ah look, they're not my lungs at all.

We laughed again.

I laughed more than anyone else.

How can you deny your own lungs?

The shadow singer began talking about America. About the great blues singers he had met, all the train songs he had learned from them. The blues were inside us all, he said. It was the same foot tapping in every country. The Irish brought their culture with them, it got mixed up with African American roots, French roots, German roots, it was part of the anatomy of America, the music goes across the world and comes back home again.

He took a small harmonica from his back pocket. He rubbed it against the front of his jacket. He placed it up to his lips and blew a mouthful of shuffled notes. The pub went silent. With the instrument held in his fingers and the light overhead flashing off the steel casing, he sang a train song. His chest filled up without losing a word, nowhere could I find where he inhaled. It was hard to believe the power in his lungs without amplification, he had us standing with our backs to the wall.

He left the harmonica behind on the bar counter. I brought it with me. I was keeping it for him.

When I got home, Helen was sitting with her knees up in the armchair. Spread out on the table was a series of photographs. They were printed in large format, black-and-white, done professionally with white borders. Moody, natural light, out of focus wallpaper, the edges of a plant maybe. In some of the photographs, she was wearing black leggings, the V-neck of her T-shirt revealed a spray of freckles. In other photographs she was wearing a white blouse, staring out the window. The light was coming through the fabric.

I looked into her eyes.

She had told me in advance that she was getting the photos done. It was not like me to go against her, only to encourage her. I didn't want her freedom to be my weakness. I didn't want her to be trapped in a foreign country like my mother was, not allowed to have friends, having to call my father in the office to make every decision in life, describing what a good pair of shoes looked like and why they were worth two pairs of bad shoes.

I gathered the photographs and put them away in a large envelope. I could not bear to look at them, the silvery silence around her shoulders. I wanted to erase the room in which they were taken.

I had no language for these things between us.

My wooden mouth started saying things I did not want to believe. She was there all afternoon. The photographer kept circling around her with his camera. He took off his tweed jacket. His voice filled the room. He lit up a joint and passed it to her. He began to describe each detail of her body with great precision, her neck, her shoulders, the shape of her knees, he spoke of her freckles, her weightless hands, her mouth, her lips, he spoke of the sweet breath under her arms.

I saw her with a surge of longing. I thought I would pass out. I thought I would piss without warning. My stomach was empty, my vision was blurred, I felt sick. I wanted to pick her up and crush her against me. Was it love? Was it desire? Was it pride? Was it dispossession? Some illusion of ownership? My mind was gone hard with naked body parts. A cubist mess of open mouths and spaces between legs and clothes lying around.

My teeth were screaming.

With the best will in the world, the dentist had been wasting his time. The trouble with my teeth had nothing to do with my teeth. It was never my teeth. My teeth were being falsely accused. I was holding them responsible for the consortium of languages trying to cross my lips all at once and getting nothing said. The mismatch, the misconstrued, the naturally occurring blasphemies, the last-minute retractions, the trapdoor between the words. My teeth were being blamed for all that was unspoken. For the river of emotion that never reached the room. For all the deepest meaningful things I wanted to express but which were trapped in a parallel medium. It was like blaming light particles for the silence, like time being held to account for emptiness, my teeth were innocent bystanders. They did not cause the glass breaking absence of words. By not charging me for his work, the dentist was disclaiming all responsibility for the silence, louder than ever, breaking out with such deafening force.

I walked out the door. This is what I had been doing since the age of nine, walking away from my father and his language wars, walking away from my mother and her burning cities. I turned right, past the furniture auction rooms. I came to the redbrick terraced house. The lights were still on, the room upstairs with the embossed sword design in the wallpaper, the painting of lions, the chessboard laid out.

Don't ruin us, I shouted at the windows.

My glass mouth was back. I continued up the hill, walking away from myself.

★

Where did all this doubt come from?

Did it come from my father? The doubt of nations. The jealousy of flags and memorials and trenches and stolen lands and lost wars and languages in flight. Love divided into parcels of territory. Love with borders. Love with fortified defences and checkpoints and barbed wire and watchtowers and walls ten-foot high. All the hurt minds of time, all that restless ethnic grievance since the start of civilisation frothing inside my head.

Or did it come from my mother?

Did she pass on to me the feeling of coming home and never arriving? The memory of places left behind. Her need to go back and pick up the past. Her instinct for imagining the worst? Thinking through every mistake in advance, revising every mistake behind her, unable to return.

I remembered her once getting ready to leave, packing her suitcase, telling us that she was going home, it was all a mistake. My father made her life so difficult. She sat down and told me that when she first arrived in Ireland off the boat early one morning, she stood in the empty hallway not sure if she was going to stay. She was already married, already expecting her first baby. She was afraid to take off her coat. My father had to persuade her to stay by saying there was nothing left in Germany only ruined cities. She was just a bit homesick, he told her. He kept her from going with German music rising all the way up to the roof. She agreed to stay for one night because she had nowhere else to go. In a dream that night, she heard her first baby boy speaking her language – please, don't go.

She loved Ireland. She loved us with all her heart. She loved all those things that made no sense, the words out of place, her history mixed up with ours, her language mushed in with the shadow language and some prohibited words borrowed from the street. She loved the sea, it was like being on holidays, but she found it hard to adapt. She once tried to make friends with the country by sending a cake to West Cork, but my father refused to take it with him – did his relatives not like cake?

Did she marry him to make up for something in the past? His limp? His birth deformity balancing up her own failures? His weakness giving space to her kindness?

My father must have feared her doubt. The power it had over him. The power he had over her when she didn't leave. Did he worry a lifetime that she might change her mind, his raging energy, the damp and confused country he belonged to? Is that what made him so tough and impatient, one soft foot and one hard foot, so eager to remake Ireland more like Germany, letting his West Cork accent disappear in her language? Did he devote his life to an impossible goal, turning himself into the German man of her expectations, putting on Mahler, planting apple trees, making wooden toys, paying enormous excise duty on goods imported from Germany. Limping like a man after war, carrying wrought iron Christmas tree stands under his arm that nobody could afford to buy?

Everything to keep her from leaving.

His love, his wild-hearted plans fell short in a temper, knowing that he was unable to replace what she missed most – her father, her mother, her sisters, the house on the market square. He did his best to recreate her country inside the house, we were her citizens, we knew the map of her town better than our own, we knew the way to her bakery. She sat with her back to the window in the top room listening to us speaking German, the direction of the afternoon sunlight lined up with her memory, throwing an oblong box across the wooden floor. It allowed her to imagine being at home, children playing around the fountain at the centre of the market square.

And the bells.

More than anything, the evening bells bursting into every corner of the room, under the beds and into the wardrobe, down the stairs into the kitchen, liquid bells filling up the house until she could hear nothing at all, the sound of steel took away her voice.

I thought of her singing her favourite song. The song she was not allowed to sing while my father was alive, because it was in English, his forbidden language. The song about flowers in your hair and gentle people waiting there. She had no problem using the term love-in. Her accent was like a passenger ship going straight from Hamburg to San Francisco.

Stay or leave.

The decision she had to make every day of her life.

Late one night, she told me what happened. What I already half knew as a child, what we saw in her eyes, what she had tried to tell me a couple of times before. While I was helping her up the stairs, before Greta came and put her to bed, she stopped on the landing by the copper etching of her town with the spire of the church gone grey. She told me what she had never told anyone before, none of her sisters, none of her children, not my father, not even in confession, only to her diary.

She is alone in Düsseldorf with no friends, nobody to talk to, living in an apartment block where people keep to themselves. They have sons at war, they talk about where to get food, they have pictures of Hitler in their living rooms. They admire her boss when he comes to visit, she hears him coming up the stairs, he has the authority to force himself into her room. Her objections will not be taken seriously. The neighbours smile, they shrug and make crude hand signals, they enjoy the covert story of an older, married man in a suit, calling to see a young woman alone at night, holding flowers.

He sits down and tells her she has lovely hair, he praises her modern clothes, he would like to see her smile.

The flowers in the room are toxic. She can do nothing to stop him, he is too strong, he is a member of the Nazi party and she is not. He says it is a time of sacrifice. He talks about the war, what bravery the men have shown in Stalingrad, locked in the cauldron, giving up their lives so the Reich can endure. He talks about the greatness of the Nazi empire, the endless bleeding borders. Her beauty has become part of that battle, he tells her, it is her womanhood the men have been defending with their hands and feet frozen black, faces wrapped in thin scarves stuffed with newspapers, shivering out the last Christmas of their lives, writing letters that never reach home. It is her duty to smile for Germany, for the fallen comrades in Stalingrad, for the glory and survival of their race.

She refuses to give her smile.

How can she decline, he says, she has such an ability to make people happy, why not light up the room? Look at the flowers, do they refuse to smile? Once again, she shakes her head, keeping her expression of happiness contained, her face remains full of fear. Raising his voice, he commands her to be joyful. He steps across the room and puts his hands on her face to extract a smile, with his fingers he pulls her lips apart to show her teeth.

Next morning, she is forced to face him in the office, he asks her where the smile is gone, but she cannot find it, she has already unlearned it.

Some months later, she stands in front of him once more in the office to let him know that she is expecting a baby. There is nobody else she can turn to but the man who has overpowered her. He says he is glad she has come to him, he appreciates her loyalty, he takes it as a show of love. He tells her not to speak to anyone else, to trust only in him, he has a way of dealing with this situation.

She has her coat on, waiting in the small upstairs room in Düsseldorf with the air-raid sirens howling in the streets. A deep sound of aircraft humming, followed by anti-aircraft guns, followed by whistling, the ground shaking, every sound measured to see how close it has come. Everyone else has gone to the air-raid shelters. The lights are out across the city. She waits with the sounds of falling bombs around her, until her boss comes to the door with a small case in his hand, no more than a round pouch with a handle.

He warns her to keep this to herself. What they are about to do is a crime against Hitler. He makes it clear to her that they are going to kill one of Hitler's babies. He tells her to be quiet, stop crying, lie down. With the help of a small flashlight, he takes various items out of the medical case and prepares them on the table, the shape of his hands projected onto the wall like giant gloves. She asks him where he got this stuff, he says he has it from a reputable doctor, be still, don't turn on the light. She lies on the bed in her room, with the buildings in flames around her, the fire services out, shouts along the street, people screaming their fear, grief laid open to the night sky. Her boss administers the injection like a giant bee-sting.

He tells her to lie still and wait for him.

She is on the floor by the time he returns. There is a burly man with him, they carry her down the stairs like a bomb victim. Nobody can tell the difference. They cross the street, she cannot stand, there is a house on fire, flames in the windows, the smell of phosphor and household things burning. They carry her to a parked car, she retches and leaves a stain on her boss's suit, next to his party badge. Money is passed over. She is bleeding heavily. The driver spreads out sheets of newspaper on the back seat. There is an argument, more money is passed over. Finally, the driver helps to put her lying across into the back seat and drives off. Her boss stands on the street taking out his handkerchief, not to wave goodbye, but to wipe the stain off his jacket.

She gave me his name – Stiegler.

Have I become trapped by this knowledge? I am her story, her diary, the keeper of her nightmare?

The light came across the hill to face me. The gravel under my feet was the sound of trespassing. On a stone bench, I sat down and drew up my collar. The air coming into my lungs was like a window left open. The bay was spread out before me, I heard the waves below on the beach, the mountain was shaped like a volcano.

This was the place where we walked on Sundays, nowhere else could have so much power to repair the world. It was a long way for my father to go with his limp, but he knew it made my mother happy. She looked across the blue bay and took in a deep breath. Behind us, the gorse hill with the stone eagle. Where we once heard a dog barking and my mother told us it was not a dog but an owl.

The wide bay helped her to fall in love with the country that adopted her. She pronounced the word beautiful in a way that made this the most extraordinary place on earth. The word was reserved mostly to describe children and landscape. Children's eyes, the truth in children's drawings, the colour of their cheeks, the copper glow of gorse, the white collar of foam along the beach.

This was the view that stopped her from leaving.

Was it enough to keep me?

I made my way down the laneways to the small harbour where I used to work in the summer. It held on to the smell of fish and seaweed, the perfume of women coming to buy lobster, pointing out the dark blue creature still alive with elastic bands around its claws, soon to turn boiling red. Trawlers were coming in, gulls were moving across the bay to the north, maybe a landfill site.

By the time I got back, it was bright. Helen was there, sitting in the car outside. She was parked on the street, opposite the furniture showrooms. The children were staying with my mother, my sister Greta had taken them to the cinema. We should have been alone together, but instead I spent the night walking, she drove around looking for me.

Helen, I said. What are you doing here?

I opened the car door. She didn't move.

Have you been here all night?

She stepped out of the car. She stood in the street, looking at the house where we lived as though she could never re-enter, like a part of her life had now gone into the past and she was unable to return. Everything appeared false in the yellow street light. The walls a cream coat of silicone, the windows made of black plastic bags, the door an orange sponge.

I brought her inside. I took her coat off. I put the fire on and waited for her to speak.

She sat on one side of the empty room, underneath the window, her back to the wall. I sat on the far side. We stared at each other. Outside, the house fronts were back to their pale colours, the leaves on the palm trees a dull green.

She took in a deep breath and composed herself. She turned her head to face the fire.

You can walk away now, she said.

I said nothing.

We'll be fine, she said.

Fine? What do you mean?

Me and the girls, she said. We'll make it. I don't want you to go. I love you to the end of the world. But I won't stop you.

I had no answer to that?

You never speak, she said. It's like we live apart in different countries from each other. Sometimes I don't know who you are, your silence is so hard for me. Look at you now, I don't know your mind. It feels like you have been self-deported somewhere into exile, we'll starve without words. If you don't speak you're not there.

I'm here, I said.

Don't leave me slowly, she said. Don't keep leaving me for the rest of my life.

The passengers going by on the early bus into the city could see us separated from each other, an empty football field between us. The green carpet, the fire, the poster of a stork carved in stone, the door left ajar, her knees, her feet, everything was up close.

I've got to go, she said.

She stood up and went to the kitchen. I heard her bare feet on the tiled floor. I heard the kettle swelling up. I heard her getting into the shower. She had the need to move on. Somebody had to get the children and bring them to school.

Appointments to be kept. Down the hall came the sound of water, the scent of shampoo. In the kitchen, there was a cup of tea on the table, a slice of toast still in the toaster. She came out of the bathroom with a towel over her head. She buttered the slice of toast and took a bite, followed by a sip of tea, then she continued drying her hair under the towel, bending forward with the bra strap across her back.

The radio was on in the background. Soft words telling me the time, the traffic news, a tree down in Kerry.

I stood in the door of the bathroom while she was putting on her make-up. I was still waiting for her to answer my question, holding out for a piece of absolute truth. She was staring into the mirror up close, applying some eye-shadow, covering up the lack of sleep. The towel was draped around her neck like a boxer. She finally spoke to me across her shoulder, still facing the mirror, as though she was speaking to herself. Her voice was cheerful, up-beat, full of resumption, what she was saying was like part of the make-up she was putting on.

Do you remember the river? she asked.

She continued concentrating on her eyes. She spoke as though it was something practical, something from a list of things we should not forget during the day.

Remember, she said, coming back from the islands, that time we were standing by the river in Galway? The brown water frothing? Like something you could put in a glass and drink? Do you remember saying that?

Was she trying to distract me? The whole business of make-up, the eye-shadow, the subtle colour on her cheeks to soften the few freckles, the hint of lipstick hardly notice-able. This was the story of herself she was making up. The construction of her life, the truth she was going out with.

Remember staring at the water, she said. We saw a plastic bottle trapped by the bridge? Our minds were gone to mush, watching the bottle going around and around in circles for ages. Remember that? A boy on a bike stopped to see what we were looking at, remember, I pointed to the bottle rotating. And the boy couldn't work out what we were so interested in. He kept looking at us and looking down at the bottle going around in a helpless loop, wonder-ing how we could be so happy staring at nothing?

She turned to face me for a moment and smiled – do you remember that?

Of course, I said.

I could remember staring at the water rushing by, the froth, the sound, at times we almost forgot the water was moving and the river stood still, then it resumed in full flow, louder than ever. I could not remember the boy. Or the bottle. Only the feeling of being carried along.

She put her arms around my neck. She kissed me and drew back to look into my eyes. She ran her hand under my shirt and said the words for love that I gave her in the native language – bolg le bolg.

I heard the car starting. The smell of toast, a whiff of perfume in the hall, the radio repeating the same news. I stared at the cup of tea she left behind and tried to piece together the person she was – her breath, her frown, her mistakes, her belongings, her letters, the stick of salt she got from her father, the stolen spoon from Berlin, a galaxy of memory and human fabrication.

She is an actor, I said to myself. A method actor. Trained in London, at the Royal College of Speech and Drama. She belonged to a small backstreet theatre in Dublin, worked in the Stanislavsky system, she has done Strindberg. She can fake her own story. She is good at keeping things to herself. Good at keeping things from herself.

Her family comes from a country of actors.

Her mother pronounces the word beautiful with her hand on her heart. It's given a musical lift. The beginning of a song, it makes people stop and admire the beauty of the word itself. They unite in appreciation of something that is better and more beautiful than anything ever seen before, like a piece of porcelain only brought out on special occasions.

It's in their bones, that magnetic quality, the guilt-free smile, they show the honest face and conceal the honest heart. They are good at making things up, good at not answering like they're in the witness box. They wear the truth like a coat, you can leave it open, you can fold it up and put it on the windowsill of a pub, you can bring it back to the shop and swear it was never worn once, you can get it altered, you can put it over the bed at night like an extra blanket when it's cold.

Her grandmother loved nothing better than the fun of getting away without paying, bus fares, groceries, a full chicken hidden underneath her coat like she was pregnant at eighty, she liked to tell people she was related to the Bishop in Donegal, she went to work at the Irish Sweepstakes wearing a child's pink sunglasses, one lens missing, nothing wrong, just to see what they would say.

Her mother has two oil paintings of a Dutch couple in the living room, bought for nothing at a house clearance in Donegal, she tells everyone in Canada it's her ancestors, nobody can verify this in a foreign place. Nobody around to say the gilded oval paintings are of King Billy, William of Orange and his wife, what Catholic Irish family commissions portraits of themselves around the time of the Famine?

Her uncle in London is a caretaker, he had a great career in the Bank of Ireland before he suddenly left and took up a job in property management, he calls it. The portraits of King Billy and his wife originally belonged to him, kept against rent arrears. With nothing left he decided to renounce all wealth and material possessions, the only thing on the wall of his basement flat in London is the portrait of a boy prince, which turns out to be the lid of a chocolate box.

Her aunt in Wicklow is doing her best to become Jewish, but she has run into difficulty because none of her ancestors are anything but devout Catholics from Donegal. Now she has joined a bible group instead, Rosie and Essie say there is lots of singing and shaking in their house, hands on heads.

Her uncle in Birmingham likes to tell everyone there is something he needs to get off his chest which he has never revealed to anyone, not even to his wife before she died. He keeps everyone waiting, never reveals anything. He tells us instead how he once invited his boss and the other colleagues to his house along with their wives and gave them no drink, no dinner, just tea with slices of bread and jam – anyone for more bread. Just to watch the discomfort on their faces, the relief when he laughed and finally brought out the whiskey.

Her uncle in France worked in a gold mine in South Africa where he witnessed employees being stripped and beaten, he brought the violence home to his family. He has a lonely job travelling around France as a salesman for sports clothing. He can't stop making jokes, his language is full of poetic mistakes, they love him, they think he's funny, but nobody laughs like they do back home in his own country.

The aunt with the bunch of keys tells everyone she is a trained opera singer, she gives a high note and stops with a delicate cough, patting the gloves across her chest. She was disqualified from nursing for throwing a student nurse down the stairs, twice, Helen told me. She is full of generosity and getting the better of people, pro-life and anti-divorce. She can flirt with the wall. She comes visiting out of the blue, looking around the rooms while Helen is out, asking me questions with the keys rattling in my face – we have ways of making you talk. She looks me up and down, asking which half of me is German and which half is Irish. And what is my position in the native basement, she wants to know, am I managerial, and how are the yoga classes going, how many people can you pack into a front room no bigger than a laundry basket, what about the safety regulations? The children love her, she brings sweets and she asks them all the questions I cannot answer.

She is the left-behind version of Helen's mother, what her mother would have become if she had stayed in Ireland. They have the same laugh, the same hourglass figure, the same way of saying the word beautiful, the same handbag carried on a lateral arm under the breasts to hold everything in. Two sisters measured against each other like two sides of a decision, the reflected image of luck and lost opportunities. When Helen's mother qualified as a nurse, the aunt with the keys tried to suffocate her with a pillow. When she bought a bright canary-yellow dress to celebrate, the aunt with the keys bought the exact same dress, people could not tell them apart. When she got married to a man from Carrick-on-Shannon, the aunt with the keys ran off and got married to his brother.

So – two brothers married two sisters in canary yellow trying to outdo each other. Duplicate families in Ireland and Canada, founded on a bet to see which of them got the better brother and which of them could have the most children and which was the better country. A lifelong contest between the sister who left and the sister who stayed, which of them has the highest score of lawyers and doctors, who is having the last laugh, who has the funniest stories.

The aunt in Ireland was rattling the keys to a house she never owned. Her husband walked out. She moved many times. Never sitting in her own furniture. Unfamiliar kitchens, meaningless curtains, only the tea towels with home and shamrocks on them, enamel serving trays with a cottage home sweet home. She faked her own death. She was found on her back one day, legs out, one shoe half off. One arm was laid out underneath the coffee table, some magazines swept onto the floor and a glass of water soaking into the rug. Her curly hair was brilliantly arranged to fall across one eye like a murder victim, the keys in a fallen bunch some inches away out of her hand. As they crouched around to feel her pulse, she jumped up and laughed out loud – what took you so long?

I believed them all.

They lived somewhere between truth and invention, full of twisting and joking and theatrical deflection, converting themselves into stories.

I went to work. I got the newspaper from the vendor at the station, but I couldn't read. The facts refused to transfer. I sat at my desk in the basement all day, staring at the pen in my hand, looking up now and again to see the feet of pedestrians passing by above my head. At lunchtime, I went out briefly to the park of lovers and ate my sandwich, the same tasteless two slices of brown bread with cheese.

I could not stay awake. I answered the phone in a drowsy voice. People passing by on the street could see my head down over my desk, long after everyone had gone home.

I got back late. After dinner I left the house again without a word. I turned right past the furniture showrooms, down as far as the redbrick terrace. Audrey answered the door. She smiled and brought me upstairs. She showed me into the sitting room and threw herself on the sofa. She picked up a book, not reading, only smiling and watching. One knee was bent up, her bare thigh was showing. I looked away at the painting of lions roaming free among the fallen columns, the sculpture of the man walking, cushions laid out in a circle on the rug.

The dog came to sniff me, then he curled up on a blanket near the window. The chessboard was laid out. John came in with beer and we began to play.

Nothing was said.

There was a twitch in his right shoulder. A subconscious shrug, shaking something off. It made him look guilty. Maybe a bit homeless. One of those fidgety movements that actors put on in Beckett plays. A quirk to make themselves look more idiosyncratic, more internal, happier having their sandwiches alone in graveyards, they should try a day underground in a ghost language.

Audrey got up to answer the phone.

She had begun offering yoga classes. In direct competition with Helen. She wanted to take Helen's place. She wanted to have Helen's voice. In her London accent she said all the things Helen said, what yoga was good for, weight loss, lower-back pain, fatigue, migraine, menstrual cramps, insomnia, everything you can think of, really. She took down a name, gave the details, the number of sessions, payment in advance, bring a towel and some light clothing, leggings are best.

She put down the phone and disappeared into the kitchen, into the bedroom, it was hard to tell.

The dog got up and followed her out.

I was unable to concentrate. I made poor decisions. John looked up from the chessboard and caught me shrugging my shoulder. It was not my intention to mock him. The more he stared at me the more I shrugged.

If only I could speak my mind. If only I had brought the mouth carving with me. I could have placed it on the chess-board, right in the middle, in between the pieces, the open mouth facing him without fear – I didn't come here to play chess. I'm here to break something. I'm here to cut you off.

He got up and went out to the kitchen for more beer.

While the room was empty, I stood up. I saw the phone on a small wooden table with a green library lamp. Beside it, the notepad with the recently entered name and phone number. There was a letter opener lying next to the pen. I picked it up like a dagger in a Shakespeare play. I grabbed the cable connecting the phone to the socket in the wall and began to cut the wire. It felt like cutting through the rubbery tail of a rat. The letter opener was not sharp enough. It took ages, it squeaked, like the animal was alive in my hand, refusing to die. It produced a small ring, somebody calling in response to the ad in the paper and changing their mind at the last minute. Maybe a journalist with some news story, not all that urgent.

Was this my only way of speaking? The letter opener turned into a utensil for communication? It was hard to know if what I was doing even mattered. Would it be noticed? Would it make any difference? Maybe it was nothing more than a symbolic gesture I was after, severing contact, putting an end to this treacherous friendship.

I looked around and saw the dog standing behind me. He had quietly come back into the room without me hearing a thing. He stood no more than two feet away, his eyes friendly and hostile at the same time, as if he was expecting me to give him something, an explanation for what I was doing.

The silver dagger threw back a flash of light from the big window. I saw my reflection. I was being watched by myself, standing in a large room with a weapon in my hand and the dog a witness. I heard them talking to each other in the kitchen. Her book was left upturned on the sofa, the roof of a cottage. A dip in one of the cushions where her elbow had been. The chessboard was stalled in mid-game. I was unable to get back to my chair while the dog blocked my way. Without altering my position, I reached over and replaced the letter opener beside the notepad, neatly in line with the pen. The dog watched every movement with a tilt of his head. I tried to move but he moved with me. I remained in that helpless situation for a moment. All I could think of doing was to point across the room and the dog finally walked away, returning to his place by the window. It allowed me to get back to the chessboard. My face was red, my teeth were clamped.

I could not stop shrugging.

John came back, we resumed playing. A loud fizz of beer bursting inside my ears.

The remorse was instant. It was one of those things that felt right for a moment and triggered off the inevitable supply of guilt. Only a failed artist will act out his rage.

I began thinking about war.

My mind could not hold back the images of houses on fire, people running, sirens whining, the ruins of a bombed-out building. I did my best to snap out of it, but the uncensored run of details kept coming. I found myself thinking of a book in which a couple make love in London during the Blitz, a bomb destroys the house around them, they walk away with their faces white, hardly sure they are alive. Or maybe love in wartime made you more alive than ever. I remembered the apartment block where I lived with Helen in Berlin, the days people spent in the basement taking shelter from the bombing raids numbered on the walls. I remembered my mother standing in the garden with the laundry basket looking up at a low flying aircraft passing overhead. The terror in her voice as she told me how the sound comes from under the earth, it's only at the last minute you can tell it's from the sky. I remembered the photographs I had seen of Berlin in the library, an open mouth full of bad teeth, nothing but screaming stumps.

I thought of a town destroyed by a car bomb. At a wreath laying ceremony for the dead of the First World War. I thought of my father banning the commemorative poppy from the house, even though his own father died in the British navy. My German grandfather was on the opposite side of the same war, two grandfathers fighting each other without ever meeting. Will the first world war ever come to an end? Soldiers underground in Ypres and the Somme fighting the same battles into infinity, never allowed to be dead, forced to die over and over, every year. It must be the hardest thing, grieving for your enemies. I could only imagine a time when the Remembrance Day poppy would take on a more forgiving blend of colours. Poppies with a mixture British and Irish and German flags together, a wreath of combined enemies laid at the Cenotaph.

I thought of a story I had read about two lovers somewhere in America secretly meeting in a bar one night when a man sitting beside them takes out a small box containing the remains of a human ear. Every love affair leads back to a silent moment of cruelty deep in the green foliage of Vietnam. The man with the shrunken human trophy was letting the lovers know how close they had come to being immortal. He was showing them how much they were still alive, how human, how full of body parts we all are.

I stood up and said I would let myself out.

John smiled and shook my hand, he didn't get up.

The dog followed me as far as the door, then he was called back with a click and I went down the stairs.

It was not until I got all the way down and reached the hall that I heard Audrey calling after me. She stood on the top landing, her face was framed by the bend in the bannister rail, a floating head, her hair hanging forward. Her eyes seemed full of tragedy, concern, maybe regret. Like there was part of the bargain not fulfilled. The exchange was incomplete. I was running from an unspoken promise. Her voice took the shortest route, falling through the stairwell like a coin dropping straight down with a spinning glint. Bouncing on the floor of the hall and rolling towards me, coming to a stop at my feet.

What have you done?

I didn't reply.

I heard them talking to each other. The light was spilling down the stairs. Her face was replaced by his face in the bannister bend. He called down, telling me to come back. His voice kept me in the hall, trapped by my crime. The bark of the dog echoed through the house. I heard his feet coming down the stairs, his speed of thought leaping the last half dozen steps, sliding along the polished wooden floor.

I heard the door closing behind me, I heard it open again, I heard the steel gate clang in my hand, I heard the dog running along the gravel path.

I heard my name called after me. My name catching up, hurling itself in the shape of a dog through a gap between two parked cars, following me in a panting run as far as the corner. I continued running. I slowed down along the seafront. The streets were full of accusation. The lighthouse was pointing the finger. The beam went searching all around the bay and came back each time to point directly at me.

Helen was in bed when I got back. She didn't ask me where I had been. I told her nothing. Talking would have turned our love into a courtroom.

Audrey continued teaching yoga classes, poaching clients. She had the edge, a big room with lots of space, good heating, good art, the chessboard laid out on a side table, cushions placed around the floor. No loud buses passing close by only metres away outside the window. We saw her on the street, walking with her head high, the dog didn't recognise me. At the furniture auction, she put her hand up for a Persian rug, we heard her name being called out.

I brought the hard-backed envelope with the photographs of Helen to work with me. They became part of the native basement production line. I arranged meetings with graphic designers and printers to get the yoga brochure made up. They must have heard the emotion in my voice while I was talking about the size of the print run, the density of the paper, card or laminate. A choking sensation rose in my throat when they made helpful suggestions on typeface, the spacing around the main image, bullet points on the back. No matter how much I tried to deepen my voice and make it sound more commanding, it remained in the upper ranges, elated, over-excited, short of words. The people I was doing business with were the greatest friends I ever had, I wanted to embrace them, the price didn't matter.

It was clear that the person in the photographs laid out across my desk was somebody I loved and could not afford to lose. I wanted this to be the best brochure ever printed. To me it was a piece of art.

They came back with a mock-up for my approval. There was a problem with the first batch, Helen too black, Helen too pale, Helen with demonic eyes like a burned-out rock singer, reject brochures on the floor of the printing works with people walking on her face. When they delivered the finished product, I sat at my desk for hours holding the brochure in my hand, she kept her name – Helen Boyce.

Some months later, in the supermarket below ground, I ran into Audrey by chance. She was with her daughter, Lucinda. It was the London voice that made me look up. We were both going for peanut butter, crunchy, but she changed her mind and smiled out of politeness, withdrawing her hand. She caught me judging her by the items in her shopping basket, oven chips, pet food, my basket included cartons of juice with straws, a couple of intimate things Helen asked me not to forget, the lives of shopping baskets.

By then, her husband John had gone to live with a young Polish woman, we heard.

Was I part of their break-up?

The redbrick house was sold, she had gone to live in a new suburb. She must have returned in a moment of nostalgia to do her shopping near the sea, unable to drop the established routes. I was the last person she expected to see. The lighting in the supermarket was bad, the music was disturbing. She hurried away into detergents as though I was going to do something, when all I wanted was to wish her well. The words refused to come. My mouth was left at home.

I kept the shrug. I found myself shrugging for no reason at my desk in the basement, shrugging at lunchtime in the National Gallery as I opened the package with the two slices of brown bread and the slab of cheese. Shrugging furtively as I ate the sandwich with the gallery attendant keeping an eye on me. I was spending more time there, sitting in front of a nude bathing scene, a religious scene, the painting of a small girl sitting on the ground listening to a piper in another century.

It was a defensive thing. Shaking off the onlookers. Shaking off my doubt, my history, my languages, my family, my brothers and sisters, our open faces, our emotions on the surface. I was shaking off the people we were, our slow knowledge, the mixture of countries we came from.

Over time, the shrug gradually moved into my legs. It was hard to sit still, I was full of restless, electrical jolts. It kept me walking like a truant around the city, away from the dead basement.

Was I taking on my father's limp?

I was so busy shaking him off that I was becoming more like him. In the same way that Irish people were busy trying not to be British, and German people were trying not to be German, and British people were doing their best to stay British, I wanted to undo everything received from my father. I made sure not to wince. I taught myself not to inhale through my teeth, not to stick my tongue out the side of my mouth while concentrating, not to take fright at leaves moving in the street, not to pick up the phone as if it was a gunfight. I was the sum of things I could not allow myself to be. My aim was to appear less conscripted to where I came from, more the touring singer of sad songs I used to be in Berlin.

All these parts of myself I was avoiding.

I had no myself.

I became an impersonator. The emptiness of my composite being longed to take on the mannerisms of the latest person I met. I appropriated other people's traits, I took on a borrowed posture, anything to escape my own biography.

For an afternoon, I was the sales representative from the printing firm, his wink with both eyes was a natural piece of trust. Another day, I played with my watch, taking it off and putting it back on again, like the recording engineer. Getting off the train one morning, a man in front of me had such a fine rhythm in his walk, I followed him as far as the Custom House, I longed to slip into his place, sit at his desk, go back home to his family at the end of the day. I stepped in and out of lives, sampling human features like trying on a suit, constructing the person I wanted to become. I gave an outdoor yelp like the shadow singers did at the recording studios. I stamped my foot like a horse to show how much I loved the music. Whenever I was dealing with people who spoke in a Dublin accent I instantly broke into a Dublin accent to feel included. I wore clothes that matched the time, a second-hand jacket with a copper sheen in the fabric.

I admired the laughers. A man who laughed like a machine gun. A woman who spun like a washing machine. Another man appeared to be choking on the same piece of bread every night. The most powerful people were those who had the ability to withhold their consent, allowing the joke to die in thirst before their eyes, those who never laughed at themselves. My laugh was more like capitulation. Blushing like an animal betraying itself, turning red to announce my own fear, guilt, my slow mouth.

I did my best to get into the character of the country I was living in. I taught myself to speak without saying anything. I practised friendship. I found ways of slipping in and out of conversations unnoticed. I had no need to brag about being a good loser. No need for a great exit line.

I was the man who left the pub early without a word. At home, I had begun working on a new carving. This time it was an ear. Mahogany. Much harder wood to carve. It was not easy to get it anatomically correct. It took a long time before it finally went on display beside the carved mouth. It heard everything. It heard what people were thinking. What they were going to say before they said it. People in packed bars all around the country speaking with the sound turned down. It heard children asleep. It heard a book being read. It heard music coming from a long distance. Wind across the bogs. Water running by the side of the road. Voices underground.

What makes me so badly need friendship? I am either inside or outside, pulled into the sphere and left out again? Always arriving, never arriving. I step too close, not close enough. I find myself looking in, watching instead of being. I trust the story of a life more than the life itself. I trust the furniture in which a person has been sitting, the empty glass, the remains of a smile, the mark they leave on me.

The safest places are those where I am alone. I long to be unseen. Unknown. Unexplained. Un-found-out. In the park of lovers. In the National Gallery. On the streets, in motion. There is nothing better than the freedom of walking through the city, new and unrecognised.

Across the river at O'Connell Bridge where the photo of my father and his brother was taken by a street photographer, my mother's family said they were hoping it was the taller brother on the right. Past the woollen mills where she brought her sisters when they came over to visit. They turned the shop upside down, burying their faces in handwoven blankets, inhaling the wool like mountain air. The German excitement in their voices. Multiple packages tied up with white string carried under their arms as they went on a tour of cafés to find the best scone in Dublin, not the floury scone, not the papery scone, please, not the scone from yesterday heated up again.

Can I escape the landmarks of my childhood?

My former school, for example, with the railings and the basement pit full of rubbish and rat poison, where they once got my brother. Railings running alongside like a bad companion, muttering in my ear. I try to re-imagine the streets like a city planner, removing all the railings, how open the place could be, how calm and trusting and European. I satisfy myself with the thought of all railings being collected and brought out to be erected as a tower in the Phoenix Park, a monument of discarded separation.

Somewhere beside the Zoo, with the old signs with the finger pointing, left over from the empire. The empire in which my father grew up, my grandfather enlisted in the navy, before the landscape of West Cork lost its memory. I miss the country before I was born, I miss the place we come from, I miss the world before it was discovered.

Where possible, I avoid the General Post Office on the main street by going parallel along a side street, happier passing the spot where the uprising came to an end. I am more comfortable with surrender. Losing is the only way of winning. I have no interest in Croke Park, the national sporting arena, I am no better than my father in contest. Crowds make me feel excluded, or maybe they impose on me an obligation to be included – you have no right to be alone.

On the street of national surrender, I listen to the voices of the fruit vendors calling out the prices of oranges and bananas. I stand among them, at one of the stalls I buy an apple, the woman is disappointed, she wants me to take a dozen. I look at pears individually wrapped in paper, trays of tomatoes displayed at an angle with the price per dozen written out by hand. A bargain called out like the words of a song across the street, the echo coming back from the other end, a better offer. The vendors carry a range of traditional produce – oranges and apples, bananas, lemons, grapefruit, along with potatoes, cabbage and other vegetables. Year by year, they add a new fruit like kiwis. Now they are being joined by merchants selling varieties of fruit and vegetables never seen before. There is a demarcation in trade, the traditional vendors stick to their customary range of exotic produce while the newcomers bring in items such as plantain, chillies, lemongrass, lots of things for which there has previously been no demand.

At one of the stalls I get a strong scent of strawberries. I remember that smell all over the bus, the day my father brought us to the market early in the morning to buy fruit for making jam, boxes on the seats going home, the passengers smiled, the conductor took a raspberry. The labels on the jars had the name of the fruit abbreviated in German.

I walk to the central sorting office, with the looping railway line overhead. I stand watching vans driving in and out under the vast roof of the postal warehouse. I know the place well from a previous job at a newspaper where I had to collect a bag of mail every night at twelve o'clock, letters and cards from readers around the country emptied out on a wide table, entries to the crossword competition, entries to the spot the ball contest, cranky letters to the editor.

At one point, I find myself looking for Prussia Street, only because I like the name, it sounds promising, like it might be inhabited by people from another part of history, soldiers from Frederick the Great's army of giants. I have no idea how to get there, I would need directions.

At times, it feels as though I am making the city up out of my head. Creating streets that never existed before, a narrow alley of redbrick houses, no cars. The washing lines are out, every door is open, children on the street, a dog barking at me. I must look out of place, the women ask me am I lost, love? At the corner, I pass the wreck of a burned-out car, orange in colour, the springs in the seats showing. There is a Madonna and Child painted on the gable end wall, she has rosy cheeks, the child's face is larger and more adult looking, with penetrating eyes. At a corner pub, the men sitting at the bar turn to look at me when I go inside, it feels as though I have walked into somebody's living room. The barman asks me if I am all right. I tell him that I am looking for the rail yard.

One of the men wants to know if I am a tourist.

I hear them laughing.

At the rail yard, I speak to the man in charge of rolling stock about the possibility of buying a section of disused track. I explain to him that I want around two metres of track and a buffer stop, also one of those signal towers with the flap coming down, could I acquire one of those? I ask. One of those worthless projects I've had in mind, building something that has no function. He wants to know what it's for and I tell him it's for my children. I am going to buy a house and I am planning to put in a piece of railway in the front garden, allow it to get overgrown a bit. He doesn't say – you must be joking, railway tracks, in your garden? He can see that I'm serious, he takes my name and address, he will come back to me with a price.

My walk is getting me nowhere. The streets are unreliable. I am achieving nothing. Escaping nothing. Standing with my reflection in a pharmacy window at one point, I think – Dublin is like something going on behind your back.

I come across a house being renovated by the canal, the door is open, a cluster of names and bells, it must have been in flats. There is a yellow skip outside full of building rubble

— bits of splintered wood, a door at an angle, window frames, radiator units, a bath filled up with used bricks. It amazes me how much can be put into one skip. A worker comes out carrying a section of plywood partially painted blue, the unpainted patch must have had something leaning against it. He throws the sheet onto the skip and goes to open the boot of a car. I see him take out a can of beer and drink from it, the angle up to his mouth tells me how much is left. He waves his arm, I think he has seen me, but it's the truck coming to take the skip away.

I stay to watch the skip being removed. I hear the chains being attached. The front cab of the truck jumps a little as the weight of the skip is raised up on the loading arms, then it is slowly brought into position over the back of the truck and set down, sinking on the wheels. Green netting is thrown across the top and the truck drives away, leaving behind a new empty skip. There is something about the sight of disposal that appeals to me, I could stay watching all day, I draw a feeling of satisfaction from the idea of things being cleared out.

Disposal and clearing, I love that.

Crossing over the river again by the last bridge before the sea feels like a re-enactment. Every journey is going back over a previous one. The city is a repository of myself in past versions. A composite map of my route to school, to work, to the German library, to the National Gallery, the various interlinking pubs, would look like one of those long exposure photographs at night with a cluster of tail lights frozen in swaying red lines.

My route leads me up along Pembroke Street to the laneway with the small theatre. The theatre Helen belonged to. A small drama group with an improvisation school, no more than thirty seats in the auditorium. It's the last building, a flat roof, you could hear the rain falling during *Miss Julie*. The applause was like more rain. All the people in the audience gathered around after the performance with cups of tea and glasses of wine. The foyer was so small they had to keep their elbows in. Helen smiled and talked to everyone on the way through. I stood waiting for her to come out, she was wearing a black velvet jacket with the line of fake fur.

I have reached the end of the city. It takes me no further. The buildings are unchanged. The sound of traffic is no different, the lights, the windows, the succession of doors, the nearest pub, the direction we took. Our lives sneaking off down the street arm in arm.

Too late.

By the time I woke up, Rosie was on the floor in the hallway. She was trying to crawl but not moving. I got her up onto her feet and brought her into the front room to Helen. I ran to get the sick bowl and couldn't find it. Made a terrible clatter of pots and came back with a plastic container, but it was too late, she had already been sick in her bed. I wiped her face with a warm cloth. I gave her a sip of water to take away the bad taste in her mouth. Helen had her cuddled in her arms, saying everything was fine, telling her to think of something nice, the time she was a baby and we once stayed in a castle near Munich, she slept in a rocking basket from another century.

I went to change the sheets on Rosie's bed, I opened the window, I propped her mattress up vertically to dry, the dog next door must have heard the noise, he was barking. New sheets, new pillows, I dragged Essie's mattress into the front room, we could all sleep together, the stuffed toys came in as well. I went back to find where the sick bowl was, it was out in the garden, they had been using it to make perfume. There was a snail floating on top. I picked it out and transferred the perfume to the plastic container, then I brought the sick bowl into the front room, for the next emergency.

Why was she getting sick so often?

We took them to Glendalough the next day, but Rosie stopped speaking. She didn't want to hear any stories. She didn't like the mountains, didn't like the round tower, didn't want to see the lakes. Didn't want me to be the catcher when they climbed on the low arm of a tree. She got sick again in the car on the way back and I stood holding her by the side of the road. I bought a roll of kitchen towels and some disinfectant in a petrol station, the car smelled like an ambulance, we stopped for something to eat but nobody was hungry.

The barman left his thumbprint in the sandwich.

Helen made everything better when we got home, she set up a theatre for them in the hallway, by the public phone, props dragged out from the kitchen. Rosie was back to herself again. It was a big production, the play about a wedding in the lighthouse. The front door was open, the audience passing by the gate, the people upstairs crossed the stage on their way out.

Helen allowed them to use her clothes, her little black jacket with the fake fur. All those untouchable things from before she was a mother, things we kept out of sight, from ourselves. The bells, the broken snake, the stolen spoon, the weeping stick of salt from a Canadian mine, the detached plait of her hair made up when she went to boarding school, still intact, not a day older, like an amputated limb. All her Carnaby jewellery. They were dripping in necklaces. They put on wide summer hats that Helen wore in the Ontario heat but never found a reason to wear in Ireland, the wind would take them way.

The crêpe-de-Chine powder-blue skirt.

A full costume rehearsal of plundered memory. They wore everything with artistic innocence, defacing all previous meaning, they were borrowing her life, her backstory, stepping into her shoes.

I took a photograph of them by the door.

Children dressed as grown women. Rosie was the image of her grandmother in Canada, full of drama, one shoulder pressed forward, hands pointed flat out on either side like a dancer. Essie was looking straight and open, hands clasped, more like my mother, ready to ask what you were thinking. Rosie born in a hurry the night after visiting the Berlin Wall. Essie born with a birthmark on her forehead in Dublin. They both sang in Irish voices on the cassette tape, we sent it to Canada for St Patrick's day – do you love an apple?

★

My true character caught up with me each time I was back at my desk in the basement, transparent and found out. The footsteps of people overhead on the street. My restless legs, my broken-bottle mouth, the pressure in my jaw reaching into each eye socket, like somebody hanging on to my cheekbones by the fingers.

You need to get out of that basement, Helen said.

I sat across the desk from the commander, telling him that I needed time off to write. He understood my request and asked me what I was writing, I had no idea, maybe something about glass.

He wanted to know what language I was writing.

English, I said.

The language of the street, he said.

It was the only way I could find a place to settle down, I explained, my feet were not my feet. In English, I might be accepted on the street, the language that made people welcome around the world.

The word for good luck in Irish means carrying a trophy. To wish somebody well is to put them on a rising road. He spoke about letting a trapped animal go free, what you said in the shadow language to a person in great thirst, what a couple in love might say to each other.

Write like a man on a bike with no brakes, he said.

He was surrounded by newspaper cuttings, a heavy fall of leaves. He kept me late. He opened a bottle of wine. We drank together from plastic cups. The desk lamp flickered, he tried to fix it, but the brass fitting scalded his fingers, he called it a right buffalo. His stories went on long after the traffic slowed down outside. The park of lovers was gone dark. He asked me for a song and I sang like the living dead.

After that, I began to write down everything that was happening in order of life moving on.

The excitement in the house when Helen's uncle arrived from London. Uncle Jerome. I wrote down how I went to collect him from the boat. He had travelled through the night. It was cold, he was dressed in a good suit, no coat, his shoulders hunched. He carried a small sports bag under his arm. Helen had breakfast ready for him, rashers and sausages and black pudding, toast and strong tea. He wasn't all that hungry after the crossing, he handed her a bottle of whiskey and she poured him a glass. She closed the door to keep the smoke from drifting up the hallway into the yoga room. I could see how happy she was, he talked without stopping, he sat in the armchair with Rosie and Essie clasped on either side, how great it was to be home, he said.

When she was eight in Birmingham, Helen once sneaked into his room to steal a bit of his aftershave, so she could remember him when he was gone.

He wore sideburns, I wrote. His hair was receding, pinned back over his ears, sitting on the collar of his shirt at the back. He wore a blue tie, he carried a manicure set in his top pocket, he perfected the London accent, he could live under cover and only be Irish when he needed to. He had a long nose and his teeth came forward a bit, he spoke like Rick in Casablanca, full of altruism, something that was gone out of fashion. It was the mark of his time to do the right thing, let the girl go, leave all that happiness and luck to someone else, better off with nothing to lose.

He had been in love with a teacher from Achill Island, she was mad about him, they said she was a painting on two feet. They were the most perfect couple, engaged to be married. He was on the way to becoming a bank manager in Mullingar, then he found himself in a hotel in Donegal where his cousins came from, late one night he bet money he didn't own at a poker game. The cards were against him. The daughter of the hotel owner recognised his distress and stepped in to pay his debts, then he did the decent thing, he married her instead of the person he loved. He disappeared off the face of the earth and left his belongings, his books, his country, his aftershave, a note to the woman from Achill he loved more than anyone in the world. He took up a caretaker position in London and lived in a basement flat in Knightsbridge with the woman who bailed him out, in return for her kindness.

His fiancé from Achill moved on, she got married to somebody else in Dublin. Like all people who emigrate, he was the one left behind.

Only the song left over full of recurring pain.

He sang his heart out at nine in the morning, the precious days of September dwindling fast. He fell asleep in the armchair and we left him alone, we got his shoes off, I took the glass out of his hand. When he woke up, we brought him for a walk by the sea, he stopped off at the pub on the corner, we had a hard time getting him out. Helen took him by the arm as though he was being arrested.

We had no room to put him up, so we brought him to my mother, he stopped to buy a bunch of flowers. She welcomed him like a visitor from home. My little brother Emil stood in the doorway with his bike, my sister Lotte carried his sports bag upstairs. Greta made dinner, he didn't eat much, only the soup. He got the hiccups, Rosie and Essie counted on their fingers, fifteen in all, he leaned forward and drank water back to front, then it stopped. After dinner, they performed their ballet for him, he even tried some ballet himself, shuffling on silent feet, like somebody hurrying across the road.

He got my mother to drink whiskey, I wrote.

They sat in the front room and maybe it reminded her of her father. It was the smoke, the sound of whiskey being poured, the link she made as a child between happiness and the smell of alcohol, the talk and the laughter it brought out, the stories keeping people up late. Before the crash, before the stationery shop was closed, before the family went bankrupt and people stopped coming to visit and they no longer got free tickets for the cinema.

Uncle Jerome told stories about London, the apartment block where he was the caretaker. He took in their complaints, their opinions, their cats, their flowers, their husbands locked out, notes from lovers, he was a psychiatrist and a friend, he helped them with the crossword, told them what was on TV, gave them his teabags, got a bottle of whiskey from them at Christmas. He knew their history, the Kurdish freedom fighter, the Iraqi former diplomat, the old Jewish woman who had escaped Nazi Germany. A Bulgarian man came down late one night in an agitated state with the fog around him at the door, entrusting him with a sealed envelope, a dead letter, the police found his passport, money, clothes, a gun, photographs of his wife and children back in Sofia.

My mother asked me to put on some music.

I unlocked the gramophone and put on one of her favourite pieces, a short piano introduction followed by a deep male voice – a stranger I came, a stranger I will go.

Uncle Jerome got up and asked her to dance, she smiled and shook her head.

It's not for dancing, she said.

Of course, it is.

He held out his hand. He didn't know what was being said in the song, but he heard the words coming from the singer's heart and insisted on pulling her out of the chair. She had to laugh because it was a bit foolish being swung in a gentle circle around the room to words that were more for listening, about love and wandering, remembering journeys in winter, the road you must go, the road no one returns.

She turned into a girl, she was out of breath and had to sit down, laughing. Uncle Jerome bowed with a sweep of his arm and said the word in German for thank you. He told us he was an Irish count. We believed him. He placed his hand on the mantelpiece for support and laughed with his head back.

I never saw my father dancing.

Dancing produced nothing, it had no destination. My father never made those sweeping gestures, he didn't drink, he didn't throw his head back, he made speeches and spoke with great fervour about how things could be improved. When he listened to music, he stared at the floor with a frown.

To demonstrate the depth of his feelings, my father built a gramophone. It was enormous, it took him over a year to finish. Four separate compartments, components imported from Germany, the finest quality needle ordered in from Sweden, arriving like a piece of jewellery in a small box with velvet cushion interiors. He built a single speaker in one corner, the size of a wardrobe, a triangular shape with cavity walls full of oven-dried sand for solid sound, chequered speaker gauze throbbing. People on our street understood the magnitude of his project. The volume of music he played to keep my mother in Ireland could be heard six doors down, we had the Vienna Philharmonic orchestra in the front room, dancers in costume bowing and taking the arm. The walls were swaying, the furniture moved, vases, ornaments, table lamps, photographs of our dead relatives, pictures of my mother's town, the stationery shop, the paper factory, floating up to the ceiling. The sound was so pure, my mother said, you could hear the sheet music being turned.

This gigantic record player was my father's sweeping gesture, I wrote. That was his exaggeration, his overstatement, his love so close to his fury.

We left my mother and Uncle Jerome sitting in the front room with the side lamp on. Greta said it was after midnight by the time they got to bed. Uncle Jerome sang a train song on the way up the stairs, he went down on one knee on the landing, his arms out, my mother held on to the bannisters, laughing. Lotte showed him to his room, they had the bed made up for him. It was my room, the window leading out onto the flat roof where the beehives used to be. It was my bed he slept in, with the heating pipe in the corner and the Chagall poster on the wall and the books of Russian poets. He took my place. He took the fear out of the walls.

He coughed a bit, Greta said. His light was on for a while. They heard him laughing and talking in his sleep as if the room was full of people.

There was sweeping exaggeration in everything I did after that. I began phoning estate agents. We went to see run-down properties that few other people seemed interested in. Rosie and Essie ran around the empty rooms, hearing their own echo on the stairs. Helen remarked on the lives of previous occupants, the faded curtains, the bits of broken furniture, stains and smells left behind by people who came to the end of their lives, soon to be replaced by a new family.

I bought a house. My solicitor did his best to hold me back, but I panicked and agreed with the asking price, the building society accepted the inflated figure I gave them for my salary. It was a time of exuberance and risk.

On the phone to her mother, Helen described the house we bought as though it was in Canada. It was on a corner site, it had a big front garden, not on the bus route. One of the bedrooms at the back looked out over the sea. Rosie and Essie would be able to see the lighthouse when they went to sleep.

It was built on a slope, the house was back to front, the hall door was blistered by the sun, the back door was dark. It needed to be rewired, the fireplaces in the bedrooms would have to be blocked off, it had no heating, no curtains, no light fittings. The roof had no insulation. We sat in the car in the evenings looking at our future. We walked down the slope to the front door, we stared in the window at the empty living room, a faded estate-agent brochure, some dead flies on the windowsill.

In great bouts of exaggeration, I set out to put Helen's business on a sound footing. I looked for decent premises to accommodate the yoga courses. The small front room in a downstairs flat was no longer adequate for the size of her classes. She was getting a lot of new clients. Brought on by the contract she had with the radio station, a slot every morning, teaching listeners how to relax and do shoulder rolls while they were sitting in traffic.

I looked at lots of commercial premises and eventually came across a studio space in a terraced house. It seemed perfect. It had a side entrance, changing areas, bathroom, cloakroom, a big room with a concrete floor. There was plenty of parking. I spoke to the owner. His name was Bardon. He lived upstairs, he had corrugated white hair, he wanted guarantees, he didn't trust me until I told him where I went to school. I let him know that I had a secure job in the native basement. We would be great tenants, I promised, absolutely no parties, it was not residential, to be used for yoga only, quiet people breathing in and out, I said. I told him I came from the area, I gave him the address where I grew up, I had just bought a house close to my mother.

He wouldn't go down on the rent. He wanted me to sign a three-year lease, he used the word copper-bottomed.

He promised to put in a carpet.

The place worked out fine for the time being. Helen would have preferred a wooden floor, even with the carpet, the clients needed to put down towels because the concrete floor felt cold. There was plenty of space. They could stretch out and do the folding crucifix without touching each other's hands. The problem was the damp. The heating made things worse. The place smelled of mildew, you got it coming in the door. Helen had to spray the corridor and the main room before the clients arrived, the heavy air of perfume and human breath. There was condensation on the walls. The carpet had the thickness of corduroy trousers, rubber backed, it began sweating underneath. At one point, Helen called me to say there was something growing in the corner. I went down to find a section of the carpet covered in mushrooms. I got the hoover out and mowed it like a lawn.

I complained to Bardon upstairs, he came down and told me to open a window, we had the place overheated.

It was never going to work. Already, we began talking about somewhere more suitable, a brighter, more inviting kind of place in a better location.

I took more and more time off from the dead basement, not getting much written. Searching for better premises, with a secure lease. Helen was talking to potential investors. It all looked promising. I avoided those meetings. I showed too much enthusiasm. My words were warped with idealism. Ecstatic ways of describing the business potential – immense, out of this world, it's going to be an edifice.

Our view of the world was full of reckless belief. I trusted Helen, she trusted me, I believed her, she believed me, we talked each other blind with optimism. I was doing it to set her free. She was doing it so I could speak.

I had no idea how to measure the future. My ambitions were born incoherent. I had grown up inside a preposterous family venture. My childhood, our German-Irish home in a seaside place in Dublin was a giant exaggeration, full of overreaching and unreasonable calculations. My mother and father backed each other up with misguided courage that never matched the country we walked in. Their expectations were fantastic, like building plans that got swapped for faraway places.

I ignored the episodes of doubt breaking out in my teeth. I shaved off my beard. I felt the cool breeze around my chin as I walked around the city at night.

One day, I persuaded myself to go back to the dentist. He was nearly in tears when I asked him to take out the dead tooth. He flicked his head towards the chair. He began to examine my teeth once more. He spent some time admiring his own work, the crown he had put in, it was like asking him to remove a priceless piece of art. He smiled, holding his little stainless-steel mirror in the air as he explained to me once again that it was no longer part of my living body.

Blaming a dead tooth was like blaming a piece of furniture. It was as dead as a dead tree, how can a piece of oak feel pain? What I was experiencing had to be caused by something else, something missing in my life, perhaps, some grief I could not speak.

You want it removed, he said.

Please.

He said nothing more. He gave me an injection and went about the extraction with sad resignation. Like he was removing a language from my mouth that he loved, we both loved. He handed me the extinct tooth with some blood attached, said I should bleach it if I was going to keep it as a souvenir. His eyes were full of restraint, once again he would accept no payment, for what, for something gone, something missing? I carried the tooth in my back pocket. I practised smiling sideways to cover the gap. I experienced phantom pain from time to time. Pain where the pain used to be.

By the time I get the keys to the house it's summer. Helen is in Canada visiting her family with the girls, her mother booked the tickets. I drive back from the solicitor's office with my elbow out the window, wearing my billowing white shirt.

This is my turn. My sweeping overstatement, my great family extravagance. I carry fantasies of arrival. Fantasies of home and never moving again. Getting to know everybody on the street, trading bits of gossip, watching cookery programmes on TV, inviting people for dinner, staying up late and singing my heart out in my own house.

I park the car down the sloped driveway. I get out and turn the key in the lock. Closing the door behind me, I listen to the silence inside the house. I am happy to stand in each room and allow the walls to get to know me, gently letting the wooden floors get used to the weight of my presence. I hear the creaks. I feel the handshake of door-knobs. I open the windows. The dusty stillness of the rooms begins to move with the noise of traffic entering from the street. A draught comes in to flip the estate-agent brochure off the windowsill, bringing the house to life. I hear my feet on the stairs. I stand in the children's bedroom watching the sea, the lighthouse will be coming on for them at night, ships will cross right by their beds.

Filling rooms is like writing a book. I get bits of furniture from the auctions, things given to us by my mother, I hang the glass art angel from Cologne up by the door. I find second-hand curtains for the bedrooms, a bargain mat for the hall, a wicker chair for the bathroom.

The carved bass mouth is there on the mantelpiece. A voice going right through the house, speaking encourage-ment. Beside it, the carved ear listening to me working.

I have put in the heating, I've connected the phone, I rewired the house, somebody helped me with the fuse board.

My lungs are full of dust. My eyes are red, I eat a sand-wich that tastes of varnish, I drink mugs of tea with the scum of sawdust. I get to know the faces at the hardware suppliers. I love building materials more than words. My hands buzz with the grip of drilling. My hair, my face, my arms are caked to the elbows in bits of cement, sealant, emulsion, my mind is under the floorboards. I can't help laughing at one point because I find myself using the sick bowl to mix a bit of plaster.

3

It was the morning of their school concert. Helen got them dressed. Their grey chequered uniforms and blue cardigans were too big, intended to last an extra year or two. There was trouble because Rosie wanted her hair not to be done in plaits the same as Essie's, some screaming in the kitchen. Essie ran away into the dining room and took it out on the piano. Two of the most vital keys were out of tune, bruised notes undermining a piece that was meant to be played with vigour. The piano had been left to us by the aunt with the bunch of keys, when she moved her family into a house too small.

Helen stood at the door waiting.

She wore a peppermint dress, her tweed blue coat, a bead necklace from her mother. You rarely saw her using more than a touch of make-up, that morning her face was a shield, you couldn't go near her. She didn't talk. She didn't eat much. She kissed them goodbye, said she would do her best to get to the concert – we'll go somewhere nice afterwards.

Good luck, I said to her. It sounded more like farewell. Everything in my words began to contain the accidental opposite of what they were intended to mean. Our eyes avoided each other.

She was going to a meeting with the investor, he was bringing his lawyer with him. They wanted to see the accounts. She carried a bright red ledger under her arm, a schedule of bookings, takings from the café, bank statements, the outstanding debts, a list of creditors. It was me who kept the books, I should have been there to explain them, but that would not have improved anything. Through the venetian blinds in her office, you could see her laying out the documents across the desk, they sat on either side, ready for the audit.

The assembly hall was full. The man sitting next to me was from Chile, his accent was soft, he told me his wife was a translator of European trade and legal documents. Everybody was talking, mothers and fathers, grandparents, all reaching like periscopes over each other's shoulders to admire their own. Rosie and Essie were standing in line by the stage. Essie saw me waving. Rosie was saying something to the boy next to her, he laughed and elbowed her, she punched him back. The man from Chile had a camera with a zoom lens, his daughter was in same class as Rosie, he took some shots of them together, said he would send them to me.

The high wooden ceiling had heavy exposed beams, there were three tall stained-glass windows facing the street and plaques along the walls in memory of sailors, this is where they met and prayed with their families after they returned from their journeys. A balloon had become trapped beyond the wooden beams, some cobwebs that could not be reached either, the floor was white marble with black dots. One of the teachers clapped her hands, she had curly hair, a round motherly face, the noise died down. The junior infants were first to come on, all waving, in their faces you could recognise their mothers, in some of them you could see exactly what they would look like when they were eighty.

They sang a song about happiness. One of the girls sang louder than all the others, one of the boys kept pulling at his blue tie, another boy stood with his hands over his eyes and had to be reunited with his mother, a girl in a dream suddenly joined back in with the chorus – happiness. The applause lasted a long time, mothers smiling at each other, shaking their heads, one of them said the word – hysterical. After the group filed off again, one boy was left on the stage as if he was lost on the street, he had to be led away by the hand.

When Rosie and Essie came on, they didn't see me, they were looking for their mother. A man sat down at the piano, his girlfriend was the teacher conducting the group, they sang – here comes the sun. I had heard the song in the house for weeks, but I was euphoric hearing their voices in a choir together singing about the long winter coming to an end and the sun arriving at last, something overwhelming about children telling adults everything is going to be all right.

I was worried about Helen. Under questioning in her office, trying to explain a set of financial records she didn't have much control over.

The concert finished off with happy birthday. It included an extended list of names, all the children with birthdays falling in that month. They served tea and sandwiches and cakes afterwards. Paper plates got mixed up, left behind on tables with nobody claiming them. I had some tea. I continued talking to the man from Chile, he said he missed the weather. He invited me around to visit him, he sat on his front porch every evening with a beer, even in the middle of winter, looking at the cars going by, waiting for the sun to go down.

We called the investor only by his full name – Maurice Delaney. He liked to crack a joke when he arrived, placing people at ease, some comment about himself not being fit, sometimes it was the joke about the man with a stammer taking the piss out of the man without a stammer. So much depended on him, we laughed, we wanted him to be happy. He used aviation language, gave the impression of a pilot in control, busy but relaxed, patient to a point, he had the habit of looking at his watch while you were talking. He clapped his hands to let you know when a meeting was over. He never made notes, preferred to keep everything in his head. His smile was not thrown around aimlessly. His eyebrows were shaped in arches, something boyish, affectionate, a deep voice, like somebody on the radio, the way he said the words – up and running.

We were never invited to his house, he never came to ours. No obligation for us to be socially compatible, he didn't want friendship to unbalance business arrangements. I never found out what music he liked. Once I heard him driving off with the car windows down – the power of love – I would have switched that off. He wore a yellow shirt, but that was fine, no need for us to be identical.

We didn't know much about him, only that he was a good businessman. He had business interests in France as well as Ireland. He had grown up in Singapore, to Irish parents, his father was an architect. He came back and went to school in Ireland, he graduated in business studies in Austin and lived for a while in Texas. That's all we were told. His private life never came up, it had nothing to do with me.

Early on, after the business was set up, he pulled me aside one day to let me know how much he valued my honesty, he used the word partnership. Holding me briefly by the elbow in the car park at the side of the café, he said he admired me for staying at home to take care of the family, not abandoning Helen to run the whole show by herself like a lot of other men might do. It was the flight plan for any good business, he said. His male-to-male tone made me feel approved.

You're a good man, he said.

Perhaps he was trying to figure out why I agreed to be a good man, what was in it for me, or was it a warning, reminding me to remain a good man?

In the office that morning, the investor became agitated. He had no time for his own jokes. He ignored the plate of pastries Helen served on her desk. Out of politeness, the lawyer took a cream doughnut, he was an older man, there was a softness in his eyes, from Kilkenny. White icing sugar on his suit, some cream on his face, Helen handed him a box of tissues.

The information was laid out on her desk, bank statements, invoices paid, invoices unpaid, the ledger was full of numbers, like scattered tea leaves she had no idea how to interpret. I had spent a week going over them, hoping they would look better. My experience of bookkeeping came from my previous job in the native basement, where music and language had no price, the total mattered only in relation to what was lost.

Our projections were unrealistic. Even if the café was packed all day and the classes upstairs were going right through the night, the figures would never have added up. The business held no profit. Helen had given a personal guarantee on the rent for ninety-nine years, she had borrowed to meet her portion of share capital. We were tied up in debt. Any advice I gave her was not based on sound commercial principles, but on the memory of a café we used to go to in Berlin.

Maurice Delaney took no part in the running of things, his development company carried out the necessary alterations on the premises. Capital acquisitions were installed on credit – the most up-to-date Italian coffee machine, the furniture, the lighting, the sound system, the showers, the sauna, lounging chairs in the changing rooms, mirrors like in a theatre dressing room surrounded by lights. There was a wonderful neon sign over the door which took me ages to get designed – The Fitness Café. All in all, the place turned out well, people said it was classy.

Every figure was being questioned, each entry in the bank statements cross-checked with the takings. It was as if they were scrutinising not only the trading results but the validity of our lives, our family, everything we stood for, what kind of people we were. The figures would reveal more about our attitude to the world than they did about the short history of the business. After some quick mental calculations, the investor said the books were a disgrace. Were we giving the money away, he asked. Feeding the people of Dublin cake for free, yoga for nothing, the accounts were littered with contradictions.

Christ, he said, you haven't even paid the architect.

Helen said she had offered instalments.

He lost his temper. How hard was it to keep proper financial records? Any girl in national school would do better.

It's as simple as cleaning the toilet, he shouted.

Helen tried to explain.

This is not just incompetent, it's fraudulent.

Maurice, please, the lawyer said.

He put his hand on the investor's arm, maybe to remind him of his luck, his portfolio of properties, how easy it was for him to give Helen a break, not to turn her out like a criminal.

Her mind went blank.

She was expecting another baby. She was beginning to show, her breasts were enlarged, she walked more slowly, she was on the phone to her mother a lot. It seemed like an act of disloyalty, betraying the ground rules of business. This reckless family pact myself and Helen made one day with the afternoon sun central across the floor of the front room. Turning our backs on the calculated world. In the middle of a recession, quitting my secure job at the native basement to write a book while she was running the business and having another baby. We were avoiding the truth, as if the book and the baby were timed to come into being at the same moment, to save us.

Her diary was full of proof that being a mother didn't take her mind off running the business. She was highly organised – the staff, the roster, deliveries, maintenance work to be carried out on the showers, somebody coming to look at why the mirrors were getting steamed up, a dehumidifier was needed. Things had been scribbled in by the children, they got into everything, it wasn't Helen who wrote in the giant phone numbers, or the word *Vagina*, misspelled.

Unbelievable, the investor said.

Helen put her hand up to her mouth. She made a small gulping sound, then she threw up. A gush of thin vomit splashed across the accounts. There was no sick bowl. A tinted mush of toast and raspberry jam and tea spread out in cloudy smudges on the page. Mixed in with the mess of numbers, no mathematical logic, the totals began to dissolve.

The investor looked up thinking she'd got sick deliberately across the books to disguise them. The twin bridges of his eyebrows were up. He didn't believe her puke. To him it was a clever twist to divert attention from the appalling trading balance, he recoiled with his elbow up for a shield.

Only when she apologised and put her hand on her belly, did he finally back off. There was an alarming sense of help-lessness in the room when they realised she was pregnant. The lawyer ran out for a glass of water. The investor was no match for a coming baby – you should have told me, he said. He sighed at the futility of the day.

Helen's friend, Martina, was waiting for him. She sat at one of the tables in the café reading the paper. Her espresso was long finished. The remains of a chocolate cake scribbled on a plate. She wore a scuffed blue leather jacket. Her T-shirt had the faded name of a rock band across the front. She wore canvas slippers, not designed for running away, her nails were painted black, her hair was tied up with rope.

She is from Kerry, a single mother. She has a boy a little younger than our girls. The father is Spanish, a building worker she met in London, Helen told me, he went to see the baby at the maternity hospital, then he disappeared, Martina came back to live in Dublin. She is a great singer. She once tried to make it in a band, getting a few gigs in London, not earning a lot.

Maurice Delaney sat down at Martina's table, she didn't get up. She made a clip-clop sound with her mouth. What children do to imitate horses. She put her hand on his arm, she made him laugh, they left in his car.

He was possibly a lot more like me than I was willing to

admit. Apart from his shirts and his choice of music, the car he drove had a walnut dashboard, he may have had the same unstructured way of thinking, angry with himself for being so human, caught in a struggle between wanting and having, things you cannot own. He may have been misled into thinking this moment was positioning him at the centre of the world when it was really outside his control, he was lured into this hopeless scheme of existence with his eyes open.

The senseless set of financial records were left open on the desk in the office, a frightening representation of how false life can be. If you allowed yourself to think in that self-questioning way, everything turned to puke. It may have occurred to him that he had been shouting at Helen when he should have been thanking her for introducing him to her best friend. The business may have been sick, but it brought him great luck. Could he not count that as a dividend instead?

He is mad about Martina. She has no money, she works part time as a receptionist. The fact that she is a single mother gives him the feeling he can rescue her. He likes her eccentric clothes, the way she speaks to the taxi driver, the questions she asks the porter outside the Shelbourne Hotel. There is a husky trace of late nights in her voice. Over dinner, he orders the most expensive bottle of wine, she picks it up and drinks it by the neck. Her motherly calmness mixed in with her underground principles. She still goes to open-air rock concerts with her five-year-old boy on her shoulders, she still carries emergency food in her bag, sitting on a park bench to eat crackers and cheese, an apple sliced into small boats with a penknife.

Martina is a good listener. She brings out the rogue in him. He is happy to waste time and stand in front of the gates at Trinity College for the sake of being there, he loves the smell of the streets. He is unable to take his mind off her convent skin, the tattoo of a gecko on her left shoulder. Her smile reminds him that he only has one life, this chance of big love may not come around again.

Helen embraced the girls with furious affection. She let them feel her belly, she had cream doughnuts for them. We could not talk about what the investor said, we didn't want them to hear, we were protecting them. Your anxieties will get into their dreams, Helen said to me whenever I was trying to be honest with them – let them be children.

We drove down to the small harbour and sat in the car having a ham sandwich, the cream doughnuts, drinks with straws, listening to a song on the radio that Helen remembered from being a child in Birmingham. The seagulls were lined up on the pier waiting. One of them landed on the bonnet of the car and the girls shrieked, he slid around on his yellow rubber feet and lifted off again.

Back home, we took our eyes off each other with work. Forced to stay apart in our worlds, making noise, drilling, sanding, putting on the washing machine. I heard her getting sick in the bathroom. I held her arm, but she waved me away – it's all right, thanks. I found a way of hiding the speaker wires under the floorboards to prevent people tripping over them. My thoughts were routed along the heating pipes, with the wiring circuit, the flush-mounted sockets. It made me feel relevant, necessary, obsessed with straight lines.

We lived in a state of revision.

The girls sat at the table drawing pictures, the biscuit box with the colouring pens emptied out. Essie had the new baby arriving in a boat, Rosie had it coming from another planet, a pregnant spacecraft flying past the moon with the baby waving. They folded the pictures into an envelope and we posted it under the floorboards, a letter to the future.

Helen brought them upstairs to bed. They sat watching the evening coming across the sea. The lighthouse beaming softly into the bedroom, onto their faces, onto her belly. With their elbows on the windowsill, I heard them counting the seconds between each lighthouse beam. At my foldable desk downstairs, I tried to stop the circular pattern of failure and wrote down a description of the landscape under the floorboards, the safety beneath the room. The room light coming down in lines through the gaps, the pipes expanding, the wires pulsing, the foundations like huge hands holding. Nothing moving, only a spider crossing the letter with their handwriting.

Everything was down there, waiting quietly in the space between the floor and the ground, stored in the granite crust, in seams of quartz, in the water table, in the deep past at the centre of the earth.

It was the only way I could remove myself from this financial uncertainty. Immersing myself in memory. For a while each day, I stepped outside my life by writing down everything I remembered.

A house in Germany, four storeys high, the façade is brown, maybe grey, faces in the windows, somebody dropping a key down. The architecture is familiar to me. I know how many floors to the top, the smell of roast pork on the way up and a dog barking behind a door. A place I associate with my mother and father being happy, both in tears laughing at something.

The house is in the town my mother came from. Where we went to visit the aunt whose husband didn't speak, he was in Russian captivity for eight years. When he was released in a small town on the east German border, there was a brass band on the platform to welcome him. He started an industry of bow ties in one of the rooms, we were told to pick one each. Another uncle who came back from the war and kept revising his life, over and over, wishing he could rewrite history, telling everyone how mistakes could be avoided, how to put oil on a bicycle chain, how to eat a sandwich. I thought of the aunt whose husband ended up in American captivity after a gunfight in which a bullet travelled like a high-speed mole through the ground beneath him. He once told me he could never forget the taste of soil, he picked up a piece of earth to sniff it.

I wrote down the story of the aunt living in the house below the castle in Salzburg, she got married to her husband by proxy, he stood saying yes in front of a senior officer in the Crimea, she said yes in the presence of a lawyer on the street where Mozart had lived. Her husband never came back, she got one letter, one visit back home, they had one daughter. After the war, people came to say they had seen him in captivity, she continued waiting for him.

Helen's way of escaping the pressure is to call her mother in Canada. The phone is in the small breakfast room, next to the kitchen. She can sit down in a proper chair, with her feet up. There is a gas fire, the white element turns orange and blue while she tells her mother in Canada that everything is going great, business is thriving. The children are doing swimming lessons, and jazz dancing as well as ballet, art classes twice a week. She has been to the obstetrician, she's feeling very well.

I hear her say that I knocked down the wall between the living room and the dining room, the house was full of dust for a while, a big yellow skip outside for weeks. All by himself, she says. It was not a load-bearing wall, I want her to add. It's fortified with a steel lintel. So much space, she says. All one room now, even though it still has two doors side by side, you can take your pick, separate light switches for each part. She wants to know why houses were built with so many doors and small rooms, her mother says it was to contain the heat, people used to be terrified of draughts. And being overheard.

Listening to Helen talking to her mother, I can tell there is snow in Canada. It comes across the lake, her mother's house is the first to get it, lake effect snow. The waves are frozen. Everything is white, the streets are deserted. The

156

town is unrecognisable, the road signs are illegible, the courthouse is a solid block of ice at the centre of the square, trees with white arms up. A neighbour came to clear their drive, the sound of the shovel made the world seem like the inside of a fridge. The snowploughs are out, banks as high as houses, cars left submerged. They are spreading salt on the highways.

Her mother is the woman who looks at the frozen lake as she steps into her car. She drives through unfamiliar streets. She imagines streets that don't connect, she is surprised to find herself passing by the ice rink. The spotlights and the country music playing over the loudspeakers, people skating anticlockwise like the traffic. Some of them are wearing coloured ski-suits, some of them have mastered skating backwards, they leave handwritten twirls on the surface.

She carries on, driving out onto the main highway, some cars have been left abandoned by the side of the road like white humps. She turns off onto one of the rural routes still covered in snow, white as a field, only the telegraph poles with lines like skipping ropes to guide her.

She wants an end to the argument.

There has been a fight. Nothing but silence between herself and her best friend Nessa. Have they come all this way to Canada just to avoid each other? Going to different hairdressers, circumventing each other in the shops, not waving, not talking, close as sisters, fighting like they were at home.

The rift came about when Nessa stopped paying her housekeeper from Jamaica, complaining about the ironing not being done correctly. The housekeeper went to Helen's mother and asked her to intervene. Nessa came over to Helen's mother and told her not to interfere. In a rage one afternoon, Nessa called the blue room Helen's mother had brought over from Birmingham a heap of junk – tankards, really, only a farmer's wife keeps tankards. Helen's mother ended up telling her only true companion to bugger off.

Nothing cuts like a lost friendship.

The white landscape is meaningless. She drives through the snow to visit her friend, this can be repaired like a marriage. She intends to walk straight into Nessa's country house and demand a drink, they will laugh it off. She picks up speed to get over the railway crossing, but the car hesitates. On the tracks, the wheels begin to spin, no forward, no reverse.

She steps out and leaves the door open.

There is a house nearby, some dogs barking. She is not a walker, better at entering rooms. A trail has been dug out from the road to the house, but it's half covered in snow again. She moves sideways, hands out, her shoes sliding on the hardened ice. She stops to call out. The dogs come running, black and barking, not along the track but directly across the snow bank, swimming and snapping, saliva flung across their backs. She is a piece of immaculate fur, unable to run away.

The owner comes out pulling on his parka. He calls the dogs back. She points to the car on the tracks with the pink exhaust fumes.

Got to get my boots on, he says. Got to get my mitts on, got to get the Klondike.

Two planks under his arm, he has done this before, he knows by the sound of the hooter how far away the train is. He takes off one glove to show her the missing finger. He has a friend who lost his foot, another friend who coughed up his frozen larynx. He begins digging, gets her to hold the un-planed wood in her thin burgundy gloves. His breath is an engine. He frees the wheels and kicks in the planks, tells her to get back into the car – you got no hat, lady.

She drives away and hears the train hooting behind her. Her face is a mask when she gets home, her eyebrows white, her blonde hair a crystal gauze. She reaches the house and parks the car in the drive. The snow has begun to fall again. She remains motionless at the wheel, staring ahead, unable to open the door and go inside.

Her thoughts are frozen. She is trapped in the life she once had back in Birmingham, before coming to this winter in Canada. She remembers the city of happiness, the city of her best years, the city of singing and joking and not being mean with the drink and shoes thrown into the fire and brothers chasing each other across the lawn at night and no harm done. The city of great friendship, before Nessa went to live in this town by the lake in Ontario and everything slipped into memory. The city of great times became the city of unbearable loneliness, the city of fog coming up the stairs and people at the door with leaflets, campaigning to keep England for the English, warning about immigrants moving into the neighbourhood, she had to deny she was Irish – always say you're from London.

Was that the reason for leaving? For deciding to take her ready-made family away and follow her friend into the future as though they could not live apart. And now, here they are, living within shouting distance across the snow and the landscape so quiet.

Behind her, after she went to live in Canada, it became the city of blood. The city of interiors ripped out of pubs. The city of young people crying and calling for help. The city of people counting children and people phoning each other throughout the night, days later, weeks later, reading the names of the dead published in the papers. The first of the bombs went off in a bar she had seen many times on the way into the city on the bus, young people going in dressed in the latest clothes, bell-bottom trousers, high boots, fur-lined jackets. Many of them were trapped underneath girders which had collapsed with the force of the blast, some had their clothes burned from their bodies. A warning had been given in advance of the explosion, but it came too late. The second bomb went off ten minutes later in a pub the police had just begun to clear, it had been placed at the bottom of the stairs, next to the entrance. Some of those killed were thrown through a brick wall, they were said to have been stacked on top of each other. Survivors spoke of a deafening silence, before the crying started, before people came to help and the rescue services arrived. Twenty-one people were killed that night and one hundred and eighty people injured.

It was a time of great distance in the world.

She left messages, notes pinned up by the public phone in the house where Helen lived in London at the time – call your mother. She checked the newspapers, some of the names were Irish, some of the faces seemed familiar, they could have been us. She saw the images on TV, the injured being carried away, the blood so black in the photographs.

By now, the snow has already covered the windscreen. She gets out of the car and walks up the steps onto the porch. The heat inside the house makes her cry. She stands in the hall as though she cannot recognise the surroundings, has she made some mistake, has she got the wrong house, the wrong country, the wrong family around her? They bring her into the kitchen. They prise her shoes off one after the other like pieces of porcelain. They peel off her thin leather gloves, blowing warm family breath across her burgundy hands. They put her sitting a few feet away from the stove, staring into the flames, she is so cold she cannot speak. They leave her coat on. They bring the glass of brandy up to her mouth, just a drop or two across her lips.

There was a man sitting in a car outside the house. The girls had been asking what he was doing out there all day, staring ahead in a dream, not even the radio on, looking up at the windows of the house every now and then. What was he waiting for and why was I refusing to answer the door?

I was upstairs reading a book about the first people of Australia, the routes they had mapped out across the bare landscape in songs. You might think there was nothing to recognise but they knew every individual rock, every bone, every dead snakeskin, the black marks of previous fires. They could sing their way along a list of signs full of ancient memory on the ground and I thought it was similar for the people I knew in the shadow language, out in the west of Ireland, every rock had a story, they could speak their way home.

Helen was on the phone, laughing. Her mother was telling her funny things about Canada. Listening to her made me forget there was a man outside on the street waiting for me. Her voice seemed to physically pick the house up and relocate us all to Canada. It filled me with optimism. It made me believe there was a way out of all this.

I looked out the window. The man in the car was gone. His disappearance was a relief, like the rain stopping. I took the opportunity to go for a walk. I walked through the grounds of a girl's secondary school with the hockey pitch lit up, where the students had written up – Miss Foley has a dick. All the way as far as the golf course, they had a problem with rabbits, the clubhouse had a view of the mountains, some people standing at the bar, it was full of warmth.

On my way back, I came along a street with no walls or fences around the front gardens. They had no gates, each with an open driveway for double cars. The houses were single storey, with unusual designs, wooden features alongside the brickwork, front doors to the side, windows with no curtains. You could look right into the living rooms uncluttered, lamps on, people not bothered being seen from outside.

It gave me the feeling of being in Canada. As I passed by these houses and saw the warm interiors, I felt safe. I was in the town by Lake Huron where Helen's family lived. All I needed to do was continue down to the salt mine where the giant salt ship was being loaded, it was daytime there, the sun would be going down twice. The red glow across the water would turn the unpainted hull of the ship bright copper red, the columns of the grain elevator pink. Over the railway tracks to the wooden bridge and the mouth of the river, you could be alive a thousand years ago.

Walking back by the cluster of shops, I came around the corner and saw the lights on in our house. It looked warm and cosy, but then I discovered the man was back. He jumped out in front of me. He must have parked his car out of sight and waited for me, hiding in a hedge. When I came to the gate he stood in front of me and called out my name. He asked me to confirm that it was me. He handed me an envelope with a writ. He apologised for startling me. He said he was obliged to give it to me in person.

I got to know a lot of creditors.

Some of them were courteous, understanding, but unyielding. Some were cold and uncaring. They could see it was a waste of time, there was no money in us. Because Helen was so busy teaching and running the café, I took the job of debt management, she referred them on to me. It gave me an insight into what people were like, money brought out the true character. Some had to be avoided, some wanted only to be listened to. Normally, I offered them coffee and cake. Some were quick to raise their voices, it was embarrassing for Helen, so I dealt with them in the office. In the space of a morning, I could go from being let off the hook to being hunted and empty. More often it was not the severity of the debt that mattered but the human interaction, a look in the eyes, the hand movements, the wording – don't give me the run-around.

It told me a lot about the ground I stood on.

The coffee machine was the first big crisis. Two brothers sat in the café one day, they gave me until close of business, if I didn't pay them in cash they would take away the machine. They were absolutely within their rights, though I had no idea how to come up with the money. The whole-sale coffee brothers. It was hard to tell which of them was the elder. I explained that we would soon have the finance in place, we were going for another loan, but they were not interested. They kept looking at each other, either one of them on his own might have given in, together they were unrelenting.

All I could think of doing was to sell the car. I spent an hour hoovering the back seats, got some air spray to make the interior smell like new. I drove around from garage to garage trying to get a good price. They could see that I was a bit desperate, so they didn't offer a lot – you're taking a terrible tumble, one of them said. It was a good Italian car, white, chrome frames, full of comfort, green tinted windows. We had done some great trips down to West Clare, the rocks turned blue, the seabirds were silver, turquoise foam along the shore, everything was enhanced by the tinted glass, our country looked so cinematic, more like Italy.

What option did I have? I agreed on a half-decent price and made the handover. It was the strangest thing, trading down. I exchanged our respectable car for a small, lime green Japanese car.

How easy it was to lose your standing in the world. People saw me pulling into the car park in a heap of shit, the windows were steamed up, the seals were perished, a line of green moss, the heating was no longer working. They wanted to know what happened our nice Italian car. I joked about it, saying it was nothing but a status symbol, we were scaling down, the replacement car was more ecological, low on consumption. Rosie and Essie found a rust hole in the floor, they could see the road speeding by underneath. The car left a black stain of oil on the driveway. What I hadn't noticed at first was that the front passenger door could not be opened from the inside, I had to go around each time to let Helen in and out.

At least we still had the coffee machine.

We discussed the future of the business with the investor, there was a further meeting in the office with his solicitor. The bank repayments had fallen behind. The rent on the premises was in arrears. For Helen, the most important thing was to make sure that staff were getting paid. I made a poor impression at those meetings. Too eager, too prescient, like the whole enterprise was a novel. I dreamed up the most fantastic plot, more loans, more capital investment.

Most of the time I felt disintegrated. I wanted to sleep and not wake up. I was happy staring at the lighthouse every night from the bedroom window, it was the only respite I got from my own imagination.

Helen remained upbeat.

Nothing mattered more than the coming baby. We still had to live. She had to buy a loose dress. The girls ran around the department store, hiding among racks of women's clothing. Essie spun a carousel around until the jewellery began to fly off in various directions, the shop assistant came to pick them up, asking if they were my children or was I just watching them. We had to eat. Scampi and chips. They smiled at the food when it arrived, the food smiled back. It was the meal Helen had each time before being sent to boarding school, she could never finish it, still dreaming of what was left behind on the plate, the scampi uneaten.

The doorbell rang one evening. A woman stood in the porch under the light with an expression of deep concern. I thought she had an accident on the street. She gave me her name, Marie Delaney. The investor's wife. It came as a complete surprise to me that he was married, it had never even occurred to me that he had a family life.

The girls were asleep. Helen was out working. I was reading a book about a man somewhere in America sitting in the car with his family, he finds the beauty of the red sunset a bit suspicious, it might be pollution, then he goes home and thinks about Hitler.

I asked her to come inside. I offered her tea. She would not sit down. In the hallway, she put her hand on the newel and stared at me in silence for a moment. It was clear from her accent that she was from Belfast.

You knew, she said.

That's what people said to their parents after the war, I thought. She was referring to her husband, Maurice. He had been seen coming out of a hotel in Paris with another woman, Irish eyes everywhere, the news was reported back directly by a neighbour. She wanted to know what was going on, her questions revealed how little she knew.

Where does she live?

Who?

You know who I'm talking about, don't be an asshole.

Martina, I said.

What's her address?

I was only there once, I explained, it's near the hospital, an apartment block.

Give me her phone number?

I don't have it, I said.

What does she look like?

All I had to say about Martina were good things. She was a great singer, she had a lovely way of talking to children – you don't want to put on that itchy old woolly jumper, it feels like a sheep around your neck. She had the same way of talking to adults – I don't believe it, they want you to work day and night. She turned everyone into a child. She was very loyal, she gave great encouragement to Helen.

I said none of this. Anything I might have said was evidence, everything I didn't say was more evidence.

Look, I said, this has nothing to do with me.

I want the truth, she said.

I'm the wrong person, I said.

Her eyes were on the verge of tears. She asked me what Martina's place was like, I told her it was not a bad apartment, adequate was the only word I could find.

Why is everybody lying?

Denial is not one of my skills. I wanted to proclaim my innocence, tell her I knew absolutely nothing about her husband or his private life. She reached into my thoughts to extract a full confession. I found myself telling her that Martina's apartment overlooked the back of the hospital, you could see the church from the kitchen window.

Her arms were folded.

I tried to make the place look worse than it was. My unwilling imagination refused to go into the main bedroom. I deflected into the hallway, into the living room, the guitar, the easel with a painting half finished, stuff all over the place, a long leather sofa, quite bashed up and covered with a rug. The small room where Martina's son slept, his name was José, his door was covered with the names of his school friends, like graffiti, our names were there as well.

José has hundreds of soldiers on the windowsill, I said, his mother is a declared pacifist.

Was this an attempted joke?

Marie could not help a smile of disdain, instantly withdrawn, she wanted more.

The bathroom had no bath, only a shower. The shower head kept falling off, Martina asked me to fix it the day we went to visit, she sat with Helen in the living room chatting. Rosie and Essie were in the bedroom, playing on the floor with José. There was a crack in the bathroom tiles, obviously caused by the door handle swinging back against the wall, the shower head was easily repaired.

We didn't know he was married, I said.

At this point, she got sick.

She cried and wretched at the same time. Her arm held on to the bannister rail, her hand over her mouth.

I'm sorry, I said.

My instinct was to run for the sick bowl. She had not eaten a thing in the last seven days apart from one or two croissants, a lot of coffee. It was nothing more than a sweet colourless liquid staining the front of her red jacket, her crying had more volume, she made no attempt to stop the tears across her face. I unrolled the kitchen paper, tried to place it into her hand, I started wiping her jacket.

Why did nobody tell me?

Her knees began to give way. I rushed forward to catch her. I got the scent of perfume, mixed up with vomit and sweat, like a photocopier, I thought. Her jacket was buttoned up wrong, I noticed. Her hair was an urgent ponytail. She was not wearing any make-up. I got her sitting down at the foot of the stairs. There were things I wanted to ask her, where she was from, her family, how long she had been married, did they have children, but that all seemed too personal. One of the neighbours stood at the door, her car was left at a dangerous angle on the road, no handbrake, headlights draining the battery.

In Irish, to be short of money is to be naked. It is the lender who has money on the borrower, the person without funds is left stripped. To owe a debt in my mother's language is to be guilty of it, in German you are pronounced guilty of the amount owed. Being indebted in English is to be obliged, bound, beholden, liable, embarrassed, encumbered, accountable, in hock, shy. In the language of the street, we were thousands shy.

We were naked and guilty and embarrassed.

I had to deal with each one of the creditors in a practical way. Explain the situation to them. Come up with some proposal. When there was no financial solution, I went home and put down a brief description of the day in my journal, their names, what they said, their clothes, the expression on their faces. It was the only way of removing myself from this condition of being naked. I wrote them off my back. The following day, they returned with no let up.

A man came to take away the water dispensers. It was one of those things the women loved after yoga sessions, some of the courses were full on aerobics and jazz dancing, they produced a lot of heat and human steam, they could not be running into the café asking for water. There was a basket full of used white cups beside each dispenser, some marked with lipstick.

I tried to persuade the water man to give us more time, I would send something in the post. He seemed friendly, his accent belonged to the same part of the country as Martina. It occurred to me to ask him if he knew her, but that didn't sound promising. He threw out his hands and said – sorry, I've been told to remove them. I offered him coffee, he didn't have time. I stood back to let him get on with it.

For some reason, I reverted to the native language under my breath – take the bloody things so, I said, and may your mickey remain curly.

I didn't expect him to understand or even care what I said, but he laughed out loud. He was not in the least insulted. We ended up getting into a conversation, two shadow people standing by the water dispenser, he said he played the accordion. Women came out in their leggings to get water, their necks were shining with sweat, we were talking about the best accordion player that ever walked the earth, gone to live in America.

He decided to leave the water coolers alone. He asked me to come out to the car park. He opened the back of the van, it was full of water dispensers and hosepipes and other equipment. He jumped in and brought out a case, opened it up and took out his accordion. Sitting on the back step of the van, he began to play for me. He wanted me to hear a tune he had picked up recently. He traced the origins of the reel to a shadow place on the Cork and Kerry border.

The plumber was more difficult. He was a burly man, he could have picked me up like a bar of soap. He had carried out major repair works on the showers. So far, he had only been paid for materials, his labour was not something he could take away again. He stood in the bathroom area and accused me of reckless trading. I told him I was sorry, it wasn't like that, I thanked him for doing a great job, the reason I had no money to give him was that I had to pay another contractor for an emergency job on the back door, people had broken in, nothing much stolen, only the mess they made of the place.

Two women came out of the sauna wrapped in white towels. They hardly took any notice, they continued talking as they disappeared into the shower cubicles. His eyes were only on the tiling, the grout, the silicone finishing, he seemed happy to hear water flowing. Gripped by the pleasure of his own work. More women came in, I had the feeling that being in the presence of the plumber made me invisible to them. He finally realised they wanted to get changed, he took one more agonising look at his work, then he turned his back on it. I paid him as much as I could give him, he went away happy.

One day, a woman came to collect payment for the cake and pastry deliveries. I could only give her half the amount she expected, but she said that was fine. She must have known things were not easy, people were talking about us. She accepted the money and asked if I wanted to order any extra deliveries, she could recommend a cake with a new set of ingredients, banana and toffee. We had such a perfect business combination, she said, yoga and cakes. She had a lovely name in the native language, but it sounded in my mother's language like the word for being in a hurry, when I thanked her and said her name it sounded like I was rushing her.

I felt sorry for people who came a long distance, looking all around for parking, then to be told they could have parked around the back, and for what? A cup of coffee. Some of them were disappointed. Upset. Down-hearted. Maybe they saw the sadness in me spreading to them and didn't want to stay, it was bad business making money off bad business. Often, they threw up their hands and left, saying they would be back. The representative from the glazing company that installed the full-length mirrors, for example, said he would come again when things picked up.

Some of them laughed while they were taking the world from under my feet. Some of them sympathised with me and blamed the country we were living in. It became an opportunity for them to lay into the government, the economic conditions, the history we were tied into, the schools, the island, the weather. Some of them deflected by saying it was nothing personal. Others tried to make me feel better with a kind of glorious melancholy, a companionship to be found in the collective failures of the world. If only I didn't owe them money, I could have offered to buy them a drink. I felt unequal, my smile was a lie, I had no right to be generous. No right to join them in conversation or have an opinion while this imbalance existed. I was unable to look them in the eye.

It seemed to me that this was not so much a financial reckoning but some inevitable human accountability I was facing. They had come to recoup the happiness I had taken from life. What we owed the world. Our dreams were in default. How naked and shy and guilty we had become. I could not escape the images of paradise and expulsion I grew up with. My extravagance, my billowing white shirt, the squandering rush of love with which I hurled myself into this family enterprise was being called out. They were coming to cash in. Every smile, every laugh, every word of affection had to be repaid.

The man who installed the neon sign asked me to call in one day. His office was in the city. On the same square as my former school, near the Garden of Remembrance, over-looking the maternity hospital where Essie was born. Parking the car around that area gave me a range of contorted feelings, from terror to extreme joy.

I was surprised to find him so welcoming. He asked me to sit down, his secretary made tea, with chocolate fingers on a plate. He briefly mentioned the outstanding bill and I kept apologising, then he didn't want to hear any more.

The world is full of apologisers, he said.

It was hard for me to understand why he had asked me to come all this way to let me off so lightly.

I was shrugging a lot.

He was Jewish. His mother was from Lithuania, he had grown up in Toronto. He married an Irish woman from

Limerick and came to live in Dublin, she was a barrister, there was a picture of her and three children on his desk. He was an athletic-looking man, a runner. Helen had met him running up the pier one day, pushing his eldest son in a buggy, the boy had severe disabilities from birth, he suffered terrible seizures. They often had to clutch him until the episode passed over. I was told by somebody else that he was often seen running through the city at night with the buggy, along the quays, all the way up to the Phoenix Park.

He asked me if I could play the guitar.

No, I said. Not really.

He asked me how many children I had, I said there were two girls and one on the way. He pointed to the photo of his own children and said his eldest boy was twelve, he would have to undergo an operation to straighten his spine, it required a metal support, they would need to fly back to Toronto for it. What I took from this is that they would be needing the money. But he didn't mention it. Instead, we got into a conversation about children, we compared some of the things they said, he said his five-year-old daughter kept going around the house saying everything was ground-breaking.

He leaned back in his swivel chair and asked me how far I would go to protect my family.

I smiled.

It was a strange question, I thought.

Would I die for my family? he wanted to know.

I'm a father like any other father, I said.

His Canadian accent appealed to me. He spoke fast, he didn't have the patience for small talk, straight questions, straight answers. I admired his ability to eliminate the dross of language, no rambling, no buttering, he could ask a question and answer it in the same sentence to save time. He could speak for you if there was a problem, if you delayed.

He wanted to know if I would be prepared to kill for my family. It was not something I could answer, but he pressed me on that, would not let it go. You must have a view, he said. As far as he was concerned, I had every right to kill anyone who endangered my loved ones, the history of my country was on my side. What country? I thought, no country I belonged to ever gave me justification for killing. It threw me into a spin of uncertainty, I had no answer, I shook my head.

Would you take up arms?

Never. I would not go that far, I said.

Never?

Unless I was provoked.

We both laughed.

That was a good enough way of leaving it. But then he pursued it further, as if the situation was coming soon and I had to be prepared for that crucial dilemma, would I kill to defend my family?

No, I said.

You're lying.

I would rather they came and killed us all before I did that to someone else.

I don't believe you, he said.

There was no answer. It was one of those elliptical questions that should be left to philosophers, like angels dancing on a pin, how could you predict your own behaviour?

What would John Lennon do?

He's dead.

Seriously, I said, do you think John Lennon would have killed his assassin to save himself?

He took out a guitar from behind the desk and began strumming. It was a nice guitar, I knew people who would give their right arm for it. His mouth was strained as he played. He was biting down on his lips, breathing heavily. It was a song everybody knew – Imagine. Easy, all beginners had it. Even I had mastered it, after a long time. I watched him doing his best. He struggled to get it working. He had the chord sequence right, he had the words, but there was something about the timing, he jumped in too soon, his foot was tapping to another beat entirely. He asked me did I know the song, could I show him? He handed me the guitar across the desk and I gave it a go. But I was no better, I couldn't get it going either. I was sure I had the hang of it, but somehow it was gone again. I counted the beats, but they came out completely wrong. I handed him back the guitar. We laughed. Neither of us had much rhythm.

I was late getting back to collect the children. I had the feeling somebody was following me and I kept looking over my shoulder. I was in such a hurry to get to the school, it must have appeared to people on the street that I was running away from someone. They were the only girls left in the class when I got there.

It turned out I was being followed. Next day, a man who was owed a substantial figure for installing ventilation ducts in the ceiling above the yoga floors, caught up with me – you think I can't see you.

The reason I was walking along the seafront had nothing to do with trying to avoid him. I was not feeling well, I was biting granite again. Walking was the only way of shaking it off. I had to keep moving, remembering a storybook that Rosie and Essie had, in which a boy with a stick in his hand knocks the teeth out of two crows, that's why birds have no teeth. I wanted mine out, my crow mouth.

The ventilation man had a grin on his face when he found me at the old baths with my head down. The cheque I had sent him was not honoured by the bank because he had left it two months, the funds had dried up. The ventilation ducts were of no value whatsoever, they made the situation with the steamed-up mirrors even worse, Helen had to get one of those window-cleaning swipes on a long handle to keep them clear. He said the problem had nothing to do with his equipment, it worked in all the offices, lots of churches with large crowds of people coughing, sweaty dance halls, damp basement restaurants right around the city, his testimonials were longer than his arm, he said.

I gave him another cheque and told him to cash it straight away this time. He examined the cheque, he examined me, he looked at the derelict public baths. He said it better work this time or else he would haunt the living daylights out of me, I could hide with the rats in the cubicles where they used to have seaweed baths, he would still find me.

Some of them were even more aggressive.

You couldn't blame them.

The man who put in the sound system over the yoga floors said he was not leaving any more messages. He pushed his way past me and walked right in with his ladder and removed the lot. He stepped across the women on the floor. They were in the middle of a yoga session at the time, around two dozen legs in the air, the calm, watery music came to a sudden end. Helen explained to them that there was a circuit problem, she continued as if nothing was wrong, kept describing tropical beaches, light coming through curtains, megalithic tombs. I had to go back down later that evening with the cheap pair of second-hand speakers to replace them.

Another man lost his patience completely and began threatening me, asking if I knew what happened to people's knees in Belfast. He had red hair and a black beard, I thought that was a contradiction, like myself, two people in the one person. He was owed a small amount on tarring the car park, I had given him two thirds and said he would get the rest when the job was finished, as agreed. He said he had friends. It was not something you could ignore.

The smaller the amounts owed, the more trouble they caused. Some of them tried getting it from Helen, then they came back to me with redoubled force. They started coming to the house, some of them got paid, some of them went away with hard promises, one of them called me a scumbag, one of them arrived with a dog, a terrier barking at me in the doorway.

One of them sighed when I told him I had no money even to get sandwiches for school lunches.

This is a howl, he said.

I had no idea what he meant. A howl? He turned and spat behind him. In his language that might have indicated a show of disgust, in my mother's language it meant there was a funny taste in his mouth, in the native language he was measuring the distance between himself and the rosemary bush.

The biggest problem was not knowing what they were like. I knew nothing about their families, their mothers, their backstories, their private lives. I knew them only by their names, what they were owed, what they had on me. Now and again I found out somebody liked sailing, or rugby, things I knew nothing about. One of them spoke about golf like there was wisdom to be taken from sport. One of them spoke like a priest, he was owed money for office equipment, he said it was morally unforgivable to possess even so much as a box of staples not paid for, I was in danger of losing my soul.

One evening the doorbell rang, it was two men from the Latter-day Saints, they left me a leaflet.

Another evening, I heard the doorbell ringing only to find nobody there. I was hearing things, making up creditors that didn't even exist.

The exposed location of the house, the steep slope going down the driveway must have made them feel taller. It made me look inferior whenever I answered the door. The underground expression in my eyes, living in hiding. I had brought my family down into a burrow. It seemed no accident to me that a short story had already been written about the enemy getting inside the burrow. Despite all defences, the place of maximum protection is invaded. The door is left wide open. Terror walks right in, it will make itself at home and sit down in silence with the family at the table. Everything I feared was dwelling with me in the house, my burrow was no longer safe.

The most difficult of the creditors had nothing to do with the current business but with the premises we had before, the damp studio by the seafront. Bardon. The man with white hair, corrugated. He was polite at first. He came well dressed, in a good suit, brown lace-up shoes. He stood in the café admiring the décor, the lively city atmosphere, women coming in with their sports bags over their shoulders, dressed in tracksuits and colourful runners, ponytails, sweat bands. He liked the European look of the place, the soft lighting, the beat of the music, people having coffee and cake after their sessions.

The car park was full, he came on foot.

Strictly speaking, he was owed nothing. We were forced to break the lease a couple of months early because the place was so damp, there was water on the carpet, people stopped attending the classes. He had a new tenant lined up the day Helen moved out, he didn't even repaint. Morally, he had no right to demand any money. But that made no difference, there was no hope of getting him to drop it, he had his bills to pay – please don't test my patience.

We tried explaining to him that our business was in difficulties, once things improved a bit, I would be more than happy to settle, fair is fair, I said. He had no time for that kind of language, wherever I picked it up – fair is fair? No matter how much I practised these phrases in my head, they came out false, he saw through every word. He accused me of being sneaky and full of shit, he had a way of raising one eyebrow while keeping the other one level, a facial question mark.

He said he could do untold damage to our business, his wife might spread the word among women around the area that we were a fraud. There was nothing I could think of that might get us into a friendly conversation, I knew his wife's name was Marjorie, but that got me nowhere, he didn't want a chat.

He began coming to the house. He rang the doorbell one night when I was putting the girls to bed. Insisted on having a word, inside. I didn't offer him anything. I found it frightening that he came on foot, like he didn't want his car to be seen close to the house. I told him I was busy with the children, but he was happy to wait in the living room. He looked around and remarked on how nicely I had done up the place. I thanked him. He didn't intend it as a compliment, only as proof that I could pay him what he was owed.

He confronted me with the children present. He raised his voice. The girls were afraid. I told them everything was fine. I brought them back upstairs and they stood on the landing watching through the bannister rail.

I had some money on the table in the breakfast room, it was there to pay off somebody else. I thought of paying off part of what Bardon demanded, but he had frightened the children, it would have been wrong to give it to him. I told him I had nothing, we were completely broke.

I'm sorry, I said.

He refused to leave.

I told him he was threatening me in my own home.

He thought about that and moved back out to the hall. I opened the door wide, he turned around and came up face to face. I was certain he could see the money lying on the table behind me, but he stared right into my eyes.

You will pay, he whispered – German bastard.

He pointed his finger into my chest, then he walked away, the door was left open. There was a delay before the impact of his finger threw me backwards against the wall. It felt as though there was a hand gripping my jaw, reducing my mouth to an oval nought.

The girls ran down and closed the door.

I slapped my own face. It was like a primitive religious belief that something self-inflicted could beat off what was outside my control. The grinding sound inside my head was like the fires of an opera we heard as children, swelling with emotion, flames around my mouth, each tooth a piece of melting steel. I went down on one knee, like the photographs of my father's time when men took out a handkerchief and placed it on the street, kneeling for the Eucharist going by. My pious head went down to meet the foot of the stairs, my voice creeping along the hall.

The girls asked me what was wrong. I didn't want them to know. I said I was trying to remember something. I got up and made them cocoa, they could have a biscuit each. I brought their mugs upstairs and put them on the window-sill. I sat with them, counting the lighthouse.

A while later, the doorbell rang again, I thought it was Bardon coming back. It was another man, less well dressed. He was holding a mug towards me, it had a flowery design, heavily stained, would I mind making him a cup of tea. I was so delighted he was not looking for money, I asked him to come inside, into the breakfast room. I got him to sit down while I put on the kettle, I took out a plate and gave him two of my Mennonite cookies. He was staying in a caravan not far from where the café was. I gave him the mug of tea, no sugar, just a whisper of milk. Rosie and Essie stood at the door. He smiled at them. They saw me smiling. They clung to the door frame. I didn't want him to think we were going to watch him as though we had never seen anyone eating biscuits before, so I brought them back upstairs.

Take your time, I said.

Thanks.

You're welcome.

I didn't want to be seen swiping the money on the

table out of his reach. The money I could have given Bardon was better spent given to this man, I thought. I took a note from the pile and put it under his plate, left the rest where it was.

The girls wouldn't sleep. They wanted to stay up until Helen got back. They kept asking me what the man wanted, was there a story in it for them. He was a man who kept moving all his life, I told them, he lived in different parts of the country, I heard him on the street one night singing a song – I'm a true-born travelling man.

When he was leaving, I heard him in the hallway, calling up the stairs.

Search me, he said.

It's all right, I said.

We heard the front door closing.

They wanted to sleep in the bath, I said – no way. They wanted to watch TV – no way. They kept jumping from one bed to the other, shouting – way no way no way.

I couldn't calm down either.

There was a building bruise on my arm and they asked me how it happened. I told them it was the thumbprint of a polar bear I met walking across the golf course, they examined it closely, the shape of a purple coin. The polar bear had gripped me by the arm, he was in a hurry, he asked me if I was the father of two lovely girls with pyjamas that had giraffes and zebra designs, they looked at each other. I pointed at the harbour, he was getting on a ship with three masts heading for Brazil. We were all welcome to come, our entire family, we could bring our toys.

That was no help. They started packing right away. I told them it was only a story, but they refused to sleep. I had lost faith in my own fantasies and went along with theirs.

How much did they know?

Did they pick up things they could not name? Like me, worrying about glass breaking, trains on fire, houses crumbling? Was it in their dreams? They sometimes woke up at night and crept into our room, two ghost daughters breathing quietly in the dark, inches away from my face. My love, my anger, my teeth, my episodes of panic, my inability to conceal myself from my own children.

Helen came back late. The girls saw the headlights of the car shining into the hallway and bolted down the stairs. She came in with an envelope. She put it on the hall table and embraced them, said she would give them cocoa and a chocolate biscuit. They've already had that, I said. They told her a man was shouting in the house. They said another man lived in a caravan and he ate two biscuits. They said a polar bear left a bruise on my arm.

I had a look at the document in the envelope. Another writ. A creditor going after Helen personally instead of the company. I put it back in the envelope.

All I could think of was to put on some music. Something upbeat. Nothing serious, nothing weighed down with reflection. Something warm and easy, with lots of love and sha-la-la. The live recording, with the audience erupting in a spontaneous cheer when their home town is called out. A large creature made up of tiny human voices rising in a single roar of emotion. Thousands of hearts taking off like a flock of starlings, how do they know when to change direction all at once?

The music filled the house. It went up the stairs all the way to the roof. It went out the front door, up the street, maybe as far as the shops. It went down under the floorboards with the pipes and the wiring and the silverfish, down with all the layers of dust and memory.

Helen came in. She put the girls sitting on the couch with their cocoa and home-made biscuits. She stepped into the middle of the room and started dancing.

Her eyes were closed, shoulders moving, spinal column straight. Her hands were turned flat down. Her hips were swinging as though she was standing on a flotation device. Her belly was keeping her upright, without being pregnant she might have come crashing straight into the fireplace or shot off towards the window, maybe fallen on top of the girls with their cocoa. Her body had attached itself to this big round cargo. Her arms and legs, her face, her smile, her apple breasts, the wild movements she made in circles around the room – every part of her was stuck on to this coming baby. It gave her gravity, balance, it stopped her from spinning away uncoordinated.

The stairs were narrow. She went up holding the bannister rail. Her shoes were not right. We reached the second floor and she turned to ask – is it much further? I told her it was the next one. There was a bare bulb lighting each landing, a shadow of handprints along the paintwork. We read the nameplates, a freight company, a chiropractor, chartered accountants, the national chess federation, it was at the top of the building, a small office overlooking the city.

We knew him before he became a solicitor. We met him through my friend gone to Australia. He had a broad moustache, he was on the phone when we arrived, he smiled and asked us to sit down. We waited. His office was in a corner building that was shaped like a triangle, you could hear pigeons on the roof. I looked out the window at the city lights, it was dark early, we could see traffic crossing O'Connell Bridge. A wide view of the rooftops, the lights reflected along the river gave the city a carnival atmosphere, an orange glow in the sky over the Phoenix Park.

Helen took off one of her shoes and put it back on.

We could overhear the conversation on the phone, it had something to do with finding a buyer, in perfect condition. When he put down the phone, he smiled – you don't want to buy a shotgun?

He laughed.

His shoulders were jumping. It took me a moment to realise what was funny. Helen was quicker, she said – yeah, let's shoot them all.

He was a fan of American country music. He once got an autograph from a touring country star after a concert in Dublin. The piece of paper he held out to the singer was folded over, blank on one side, on the other he had written – I owe the bearer of this note a thousand dollars. The country singer laughed in a deep country voice and crossed out the figure, he wrote in its place, a pile of horseshit. The autograph was pinned up on the wall behind his desk.

Most of the details had already been explained over the phone, I had sent him the documentation. It was laid out on his desk. He had been able to deal with some of the issues. He had managed to restructure the home loan with the building society. He dealt with the writ I had received for an electronic typewriter, it had a self-correcting feature, you could make as many mistakes as you liked, they had reclaimed the equipment and agreed to accept a small settlement for the balance.

I loved the sharpness of legal wording. I admired the ground rules, striving to be as accurate and as minimal as possible, any excess gave doubt a foothold. By then I had read many writs and demands, I could see beauty in precision. There was no need for eloquence, no need to be interesting, no need for playful language. The meaning could be so easily misconstrued, the idea was to avoid all ambiguity, get to the point as fast as possible on the least amount of words. Stick to necessity, avoid punctuation, avoid adjectives, anything that might leak emotion. I thought of various crisp legal phrases – in contravention, left with no alternative, to be brought in line with immediate effect. I felt nullified. Empty as an empty swimming pool. One of my favourite authors started off as a lawyer.

Our solicitor let us know the banks might not be the worst. He had already let them know we had no available funds. To keep them onside he made up an imaginary relative who might be able to step in with financial aid, it gave them hope, they could be asked to accept small monthly payments to pay off the capital.

We'll see, he said.

Some of the other creditors were trickier. The company that carried out the promotional work on the café was not budging. He had trouble getting anywhere with the architect, it was too late to claim the invoice should have been made out to the company, not Helen personally. The architect always wore sunglasses on top of her head, her coat had an interesting design, green with a black collar going out over the shoulders, shaped in a triangle across her chest. Her surname was the same as a native singer I knew in the Aran Islands, but she could not possibly be related to him.

Our solicitor told us to put our minds at rest, he would find a way of dealing with the rest of the claims.

The relief made me want to cry. It was a kind of friendship I had never experienced before. Nobody had ever made me feel so much at ease with the place where we were living. I looked out the window at the city, the cars and buses waiting at the traffic lights, the familiar advertising on the front of the buildings, people crossing the bridge. I was seeing everything from a new angle, from above, I wanted to ask him if we could stay the night in his office, we could sleep on the floor, watching the city, refusing to close our eyes. I wanted to be there in the morning to see people coming to work, I wanted never to leave, never to go home.

We had a short conversation about Canada. Helen told him her brothers and sisters were mostly in Toronto and Ottawa, one of them was a boatbuilder in Halifax, they all got together when she went over with the children in the summer.

As we were getting ready to leave, he gathered up the documents on his desk and mentioned one further thing. He said it was nothing, merely out of interest – how would you feel about selling the house?

I looked at Helen, she didn't look back.

It was just a thought, he said.

On the way down the stairs, she went ahead of me. I was certain she was crying, but I couldn't prove it. I couldn't ask her to stop on the landing to check. The chiropractor's door was left open, a worn blue carpet, a coat stand. A manual typewriter clacking in another room. The light fitting on one of the landings was broken. She carried on all the way down without me seeing her face. We were back out on the street and she turned to me with a smile – a glass of Guinness for the baby.

All those rehearsals, the method-acting workshops, drama college in London, the small theatre in Dublin, Strindberg, Ibsen, Synge, her previous roles all led up to this moment. She could conceal from me, from her children, from the entire world, the stain of sadness, it never showed. She continued working, answering phone calls, teaching classes, smiling a lot, she would not even give in to a cold. Nothing would keep her from going on the radio every morning to cheer the city up and tell people in traffic how to relax in the rain.

We stopped looking each other in the eye. We might have started blaming one another for everything that was going wrong. Talking straight was betrayal. We stayed false to each other. The only way of remaining faithful was to keep pretending. She remained loyal to the image of a plastic bottle rotating in a river. I stayed loyal to the footprints of a fox in a poem. Our thoughts never crossed. We sat in the car outside the house for a long time without going inside. The lights were off. We didn't even have any music on the car radio. Just a long pause between us. She put her hand on the back of my neck. I put my head down to listen to her belly, it was like a salt mine in there.

I have an idea, I said.

She waited while I straightened up and put my hands on the steering wheel.

I'll get my job back, I said.

What?

They'll take me back any time. The commander said it to me, he meant every word, they'll bring me in at managerial level.

Back to the basement?

It's not a bad job, I said.

I don't want to hear this, she said, turning towards me. I can't believe it. Don't you remember the bargain we made. I am having the baby, you were meant to start speaking.

There was impatience in the way she tapped on the glass beside her, I ran around to let her out.

★

On the phone to her mother in Canada, Helen makes a funny story of the woman who found a dead rat in the shower, running out into the café with only a towel around her and shampoo in her hair, saying Holy Jesus. She had to be comforted with herbal tea and given free classes for a year in compensation. A rubbish bin went on fire outside the café one night, it scorched the door and one of the small olive trees in a plant holder, other than that everything was fine.

She tells her mother nothing about Martina, only that she went to Paris and brought her back a blouse with the word Calvados in the design, hidden among the leaves. José came over to stay with us for a weekend while she was away. Helen never mentioned anything about the investor's wife, Marie Delaney eventually getting a hold of Martina's phone number, calls in the middle of the night – leave my husband alone.

It seemed to me that the rapid collapse of our business coincided in some tragic way with the decline of the investor's marriage. His descent was our descent. Everything was tied into his love for Martina, the anguish of his wife and family, how desperately she wanted him back.

Martina was in the city one afternoon, she had arranged to pick Maurice Delaney up outside the Shelbourne Hotel. His car was parked in a lock-up at the back of the solicitor's office. He was standing on the pavement in his blazer and tie, a schoolboy, a gentleman, a financier looking at his watch, scanning the traffic. It was a fine day, lunchtime, no wind, the pavement busy with people passing by. The hotel porter stood in his tailcoat outside the main door. The flags hanging from the front of the building were not moving much. Martina swung the car in and pulled up to the kerb, she switched down the music and pushed her bag with a Jamaican scarf attached off the passenger seat onto the floor to make room for him. She leaned forward with a smile, but he seemed not to recognise her. She called his name, gave the car horn a slight beep, a country touch, but he turned away. He was running back into the hotel, disappearing through the revolving doors as though he was avoiding her. She waited, realising how easily this could all come to an end.

A woman's voice shouting.

The Belfast accent made it easy to work out. It was Marie Delaney in the car right behind her. The shock made Martina instantly pale, as though her make-up had been removed, a shiver along her back. She was afraid in a way that she had not been afraid since primary school, the brutality of teachers in a small country town. A rush of weakness shot through her stomach, her name being called. The panic set her off at great speed, accelerating with a yelp of tyres that made pedestrians look up. Everybody watching as she raced away in her bashed-up red car, with the screeching noise of a larger car behind in close pursuit.

The afternoon was blind with fear. The map of Dublin became incomprehensible, streets appearing in the wrong order, no time for safety. The race through the city seemed out of touch with the pedestrians in their summer clothes, calmly walking across the street without heeding the traffic lights, skipping out of the way at the last minute. At the side entrance to Trinity College, Martina was forced to stop for people crossing. She saw Marie Delaney coming to a sudden halt behind her. In that stationary moment, she looked in the mirror and saw Marie Delaney's eyes. Her mouth was moving. She could lip read the words like a mimed communication between them. Each begging the other to give in, to be reasonable, cursing as they moved on again at high speed.

They drove the same streets twice, like a grid they could not escape. They came around by the dental hospital, past the chemist on the corner, back up around past the National Gallery, a closed circuit that kept returning to the Shelbourne Hotel as though they were in a race to get back to the starting point. On the street with the smallest pavement in the world, pedestrians spilling out onto the road were forced to jump back as Marie tried to overtake. The terror eventually caused Martina to take a gamble, driving down a laneway without knowing the outcome, where it would lead.

Dublin is too small. Everyone can be seen. Everything is overheard. There is talk of running way.

Helen's mother has no news on her side of the water apart from the fact that they are building a new shopping mall outside the town. She gives Helen the news about the family, how her father has given up alcohol and so did the judge across the road, a lady never drinks alone. She goes through what each one of Helen's brothers and sisters are doing, every good thing magnified, every bad thing minimised.

She says the boardwalk by the lake is being redone, the ownership of the salt mine has changed, Champion Roads pulled out, that's been a blow to the town.

And – her mother has a new friend.

Because her best friend Nessa is no longer talking to her and it's well known around the town that the two Irish women are having an almighty row, like a marriage break-up, Helen's mother started meeting another woman. They got to know each other at the hairdresser's. Her new friend's name is Vera, she is from Prague originally.

Vera, her mother tells Helen, has a great story from her childhood. How she married her best friend at the age of nine, they had a wedding in front of a large mirror on the landing, dressed in all her mother's clothes. When the Nazis arrived, her childhood friend had to leave for New York without saying goodbye. Vera stayed in Prague, her father joined the resistance movement against Hitler. She made her way to Toronto after the war when her family was expelled, she looked for her Jewish friend in New York but never found her, then she got married to a millionaire who invented snap-on tools.

Helen's mother was in the restaurant on the square one day having lunch with Vera when her former friend Nessa pulled up outside. Parking is diagonal, the car was pointed directly towards their table. Nessa got out and walked towards the restaurant without noticing her, maybe there was a glare on the windows and it was hard to see in. Nessa came in the door. It was only when she was standing inside the restaurant that she finally saw Helen's mother with Vera. A new woman, a replacement friend, having lunch at the table normally reserved for two Irish women. Nessa turned around on the spot, the waiter came and opened the door, he even went out and opened the car door for her. They watched her reversing and merging back into the slow wheel of traffic around the courthouse.

I went to see my mother. She was sitting at the breakfast table with her diary. Every morning, Greta got her up and dressed, she came down and had breakfast, then she sat at the table writing her diary. She was telling the story of her life from the beginning. Each time, she would start again, not adding on to where she had left off the day before, but on a new page. Often it began with the very same words – I was born in a strange time. Sometimes she changed it to – I was born in turbulent times. She began with her childhood, describing the stationery shop her father owned on the market square, how she was one of five girls, right in the middle, they played in the fountain in front of the house, sometimes the paper boats they made clogged up the fountain and the water came spilling over the edge.

Word for word, she wrote down the same details every day, how her mother had been an opera singer, there was a grand piano in their front room, a casement window overlooking the fountain. She had written much more when she was younger. She often wondered if it was a mistake to be the child of two parents who loved each other so much. Her father was a funny man, everybody in the town loved him, but nobody had money to buy paper, the business went down, her father closed the shop. It was not long after that he died.

When I arrived that morning, she had reached the point in her writing where her father died, she could not go any further. Normally she wrote neatly inside the ruled lines of her diary, this time the words drifted outside, they began sloping down the page and came to a stop – the scent of lily of the valley will always remind me of his coffin.

As we sat together, I could not help asking myself if I had now become just like her father, who went bust before Hitler came to power. Was I following my German grandfather in all his failure, my Irish grandfather in all his tragedy, my father in all his love and anger, my mother in all her homesickness?

My mother's memory takes the same route each time, back to the last days of the war.

It's after Christmas. She goes to visit her sister in Salzburg, carrying a parcel of food concealed in her case, people are so desperate they keep asking her to share it. Nobody knows how long the war will go on. She is meant to have reported for duty in Berlin, she had been drafted as secretarial backup to the military, she was supposed to be in the capital, ready to be sent to the Eastern Front, to stop the Russians. She ignores the orders and manages to falsify her train ticket. There is a town near Salzburg that has a similar name to the town she comes from. That gets her to the south, to the

Austrian border, from there she manages to get another ticket for the short journey to Salzburg to see her sister. She walks up from the station to the house below the castle, hoping to live there until the end.

She speaks to her sister about staying in hiding but that's not possible.

Her sister already has somebody hidden at the house. A Jewish woman dressed as a nun comes to visit from time to time, to help look after her missing husband's mother. The woman stays a night or two, then she moves to another house, always going to see the same few people in rotation, mostly houses where old people need care. The nun makes her way around early in the morning, carrying a small case with holy water, some religious artefacts, a prayer book, an ebony set of rosary beads hanging down from the waist band. She never goes down into the city of Salzburg. She never goes to any church, never returns to any convent, keeps visiting the small circle of houses with sick people on the mountain. The house cannot take up another refugee.

It was snowing heavily, my mother said.

She waves goodbye to her sister. She makes her way back down the hill with big flakes falling across her face. Snow eyelashes. Snow shoulders.

At the train station in Salzburg, the platforms are being patrolled, everyone is being questioned. They go through her documentation and discover she is meant to be in Berlin. Her name is called out along the platform. She is put under arrest, a deserter. The term for desertion in German means running away from your flag. She waits in a room at the station for hours, not knowing what is going to happen, she tells them nothing about her sister. After it gets dark, she is placed on a train, in a single box carriage with a boy soldier. The boy can be no more than fourteen. He is chained to the seat. She is afraid to talk to him, afraid to give him bread, it torments her that she cannot tell him to be brave, all this will be over soon, he will be going home again.

New Year's Eve. Some bells ringing. The snow is deep, a brightness across the world, everything is like a fairy tale with a bad ending. As the train pulls out slowly from the station, she can see the human shapes hanging, three bodies floating above the snow, their limp feet pointing down like puppets. Their heads have dropped to the side, their arms loose, their hands empty. Around their necks, they have signs she cannot read. The street light casts a golden circle around the snow beneath them, as if they are onstage, the wheels of the train make screeching sounds like the orchestra tuning up.

The boy in the carriage sees it, they look at each other and cannot speak.

In Prague, the boy is taken off, then put back on the train a while later, chained again by the feet. Other soldiers board the train, some of them tied to each other. She is made to wait on the platform, the train pulls away, she sees the boy again briefly, staring out, she wants to wave, but there is no way she can let herself do that.

It's become so cold, it matters which way your back is turned, east or west. The air is dry and glass sharp, it hurts in the ears. She is taken under guard to a truck outside, they help her up onto the step, into the back. With all that is happening, all that determination to get people back to the front to continue fighting, there is still time for politeness. The truck labours up the hill. The driver at one point has trouble finding the gear and there is a grinding sound of metal teeth, they slip backwards before starting up the slope again. The voice of the driver is like encouragement to a horse. It's hard to believe you can keep driving upwards, it must be close to the sky. They stop. In front of the castle overlooking the city. She gets a brief view of the wide river below, the bridges, the snow laid out like napkins on the rooftops. She is taken inside the castle and brought down the stairs, a long corridor with doors on either side, she is locked into a cell with a bed and a blanket.

Helen was the last to leave. She locked up the café, looked at the scorched olive tree outside and made a note in her head to get that removed. She walked around to the car park and got into the car, started the engine, turned on the lights, reversed. As she began moving out, she found a man standing in front of her, blocking the way. It was Bardon, she recognised his white hair, his face, the smile. She stopped and got out. She was friendly to him, but he wouldn't give in, he said he wanted to be paid, he was not waiting any longer.

She asked him to clear the way. She said she needed to get back to the children. She gave her word that I would deal with it right away, but he still refused to let her go. He stood with his arms folded across his chest, then he had them in his pockets, there was a plastic bag flapping in the barbed wire fencing along the back wall, she thought it was a bird.

She threatened to call the guards.

I'll come again, he said.

When she got home, I could see how distressed she was by the way she was trying to calm me down. She looked a bit pale. I asked her if she had been sick. She waved her hand and said she was well able to deal with him.

This has got to stop, I said.

Rosie and Essie jumped down from the bannister rail as though I was talking to them.

I'll find a way to pay him, I said.

Are you joking? she said. Pay him with what? For what? For that damp place. The mushrooms growing out of the carpet, do you not remember?

I know, I said.

He was ripping us off.

He won't give up.

His conscience is a concrete block, she said.

From her eyes, I could see she didn't want to talk about it any longer. Discussing it only made Bardon more present in our lives. What was the point? We had no money. The girls started climbing the bannisters again, Rosie had almost reached the top, she was stuck there. Helen had to help her down, tapping at the spaces in the bannister rail to show her where to place her feet. Our backs were turned to the hall door. We didn't see the face appearing in the frosted glass panel.

The man, Essie said.

I turned around, it was Bardon.

A blurred shape, moving across from right to left, searching for the bell. His face was illuminated by the overhead light in the porch, the warped pattern in the glass panels made him look short-sighted. He was unable to see us even though we were no more than a few feet away, standing still inside the hall, hardly breathing. His eyes were black, one of them larger than the other. His forehead was sloping away in layers of dense liquid, a pulsing creature with white hair, floating by like the crown of a jellyfish. He had no mouth, only the luminous design of a smile across his shoulders.

The doorbell rang.

Helen jumped – Jesus, she said.

Jesus, Essie repeated.

Helen got the girls down from the bannisters and brought them into the breakfast room. At the last minute, Rosie ran back up the hall to pick up a piece of pottery she had made in school, a green dish. Helen closed the door.

I waited to see if he would go away, pretending there was nobody in, even though the lights were on. Our car was parked outside. His vague shape was swaying. Opening the door would let in a flood of seawater, I thought, Bardon with giant tentacles and suckers clasping.

He rang again and waited. He swung around when I finally opened the door, staring at me with his facial question mark. His eyes were full of rage. He was chewing something, a vague spearmint flavour hanging in the doorway.

OK, I said, I want to settle with you.

It was the only way of getting him to leave us alone.

I was inventing some fantastic, last minute, scheme to get out of this. I explained to him that I had no money at the house. There was no point in offering him a bad cheque. He asked about the day's takings at the café, did Helen not bring home cash? I told him it was nothing, no more than the price of a few cups of coffee.

I don't believe you, he said.

What about this, I said?

It was as though I had just started learning to speak. There was a beginner's conviction in my voice. I asked him would he mind coming with me down to my mother's house. I would get her to write a cheque for the full amount. That would settle it once and for all. He smiled. He was happy to hear that. He agreed to get into the car, I reversed out of the driveway and drove down the steep hill.

Along the way, he began a polite conversation, asking what part of Germany my mother was from. He had been to Stuttgart, twice, he said. He still had a couple of words in German, the terms for health insurance, pharmacy, doors closing, the Germans are wonderful people.

I said nothing one way or another.

Outside my mother's house, I parked the car and asked him to wait while I went inside.

It might take a couple of minutes, I said.

Good man, he said.

I stood in the hallway. Greta was reading aloud to my mother in the front room. The door was open. Greta was on the sofa with her bare feet up, my mother on the far side in a chair with a rug around her shoulders. It was the story about a man running a recording studio being asked to cut the word God out of a recorded text, replacing it in multiple places with a new expression – a higher being in heaven. Then later he is asked to cut all those words out again and replace them with little bits of silence.

I heard my mother laugh, she had read this story many times before. It was written by an author who came from the same part of Germany as she did. He had been in the war, he had become addicted to drugs that were given to the soldiers to keep them going, a version of speed that made them aggressive and detached from reality. His books sometimes appeared like drug visions, he had the mind of an expressionist painter. He had come to Ireland around the same time as my mother. He wrote a small travel book that always reminded me of her way of seeing things, the excitement of arriving, the welcome, the time moving slowly.

I continued listening to Greta reading. I waited for the moment in the story where the man in the recording studio gathers the cut snippets of tape with the rejected Gods and puts them into a matchbox. There is a change of heart. He is finally asked to splice the Gods back into the text again and he ends up with a collection of silence.

How could I ask my mother to pay my debts?

The story must have made me change my mind. I left the house quietly without disturbing them. I walked to the car and got in.

I'll drop you home, I said.

Did you get the cheque?

In a minute, I said.

As I drove down towards the seafront, he began to apologise for approaching Helen directly, she's a fine woman, he said, very honest, very feisty.

Feisty?

He said she had great determination. We were good people underneath. It was not easy for him talking to her about money. But he had his own obligations. The four other properties he had were not yielding all that much. Getting rent out of people was like extracting teeth, he said. Not to mention all the outgoings, he had two sons going to college, they burn up money, he said, it's a bugger trying to keep them fed.

With no money to pay him, I returned to the fantasy of arguing my way out. I found myself speaking in a righteous, adversarial tone, turning the finger back on him. In semi-legal language, I accused him of threatening behaviour towards Helen, a mother of two children. He had unlawfully prevented her from getting home to her family, a pregnant woman. He had physically restrained her in the car park, it amounted to kidnapping, false imprisonment.

He laughed.

You blocked her way, I said.

I was having a word with her, he said.

You have no right to stop her going about her business, holding her hostage against her will.

He laughed again.

Come on, he said, getting angry. I was having a word, it's not my fault she got so upset.

Upset?

She drove the car at me, he said.

What?

She tried to run me down.

You're making this up, I said.

She could have killed me, he said. Only that she stopped to open the car door and get sick.

You made her sick?

The hormones, he said. She was out of control.

Without explanation, I found myself racing down towards the harbour. My mind was white. My teeth were buzzing. All self-questioning was suspended.

Bardon became anxious and asked me what I was doing – where are you going?

I hit the brakes and brought the car to a sudden stop on the pier. As though I remembered at the last minute how easy it was to go over the edge, there was no barrier to madness. I pulled up the handbrake and switched off the engine. The stillness of the harbour was hard to believe, the boats swaying, the screech of a heron lifting. A red sheen thrown back by the windows of the yacht club, duplicated in the water below.

It was the small inner harbour, where they used to bring in the coal from England, where the whelk boats are tied up.

Where lovers sit for hours at night with the radio playing softly and it seems they can never get the car started again. A place of privacy. A place of fantasy. A timeless place on the edge of the world where everything could be reimagined, where the false truth could be switched off and you could go back to the truth beneath the truth and talk about stars and planets and places in the universe that became so inaccessible during the day. Where lovers were close to danger and became immortal and woke up still alive with the sun coming up, the air held too much oxygen, there was a strong smell of diesel and fish, a hollow sound of water slurping in a cavity along the pier wall.

Why had I brought him here? To this sacred place, known for love and forgetting? Like we were going to sit there and have a long chat, man to man. I was going to speak my mind, let him have it, warn him, tell him, beg him, never again to go near Helen – you made her sick, you made her cry. Here it was, the great protest. Standing up to him. Standing up to everything that was wrong with the world.

My silence let me down. I got out of the car and stood at the edge of the pier with my arms folded. I heard him trying to open the car door, asking in a muffled voice if there was a child lock. He tried again and again with his shoulder. The car rocked with each attempt. He started knocking on the windscreen, his face alarmed.

Open the door, he called, like a good man?

I turned and walked over to let him out. I was full of politeness. I could not help being helpful.

Sorry, I said. It's a faulty lock.

Why this rush to be sorry? The inability to be bad. All my bad had been done before me. There was no bad left for me to do. I had no right to repeat history. The perpetrator in me had been removed. My role models were negative. Bad was my great inspiration. I had to be better than bad. Bad at bad. Better than better. Sorrier than sorry. Never again. I had the urge to be weak, to be soft, to sit back across the coiled-up ropes and fishing nets with my arms out in submission. The losing part of me was getting the upper hand. The winning part of me was capitulating to the part of me that was full of regret. The fighting part of me was out of place. The business part of me was guided by sad songs about people leaving. The failure part of me was making up for people never arriving.

Soft things had begun to undermine my anger. Like candles and chocolate, the smell of a match lighting up in a room, wooden toys, parcels being unwrapped with the same care that went into packing them, my mother's language, things I could only laugh at like the words to describe a bad mood — your mackerel mouth.

He stood on the pier as though he had come in from a long sea voyage, happy to feel the solid force of home underneath his feet. His fury returned with renewed conviction once he was safe. His mouth was a fist. He inhaled through his nostrils and put out his hand.

Where is the cheque?

She owes you nothing, I said.

We stared at each other like underwater men.

We'll see about that, he said.

It was the brown leather shoes I heard. Kicking some of the whelk shells. I saw him stop to urinate against a bollard. I saw him dance to shake himself. I saw him step back to zip up. I continued watching his head going along the granite wall until he got to the road, he didn't have far to go.

I felt sorry for what I had not done.

Why had we allowed ourselves to be shaped by history? By human divisions? Territory? Money? We remained contestants. He could not afford to give in. I could imagine no way out. It was the same dead-end confrontation I had with my father. He was my father. Every man was my father. We were trapped in this male rage. Men doing what men do. Not letting go. Grabbing power. Pissing. Protecting property. Striking fear into others to stop the fear in ourselves.

I stayed with the calmness of the harbour. I got interested in debris floating on the surface, thick pools of oil, trawlers double moored, the squeeze of tyre fenders as they pushed up to each other, belly to belly. A tower of fish boxes, shackles and chains, wooden pallets. A few marks along the granite wall where they cleaned off paintbrushes.

I drove away with excessive caution, like a first-time driver. The streets were empty. I got home and parked down the slope outside the house. I sat for a while going over all the things in the world that were refusing to change, all the things in myself that remained unaltered. Was this another failed-artist moment? I was trapped by the things I loved. Trapped by the things I feared. Conscripted into being a man, a father, a lover, a boy, a son, a friend, a fighter, a follower, a consumer with quantifiable needs, the man I was expected to be.

Helen was already in bed, she looked up and waited for me to speak. I sat down with my back to her.

Tell me what happened.

Nothing, I said.

She told me to get in. I took off my shoes and got out of my clothes. I felt the warmth inside the sheets and gave in to the wave of comfort. A sleepy submission drew all the strength from my arms, it made me defenceless, I found it impossible to hold on to my anger. She picked up a book and began reading to me out loud. I listened to her like a child. Maybe it was the warmth around me or maybe it was the sheer irony of the prose that made me feel so safe, back in the fold of the imagination. It was the story of the troubadour going out on his horse to fight for the honour of women. The blatant connection between the book and what was happening in my life became an absurd parable. The finger was pointing – look at yourself, the heroic knight, dressed in ludicrous bits of armour. It made me laugh at myself. I could see how futile and comical my actions were. It occurred to me that Bardon was sitting up in bed with his wife Marjorie, that she was reading to him from the same book and that he was also unable to stop himself laughing. The two of us with the covers up to the chin, we might as well have been in the same bed together, all of us helplessly laughing at the description of the most beautiful woman on earth.

*

It was time to deal with my silence. There was no point in going back to the dentist. What more could he do only remind me that emigrants were full of tears, tap on my teeth and ask if I was still speaking the shadow language. Point at the ghost of my smile and tell me that the inventor of X-rays was a German man who took great delight in photographing his wife's bones, she thought he was forecasting her death.

Our family doctor had his practice in a large house on the corner. His surgery was the smallest room. Barely enough space for a leather examination table, some bookshelves, a wash-hand basin. He sat in his chair while I sat on the leather table with my legs hanging down like a boy in short trousers. He listened to my chest, took my blood pressure, examined my fingernails, eyes, ears, tongue – ah. He checked my testicles and asked me if I was happy, was eating properly, did I drink much?

It was impossible to explain what triggered the problem with my teeth. There was no logic, each episode was accompanied by great fatigue, the wish to sleep and never wake up. Any kind of sound was enough to set it off, cornflakes, silver paper, leaves rustling, the news on TV. All the noise of the world in the papers. Should I maybe not listen to what was going on, not take things to heart? Did it have to do with remembering too much? All those things I could not forget? Something I had not yet remembered? Should I be more big-hearted? See the glass in my mouth as atonement? Reparation? I thought of the German statesman going down on one knee in Warsaw?

Medically, there was nothing wrong with me. The doctor said it was an inflammation of the nerve endings, not something you could do much about. He referred to it as neuralgia. Not life-threatening. He said it could have to do with house-dust mites, get a good hoover. Pollutants, was I doing work to the house, fumes, sawdust, cement, he spotted some hardened chunks of expanding foam on my hands.

He suggested acupuncture. Twice a week I had needles hanging from my face and hands, some in my kneecaps, it made no difference.

One afternoon it flared up while I was doing nothing but standing by the window, looking at the light changing, the first drops of rain inaudible on the glass. It had nothing to do with the mood of the day, nothing to do with money, it broke out with furious retaliation while I was calm, thinking only of the coming baby. I found myself walking in circles, running down the stairs, out onto the street, the hall door left open behind me and the sound of printing machines in my head. I lay on the golf course and tried to bite into the soft grass. They stood over me with their golf clubs, asking if I was alive, they assumed I was homeless. I made my way back. My eyes were bouncing in my head. I didn't even slow down on the street that looks like Canada with their lives on view. I reached the bathroom, my face against the cool floor, Helen's voice around me.

There was a lot of talk about healing. New words were being drafted for reconciliation – entente, rapprochement, meeting of minds, dialogue, talk about talk, taking steps, moving positions, conflict resolution, accommodation.

Talk about a new healing method where somebody could sit in a room with you and think you better. They said I should be going for help, hypnosis, past-life regression therapy. They suggested going on retreat, somewhere silent, they mentioned a monastery where I had once recorded a Christmas album in the native language, a woman with long shining hair accompanied by twenty monks, it was called the Virgin's Lament. They told me to eat melons. Fistfuls of garlic. They said I should drink yeast, sour cherry juice, fennel tea, eat more fish. I was told to love life, hum every morning, beat my chest, be a man, take up swimming, seaweed baths. Somebody suggested I should be drinking my own urine.

Martina was in the front room with Helen, the door was closed. I was in the kitchen with Rosie and Essie and Martina's son, José. He was wearing a sailor's outfit. They were having a tea party, trying to speak in Spanish to him, they wanted the curtains closed and the lights on. I had the sick bowl out, making a cherry cake, my mother told me that you drop the cherries in last, so they don't sink.

By then, the investor had found a new apartment, with a view over the water. He wanted Martina to move in with him. He was beginning a new life. He was still going back home from time to time to get some of his things, his favourite jacket with the silver buttons, his train set under the bed, personal bits that were important to him. His wife was distraught. At times she had no idea how to put cornflakes into a bowl, where the fridge was, she left the keys in the door, she lost her handbag, she was getting therapy.

One day, Marie Delaney changed.

She had regained her self-esteem. She invited her husband to a mid-morning breakfast meeting at the Shelbourne Hotel. She mentioned the word truce, asked him to bring Martina, so the whole thing could be talked out rationally. She was there early. Her brother Laurence came down from Belfast to give her support. They had the table in the bay window, the sun coming in across the room. She ordered a tiered serving of croissants and toast, marmalade, fresh scones, tea, a pot of coffee. She was herself again. She wore gold stud earrings, a necklace that looked like polished bits of coal, she had been to the hairdresser.

When Maurice Delaney came in with Martina, they were blinded by the sun at first. Marie stood up. The two women shook hands, her brother Laurence was introduced. The investor kissed his wife, grabbed her brother's upper arm in a boyish way, they all sat down. There was a pause before anyone said anything. The investor made a joke about landing an aircraft in Stephen's Green, the ducks would freak out, nobody laughed but himself. Martina and Marie sat facing each other, not making eye contact. They took it in turns to examine one another – the fingernails, hair colour, the sniff of perfume, a plaster on the heel. Martina looked less casual, she wore ordinary shoes, Mass shoes, she called them. There was a moment when the two women might have got into conversation and forgotten what brought them here and what turned them into contestants.

In different circumstances, they might have been friends, they could have sung – My Lagan Love – together. Each of them born into a different faith. Marie had grown up in Belfast with co-education. Martina had the tight rules of an all-girl convent education down south, looking at the floor, seeing nothing, custody of the eyes.

I believe you were in a folk band, Marie said.

Sort of, Martina said.

Like Joan Baez?

More Patti Smith.

Marie ordered more tea and coffee, politely asked Martina if she would like a boiled egg. Martina smiled and said, no thank you. Nobody was eating a thing only Marie, she was having a scone, the napkin held underneath, her fingernails hovering like a hummingbird to get the crumbs off. She got straight down to business, addressed herself mostly to her husband. There was nothing she could do to stop this affair with Martina, it was not her intention to stand in the way of love and happiness, she said. All she wanted to do at this meeting was to make her husband aware of where he stood.

She didn't mention the family, the home, the children, herself, the life they had built together. Nothing about their combined memory, the photo album of the wedding in Lisbon. Nothing about their honeymoon in the Alps, the romantic things he said to her, she thought he had altitude sickness. She spoke only of practical things, the business arrangements. She placed her hand on her brother's arm. Laurence was the majority shareholder in every one of her

216

husband's enterprises, the building projects, an office block on the river which was in the planning stages. Laurence pulled the strings, there was no reason for him to speak, he put his hands in the air.

Fair play, that's all he said.

The investor was faced with a choice. He could either come home to Marie or carry on his relationship with Martina. If he walked out on his family, he would be stripped of everything he owned. It was time to make up his mind. There was a softness in Marie's Belfast accent that made everything sound reasonable. The only thing she needed to add was the business with the Fitness Café. Helen was not mentioned by name, but Marie made it clear that if the investor did decide to come home and end, as she put it, this dirty little fling with a folk singer, he would need to walk away from the yoga enterprise.

Wipe your hands, she said.

A man on trial. It reminded me of how Kafka came across the idea for his book in the foyer of a hotel in Berlin where he was placed on trial by two women. His fiancée had brought another woman to act as an intermediary. They were demanding to know why he was such a hopeless prevaricator, what kind of a man was he, could he not decide one way or the other whether he was going to marry? On the train journey to Berlin he changed his mind at least a dozen times. A cup of coffee might have helped him to make his decision, but he never drank the stuff. He did eventually manage to bring his fiancée on a brief honeymoon to a spa resort, but no wedding, no ring.

Maurice Delaney was facing the decision of his life. The world seemed to be ruled by women, he was nothing more than a tragic flotilla being sent back and forth across the sea between them. He sat in the main lounge at the Shelbourne Hotel, glancing from his wife to his lover and back, they were waiting for his answer. His eyebrows were arched in the shape of self-pity, a boy being told he could not have everything in life. He was close to tears, forced into a rational corner, weighing up his commercial interests against his human instincts, the choice between his pocket and his heart.

There was doomed tranquillity in the room.

A static group, sitting at the table by the window as though they had been there since the Easter Rising, the best part of a century gone by. It was Martina who finally made the decision. She looked him in the eye. She stood up. Without a word, she picked up her embroidered handbag and straightened up, turned and began walking away across the wide room towards the door. The distance was vast. Endless tables to get around, people pulling in their chairs to make way.

There was still time for him to follow.

She continued making her way out into the foyer, past the stairs leading up to the rooms, the chandeliers, the menu for the restaurant like a precious exhibit on a stand, people gathering for lunch. The pinpoint clack of her shoes along the marble floor made an unbearable exit. She managed to smile at the porter on her way out. She went through the revolving door, hardly needed to push because it was set in motion by other people coming in, a shuffle of her feet and she was exhaled onto the street. She stood outside on the pavement for a minute or two, tall, straight, no coat, a light red cardigan loose around her shoulders. She had the confidence not to turn around. Refused to give in to the temptation of looking back to see them sitting motionless in the window, staring out as she put up her hand, getting into the back of a taxi.

I had the cherry cake ready, out of the oven, cooling on a baking grid. The cherries sank after all. Helen came rushing out of the front room. She left the door open and I saw Martina with her head in her hands. Helen got a glass of water, she picked up a box of tissues, the sick bowl was not needed. It was turned upside down on the draining board like the round back of a stainless-steel creature that moved only very slowly, a couple of centimetres every year.

It was spring. The cherry blossoms were out early. For some reason that morning, I got the impression people were waving at us. I could see nobody. It was a false perception. Unseen people at the windows, unseen people in the street, waving as we made our way down to the courthouse. It gave me the feeling we were going away.

Helen was wearing her blue coat, not closing it over her belly, her back was giving her trouble. She changed her shoes at the last minute before leaving the house.

We stood in the alleyway by the wall of the courthouse, an old redbrick building, the side door was the main entrance. People were gathered outside in small groups, men smoking, nervous family members, guards in uniform with their hats off. A woman with dark rims around the eyes shouted up the alleyway at a man going off to get cigarettes – a Mars bar, I'm starving – her voice left an echo, she had a bad cough. There was a pushchair outside the door with no baby in it.

Two guards made their way down the alley, a man was handcuffed to one of them, his arm was in plaster, his face was scarred. He looked at me with threatening eyes and I looked away instantly, they disappeared inside.

Bardon was standing a couple of metres away from us with his lawyer. His Crombie coat was left open, he wore a striped shirt with a candy cane design, a dark wine-coloured tie. He seemed out of place among the other people waiting in the alley, he made the door of the court look more like the entrance to a theatre, the opening of a new play.

Our solicitor went to have a word with them, to see if they could reach a last-minute settlement, but there was no progress to be made and he came back to stand with us again. Then everyone went inside.

Our case was called.

Bardon spoke well, his voice was steady, his words made him seem like a completely reasonable man who regrettably found himself in this situation. Nothing he hated more than taking anyone to court, he had been very patient, again and again he had given his former tenant grace to settle the debt, but there was nothing forthcoming. He was under financial strain, doing his best to conduct his business in a fair manner, he wished she had made some attempt, some gesture of goodwill, he might have found some way of coming to an accommodation with her. He had done everything to facilitate her business, he had put in a new carpet, he had made sure the heating got fixed promptly, he attended to every request, she broke the lease without any consultation, when it suited her.

With respect, he kept saying.

His appearance was that of a statesman. Somebody in the service of the nation who had been forced to take time off important duties to deal with this unpleasant matter, not of his own choosing. It was his grey hair, the white eyebrows, his good name. He addressed the judge with great courtesy. He said he had been threatened, an attempt had been made on his life, he no longer felt safe.

Our solicitor put forward the arguments for Helen. The premises had become wholly unsuitable, the conditions were appalling. His client, he said, had been forced to abandon her yoga classes, she had lost business, she had no option but to break the lease and find alternative premises.

I wanted to add more details – what about the spores in the carpet, the pools of water, the women came out with their feet wet. What about the smell of the place, the rubbery stench, we had to spray deodorant before every class.

There was no need to expand on every flaw, our lawyer made the more forceful point that the place, meant for well-being, had become a serious health hazard.

The judge asked if there was any written evidence of complaints about the conditions, any communication to relevant health authorities, there was none available.

Our solicitor concluded with a strong argument that the terms of the lease had been broken by the landlord. His dereliction had forced Helen into moving her business at great cost to herself.

I saw Helen in the witness box, it might have been only a couple of minutes, for me it was a lifetime. She looked small, holding onto the wooden structure as though she might lose her balance, even while sitting down. This was no place to smile. No place to be herself. The baby she was carrying took up all her concentration.

The judge read out the address of the premises, naming the parties to the agreement, along with the dates, he held out the lease as an exhibit, passed over by the court clerk for Helen to look at.

Is that your signature?

Yes, Helen said.

Did you sign this agreement in good faith?

Yes, she said.

What else could she say? After a moment, she spoke out. She spoke with force, without shame or culpability, she didn't use any adjectives or make any exaggerated statements. She was not accusing anyone, it was not her intention to put anybody down, she was merely defending herself and her family. She told the judge that she was doing her best, she had two children, one on the way. This man had no right to come after her for money. He may be justified in law, she said, but he has no moral right to demand anything. What he is doing is not honourable. It is wrong. I would not want my children to take a penny that is not legitimate, she said.

Helen looked around, at Bardon, at the guards, at the public gallery, at the judge. There was a pause while everybody waited to see if she had finished.

Thank you, the judge said.

He had no further questions. In the moment he took to deliberate, perhaps no more than ten seconds, it appeared to me that it was not the legal parameters that mattered but our right to be happy. The baby she was expecting. The family entity we had come here to defend. The question to be determined was not the principal sum due under the terms of the lease but what we owed the world for being alive. The air. The water. The share of luck we extracted from the earth.

Helen Boyce – judgment against her.

I saw the Irish harp, the symbol of the state, floating above the head of the judge. I cursed him and his harp like a convicted man. He gave her no chance. How unfair, how one-sided the law is, confined to the ideals of property.

I stood up.

My mouth was open. A soundless voice. It was a shock to me when the real, audible words finally flew out like a scattered bird, a crow flying across the court.

Helen, I shouted – you were great, I love you with all my heart.

My flare-up was embarrassing, hopelessly out of context and irrelevant. People turned to stare at me. The judge glanced up for an instant, then he began moving documents around. The next case was called.

It was hard to watch her coming back. As if the court had been turned around and she could no longer remember how she came in, where was the exit? She didn't see me. She walked right past, failed to recognise me waiting at the door, she looked around at the faces of the people standing outside in the alleyway smoking.

Bardon stood watching us. He held his hands out in a gesture of cheap compassion, as if to say – look what you put her through.

There was nothing to talk about in the car on the way back, nothing to say as we got home, the house was silent, as though we had come from a funeral. I collected the children from school, they must have sensed something, they were fighting. Rosie went into the front room and started screaming. Essie slammed the door of the kitchen and sat on the floor in a sulk. Helen was in bed. I spent the afternoon trying to fix a cable running under the floorboards, some disconnection, only one of the speakers working. I brought Helen up some cherry cake, but it was still there on the plate that evening, getting a crust. I offered to read to her out loud from a book, but she said she would be fine – thanks.

The news around the world was no better than ours. A solicitor was murdered in Belfast for representing Catholics. A bounty was placed on the head of an author who wrote a book blaspheming the prophet Muhammad. A tanker ran aground in Alaska spilling thousands of tons of oil.

The good news was too good to believe. There was talk of a cease fire in the North.

It was hard to stay in the house that night. A relief to be on the street. I walked past the cluster of shops, through the place that looked to me like Canada, where people sat in their living rooms without embarrassment. I went through the school, up across the golf course, the mountains were black against the clear sky. All I could think of was to keep moving. I went up the hill by the spire called the Witch's Hat, it was a folly from the famine time. I walked back around by the view that kept my mother in Ireland. I heard the first morning train below me. On one side of the bay there was a sheet of white light laid out on the water, on the other side there was a blur of rain, the distance before me seemed enormous and tiny at the same time, a limitless world inside a box.

I walked back along the route of secret lanes, an alley between two houses no more than a metre wide, by the small harbour. I came to the bathing place and stood for a while watching the waves. On a crop of rock where people dive in the summer, their bodies bending in a majestic fold before they straighten out and enter the water. I looked down into the surging tide and understood the concept of vertigo. In a book by a Czech author, I had read that the scary part is not the fear of heights or the view of death below, but the decision for life being left entirely up to you. Can you trust yourself?

How welcoming the sea is to a person in doubt.

What interested me was not so much the waves lashing in across the rocks but the water being withdrawn again. The sheet of white wash jumping up was impressive, far more dramatic every time was the furious sucking back out, each wave receding more urgently than the force that flung it inwards. It was this requisition, this payback, the demand for the return of what was so freely borrowed that I found compelling. No matter how far the foam spread in a white apron across the stone benches all the way into the changing kiosks, where people folded away their clothes, hiding watches in shoes, money in underpants, the volume of water being repaid appeared to be far greater than the amount given. I got so involved in watching this process of offering and retracting that I saw nothing but the emptying. It seemed to me that while everyone was still asleep, the earth was steadily being depleted, everything was running out, the ground I stood on was bankrupt.

The sun was up by the time I got back. They were having breakfast. I kept them out of school. I packed a small suit-case, got them into the car, told them we were going on holidays. I helped Helen into the passenger seat, she didn't want to be told any plan. I had some money that my mother gave me. I drove without knowing where I was going, nowhere far enough. Rosie said we were driving to Brazil. Essie said we were going to France first. I said we were going to Australia.

Helen smiled.

Her hands were resting on her belly, we brought only the most essential belongings. The thought that we were living on an island, that we would inevitably reach the west coast and would have to turn back at some point did not occur to me, it only mattered to be moving. We stopped for sandwiches, we gave an apple to a horse, we spotted a wild beehive in the wall. I was surprised the car kept going, it was overheating. I pulled into a garage to put water in the radiator, the fuel gauge was faulty, always full.

I wanted Helen to see the house where I once stayed in Connemara, the singer I had gone to visit, the man who refused to touch money. I thought his way of life would restore ours. His language would soothe my mouth, his singing would bring us back to life.

It took a while finding the place, the last house at the end of the road, facing out to sea. The landscape was left intact, just as I remembered, full of rocks and seaweed laid out. By the time we got there, it was late afternoon, the sun was going down. The fuchsia hedges were overgrown along the path, not yet in bloom, the house had been abandoned, the blue door left open. We walked inside and saw a few bits of furniture, the fireplace, a picture of the pope and the president. I showed them the room where I stayed, the bed was still there, covered in fallen plaster, the ribs showing in the ceiling.

We were like a family coming back after years to find our stuff scattered around. Some empty beer cans on the stone floor, things had been written on the walls. In a small window looking out over the ocean, Helen leaned with her belly against the whitewashed wall. There was nothing out there only blue distance. In the kitchen, there was a dresser with some cups hanging on hooks, a butter knife with the yellow handle partially broken off, a plate made of brown glass, some electricity bills. I picked up one of the bills and showed it to Helen, the name written in the shadow language – O'Flaithearta – final reminder. We smiled at the idea of walking away, who knows where he was gone, he owed nothing to a place abandoned, only his silence left behind.

She put the back of her hand up to touch the side of my face. She kissed me for all the people gone away. I didn't know what she was saying with her eyes, was she thinking we should also be leaving? She made a joke out of it. She threw her arms out and spun around the stone floor in a circle – at least we'll have somewhere to go.

I told the children this was where we were staying for the night. She told me not to scare them, don't worry, she said, we're going to a hotel, with a bubble bath. We tried a couple of places in Galway, they were all booked out, we looked like a family arriving out of nowhere, with no prior arrangements made. We went to the Atlantic Hotel. I had stayed there before for work, I spoke in the shadow language to the man at the reception desk, my mouth was fine.

We were at the back of the building, overlooking the car park. The light was entering like moisture into the room. There were three beds, the covers were brown, like curtain material, the sheets felt as though they had just been taken in off the line, not completely dry yet. Rosie slept outstretched, one arm across Essie's face, I moved it twice, but it sprang back into position each time, Essie slept unbothered in a curl.

There was a racoon in the extra bed, eyes open.

We stayed awake.

Helen asked me to sing a song. I said it might wake the children, the racoon, what about the other guests, next door, the hotel was silent. There was no quiet kind of singing, no way you could whisper a song, only belt it out. She said there was nobody listening but her, and the baby, she placed my hand on her belly, her head on my chest.

I sang in the ghost language.

A song about being asleep and not wishing to be woken up. She asked me the meaning of the words and I translated them for her. The sound coming up through my chest was like the engine of a boat, she said, it made her feel she was heading off to the islands.

We heard a door closing. Somebody letting us know the morning was still far off.

She was whispering. There was a brightness in her voice as she spoke about Canada. I had a map in my head of the town by the lake where her family lived. She told me how the Great Lakes were formed, they all learn this at school in Canada, she said, my sisters will tell you how the shifting ice left the lakes behind like negative mountains. The grain elevators look like some geological feature pushed up out of the earth at the same time, their reflection goes deep into the lake.

She described her sisters – Molly, Maggie and the youngest Kate. They had such a great laugh together whenever they met. It was hard to get a word in, she said. She went silent. For a moment I thought she had fallen asleep.

If we were going, she said.

Where?

She sat up as though she was talking to the far side of the room, the racoon.

I'm not saying – let's go, she said. I'm only saying, if we were thinking of going, if things get out of hand and we need to leave, that's all I'm saying.

Canada?

We could put in an application.

You want to go.

I don't want to leave, she said. The children are happy. They have their friends. Your mother, she said, you can't go, I know that, you have got to stay for her.

I didn't say anything.

No harm making an application, she whispered.

It was not something that required an answer. It was a thing she must have thought of many times before and wanted to say out loud for once in the middle of the night to put it out of her head. She said we might as well get value for money in sleep and lay down again. I had no intention of sleeping, I didn't want to find myself getting up again, having to resume.

What put her to sleep kept me awake.

I imagined walking down to the salt mine, the water sleepy, the reflection of a cargo ship, the sound of steel, out of time. The Canadian flag flying on the wharf. I would become a new person, everything would be newly said, nothing known about me, nobody following, nobody waving, nothing owed. My children would speak to me with a new accent. We would drive to Algonquin, we would pull into a service station, buy ice cream, sunscreen, mosquito repellent. I would get lost in hardware stores. I would disappear in underground shopping malls. I would find myself on the streets of Toronto in the snow, a man invented.

Would I miss my country – which country?

I thought of where we were, in a Galway hotel, the streets empty. I thought of the mossy walls, the stone bridges, the force of the river flowing, how many cubic metres of brown water pass by in one roaring night, how long has the lake been emptying itself out into the sea and it never will. I thought of the rain across the islands, the waves slamming into the cliff, the baby inside her was going to rescue us.

The hardest thing for Helen is telling her mother over the phone that she is closing the Fitness Café. She says she is looking for a buyer to take it over as a going concern, there is a lot of interest. I hear her say she has now become a journalist. The business has become too much, along with running the family and having the baby.

I have managed to put in a new phone extension beside the bed, so she can sit up with lots of pillows and make her call to Canada before going to sleep.

I hear her say that writing articles for the Sunday paper takes up most of her time now. She has begun interviewing well-known people about their lives. It's a great way of getting to know the country, she says, all the different personalities and their habits, some of them are polite, some of them are in a rush to get it over with, anything for a bit of publicity. A theatre manager she interviewed one afternoon refused to turn on the light, they sat in his office as it was getting dark, he told her he had lunch with Beckett five times, over twenty times with Pinter, once with Friel. The Archbishop gave her a slice of apple tart. The head of the Irish Management Institute told her he liked walking around the house in his underpants, she put that into the article and it caused a terrible row, his wife said they were going to sue the paper.

She tells her mother I published a short story in a Saturday paper. The story describes the palm trees that manage to grow in Ireland because of the Gulf Stream bringing mild winters. Palm trees that are not even real palm trees. False palm trees planted along the coast, unaffected by the salt in the air. Outside hotels, on golf courses, in church grounds, even in graveyards. They have long leatherette leaves that often get tangled around the rotating blades of a lawnmower.

Of course, the story is not really about palm trees. It's about a couple with two young children having an argument about where they want to live and where they belong. The story ends up putting us into more debt. There are so many things to pay off, the money I get for the story is spent three times over, once when I receive the acceptance letter from the editor, a second time when the story appears in the paper, once again when the cheque arrives a month later.

Helen tells her mother she has sent everything by post in a rolled-up baton, along with a note, the news will be ancient history by the time it arrives, she laughs, a drawing one of them made of me on the roof of the house.

Her mother has no news apart from the usual, the friendship war with Nessa is getting out of hand. Her new friend from Prague had been invited to Nessa's fiftieth birthday party. Helen's mother was left off the invitation list. Vera showed her the card with gold lettering. Her best friend from Ireland was trying to steal her new best friend from Prague.

Nobody was going to get the better of Helen's mother, not Nessa, not her sister with the bunch of keys back in Ireland, not any of the people her children got married to.

She is the Irish woman who lives in the house overlooking the salt mine. She walks into the bakery saying what a lovely morning it is to the police officer ahead of her buying a box of doughnut holes. She says she has come to collect Nessa's fiftieth birthday cake, the girl behind the counter says it was meant to be delivered. Helen's mother talks around them with her smile. She persuades them to put the cake in a large box. She doesn't want it to be put in the trunk, she watches them carefully placing it into the back seat of the car, the birthday cake for a party she is not invited to. She drives away, looking around at the cake like an obedient child. She swings around the courthouse square, there is a flaw in the clock shaped design of the town, she takes the wrong exit and finds herself going north towards the cemetery. She drives past the shrine to the salt Madonna, she ends up at the harbour, the salt mine.

Helen's mother, inventing roads that don't exist. She imagines there must be a road leading past the grain elevators back to the beach and the ice cream parlour, she is mistaken, finds herself driving out along the pier instead. The interior of the car is filled with the smell of baking. She feels the pain of being excluded, this friendship war. She cannot find a place to turn around. She pulls the handbrake and steps out of the car. The noise of the salt loading is familiar, but it's never been so close, the industrial screech, the clang of metal, the salt is getting into her hair. In between the pier and the hull of the salt ship, there is a floating collection of objects that fills her with abhorrence. She doesn't hear the red truck pulling up behind her, the man with Sifto-Salt written across his chest.

His soft voice – Lady.

What is a woman from Ireland doing on the pier, staring with disgust and fascination at the debris floating in the water, and the back door of the car left open?

He sees the cake on the seat and says – happy birthday.

She smiles and makes a joke of it – what do you take me for, do you think I'm fifty?

He gets into her car and turns it around for her, pointing in the right direction. She drives back through the town, out along the rural route, across the railway tracks where she once got stuck in the snow. She comes to the estate where Nessa lives, in along the oval drive up to the porch, no cars parked outside. She pulls up and gets out. She is in no hurry. She opens the back door of the car, reaches in to lift out the cake, steadies herself, closes the door with her bottom. Her blue leather shoes crunch along the gravel. The cake has a nice weight. She places it down carefully on the porch. She takes off one of her gloves, blue to match her shoes, with cloth buttons in a row along the side. She lays the glove down beside the cake. She steps back to admire the inspiration of this delivery. She turns and takes the same number of crunching blue steps back to the car. She puts her seat belt on, drives slowly, no dust behind her.

My mother sat in a chair by the window with her coat on. She had a light beige scarf tied around her neck and her handbag on her knees, her hands lying flat down on top of the handbag. Every day she sat there waiting. Greta got her up in the morning, she insisted on washing in cold water, Greta gave her breakfast, she didn't eat very much. She asked for more tea. Greta brushed her hair and got her coat on, tied the scarf loosely, put her handbag in her lap.

Everybody is waiting for the war to end.

She has been sent to a small garrison in Bohemia to spend the remaining days of the war. It is situated to the north of Prague around two hours by truck, the garrison is surrounded by Czech resistance fighters. She is the only woman there. The morning has been clear and sunny. An empty oil drum has been brought out to burn documents. All day the fire in the yard has been blazing, men carrying out files and throwing them on top. Bits of blackened paper flying up like birds gliding across the roof and out into the country, nesting in trees. The smell of charred paper is in all the rooms, you can't open a window, it's in her clothes, in the uniforms of the soldiers, in the coffee.

By evening, the fires are reduced to a glow. It begins raining and the glow disappears. There is a knock on her door. An officer has come to speak to her. He is polite, she cannot let him into her room. He mentions that she is the only woman in the garrison, it will not be good to be there when the Russians arrive, they are no more than an hour away. The distance to the German border is around two hours, even with the roads packed full of traffic heading west it will be hard to stay ahead. At great risk to himself, he gives her a chance to escape. He points to an ambulance parked by the main gate. She says nothing. It has been there since she arrived, never moved once. He tells her the ambulance will be going out on a call, it will instantly merge with the stream of refugees, he gives her a time, no bag, he says no more than that.

Running from the flag?

She sits in her room waiting. When the time comes, she gets up and puts her coat on, her hat, her scarf. She leaves everything else behind. She walks out into the corridor, there is no light on, she sees the ambulance parked by the gate, the rain is so heavy it leaves pools in the yard. At the foot of the stairs, she waits for a moment. It's wrong at that moment to think of her sister, of her family, of home, none of that helps, she is alone. She goes along the side of the buildings, under the wooden awning to stay dry. She gets the sodden smell of burned papers. Coming up to the door of the garrison command, she hears voices inside, the telephone ringing, officers leaning over a desk, the officer in command talking to Berlin, the words – standing fast. She remains unseen passing the window. Her eyes kept on the ambulance. The door springs open behind her, the light runs out onto the square like a bright hand searching. She pulls herself in with her back to another door, her breath stops, her body shrinking to a sheet. The flat shape of a woman in a brown coat, with a heart so loud it can be heard in the ground, up through the shoes.

The commanding officer steps into the light. He stands there smoking under the awning, staring at the sloping rain, while the voices in the office behind him continue in urgent assessment, listing off their chances, the weather conditions, the exact location of the garrison, the approximate location of the Russian lines, the time left before they will engage, no more than an hour, less than half a day.

She sees the cigarette butt flying in an arc out into the rain, hit by a large drop and extinguished instantly. The scoop of remaining smoke from the commanding officer's lungs drifts along the building like a question being silently placed all around him. He turns and stares straight at her, the thin strip of cardboard that she has become, stuck like a poster onto the door. Her face is a black-and-white photo of a woman bearing an intense gaze into the rain. The static image of an opera singer, her lungs ready to sing across the square in a voice that will echo around the doorways, into the corridors, around the rooms, under the beds, into the basement cells where the Czech prisoners are being kept, out across the walls of the garrison to their Czech friends in the town nearby, waiting for the end, pleading on the phone each night, trading safe passage for the return of their comrades.

The commanding officer reads her like the details of an upcoming concert. She can't even blink. Her breath is a voice brought short. He takes a step towards her, to make sure he's got the date right, then he is called inside, the door closes, the rain continues without the light.

It takes a while before she can move. The ambulance is far away, what seemed like twenty steps now becomes a hundred metres. She peels herself silently away from the door and makes her way back along the buildings, up the stairs to her room, she sits down on the bed, takes her coat off. She tried running away from the flag before, it didn't work this time either. She stands up and looks out the window. She watches the ambulance slowly moving away, no lights come on, the gate opens, the ambulance disappears, the gate closes again.

After I brought them to school, I went to speak to the principal. She sat behind her desk as I explained the situation to her. I told her we would have to take the children out of the school, her face had a puzzled frown. Was there something wrong with Montessori, the size of the school, the assembly hall with the stained-glass windows where families used to pray, hoping the sailors would come back? The girls were happy, I said, it was the best school for them, we could not pay the fees. She smiled and said the girls were doing well, it would be a shame to move them. She set aside what was owed and told me not to worry about the world, my ship would come in.

I didn't know how to thank her.

I drove home and started clearing the kitchen, everything had to be spotless. Helen put her coat on. We drove down to the Fitness Café together without any talking, the staff were waiting, she asked them into the office. She gave them packages she had made up, a card to thank each one of them in person. She wished them good lives and good jobs, she was sorry she had not been able to give them more security.

We closed the doors.

That afternoon, when the girls got home, they ate the entire tin of Mennonite biscuits. I checked their lunchboxes and asked them why they hadn't touched the cherry cake, they said it was full of ants. I saw the ants crawling out one by one, drunk with sugar. They had been coming up from under the sink, I thought I had blocked them, but they were finding new routes to get at the cake on the counter. Essie said the girls in her class refused to eat their lunch, they thought the ants were in all the food, the teacher had to put their lunchboxes outside the window.

I told them I had a friend in Australia, his children ate green ants. They screamed. I told them he had four children and they ate ants all the time, I said, big green ants, they taste a bit peppery, full of protein. The letter I got said they had moved from Fremantle to Cairns, his family ate outside all year round, a lot of fish. He sent me a list of bird names, full of colour. He said he hoped the writing was going well and the weather inside the pubs was good.

Not for the first time, the story of my life unfolding from moment to moment seemed to be part of a continuous report being sent off to a distant observer abroad. Each detail was staged, made more dramatic, more glorious and tragic, to be approved by my friend in Australia. I had the protection of an imaginary audience on the far side of the world, reminding me not to care so much about things left unfinished, I should be fucking off and never looking back.

Late afternoon, I walked back down to the café on my own. The place felt even more empty than before. The chairs were stacked. The lights were off. I got out a marker and a sheet of paper. I wrote a note to let customers know the premises were closed. I taped the note up on the inside of the glass door – we regret the inconvenience.

It must have been the same note my German grandfather put in the window of his shop on the market square in the time between wars. He thanked his customers for all the stationery they had bought over the years and apologised for not being able to serve them any longer. He signed his name on the bottom of the note and wished everyone well. He must have found it difficult to walk across the market square after that. My mother told me that his friend ran the cinema on the far side of the square, they always received compli-mentary tickets to every new film that was shown. From that moment on the tickets no longer came. The people of the town were afraid to be seen talking to him, as though his failure would spread to them, he was unable to make them laugh, the humour had gone out of the town. He sat for hours in the front room on the first floor, watching people passing by the shop gone silent on the ground floor. Perhaps it was his lungs that were at fault, some condition he picked up during war. Perhaps it was the coming violence, the political unrest in the streets, the slogans, the agitation, the resentment in the way people talked, the anger in the voices pounding on the radio. His health swiftly deteriorated, my mother was nine years old, he asked her to bring him a mirror when he was in bed, so he could say goodbye to himself.

I took the train into the city.

Back up the stairs past the chiropractor and the chess federation. Sitting in the solicitor's office, we went through each debt starting with the highest. We ticked them off one by one, the strategy, the likelihood of forgiveness, payment schedules. The landlords were a consortium of investors based in Athlone. They wanted Helen to pay not only the arrears but also the rent for the next ninety-nine years. The fact that we had vacated the building was of no interest to them.

We'll come up with something, he said.

It was late by the time we finished. I asked him what I owed him for all this and he laughed, he said that was the last thing I needed, him as a creditor. He asked me what I was writing about and I said it was hard to tell, maybe something to do with war. Love. War and love, that kind of thing, I said. But then I was instantly embarrassed, I blushed, even mentioning the word love seemed so uncool.

Sounds good to me, he said, like a thriller?

Yes, I said.

Going out the door he slapped me on the back to remind me that I had nothing to worry about. The people I owed money to should be worrying. His laugh was reassuring, I carried it with me down the stairs.

I started in Grogan's.

I went in the back door past the gents' toilet into the bar, through the partition, through the front lounge and out the main door onto the street again. I had no intention of ordering a drink. No interest in getting drunk. It was the feeling of being there I wanted. People looking up to see who was coming in. A man turned around to face me, he must have thought I was somebody else. A woman looked up with great curiosity, perhaps she had seen me before and couldn't make out where, the same faces will always come through the bar in rotation, in the back door and out the front.

The night was warm, the city was full of lovers, couples making their way from one bar to another. I walked through Lemon Street and came to a men's clothing shop on the corner, there was a yellow shirt in the window, this must be where the investor buys his clothes, I thought. How was he getting on, back with his family, his children?

Across the way, there was a bed made up in a shop doorway, a place with an overhang. The bed was unoccupied. A sleeping bag and a pink blanket laid on top, tucked in. The pillow was a rolled-up mat. The base was a cardboard box flattened out, from a TV. A small strip of carpet on the step.

In Kehoe's pub, it was the same sequence, in the back door and out the front. I walked into the main bar, past the gents' toilet which was to the left down the stairs. There was quite a crowd and I had to force my way through. Somebody spoke to me, but it turned out he was talking to the person behind – tickets, you must be joking.

Moving on into the front section, a woman came towards me with a pint of Guinness in each hand. For a moment, it looked as though she wanted to hand one of them to me. Two pints, two arms, two eyes, why were so many human things doubled? For aesthetic reasons, for public assurance, a mirror of ourselves. Our symmetry reflected in architecture, a monastery I once visited in Germany had two doors in the main room, one leading in and out, the other leading nowhere, onto a blank wall, put there only for visual comfort.

Leaving by the front door I found myself in congestion, people entering in the opposite direction. I stood back and looked around at the pub interiors, the ancient wooden partitions, the smoke-damaged ceiling, the wall of spirit bottles behind the bar. I saw the pint of Guinness that could have been mine, the creamy foam reaching another man's lips, the black liquid slipping down his throat. I found a way forward, past the snug where Helen once breastfed Rosie, out into the street.

I continued my tour.

The same again in Doheny & Nesbitt's. In the main door this time, past the snug. I heard the familiar bundle of voices, the crossfire of words in all directions, people laughing. People not taking much notice of who was coming in. On my way through, a man sitting at the bar gave me a nod. It was no more than a minimal movement of the head. Enough to stop me. Maybe we knew each other. No words necessary, just the angle of the forehead altered a fraction and returned to starting position. His face didn't change. His expression didn't move. I was mistaken. I had picked up an unintended nod.

The barman held on to my eyes for a moment, but I kept moving. Back outside I stopped to get my breath. Another night, I thought, you could do the same route and everybody would know you. They would all be nodding, talking the whole night, holding on to you in the street after closing time.

We were in the park that afternoon, across from the native basement. All the lovers were out. Lying on the grass with their sandwiches. Rosie and Essie running up and down a small green hill. I had a view of the building where I used to work, also the German library, and the National Gallery. The grass was still a bit damp that time of the year, but the soft voices of lovers made me want to sleep.

Helen was still working. She was determined to get as much done as possible, to the end. She had arranged an interview with a composer, a professor of music at Trinity College. It was important to her to meet the deadline for the Sunday paper. The composer said he wanted his music to be experimental, he saw himself as an agitator, producing sounds that people had never regarded as music before. He seemed not to notice that she was expecting a baby. The contractions must have begun right there in that fusty room with three cellos and two violas and stacks of yellowed score sheets. Whenever she stopped making notes and shifted with discomfort in her chair, he looked surprised, she said sorry, then he continued talking.

It was late afternoon by the time we got home, I made the dinner and she sat in the front room writing her piece on the composer while it was still fresh in her head. We were sitting at the table when her mother phoned to see if there was any news. Her father came on the line, telling her that she should be at the maternity hospital.

Go, right now, he said, this minute.

The plates were left on the table. I got her into the car, the girls jumped in, Essie had the window rolled down, shouting – the waters have broken. I drove like a car chase. I got into a race with a taxi. She was counting contractions. I was forced to stop for petrol, the fuel gauge, I couldn't trust it. I put in enough petrol to keep us going. I had to jump the queue to pay. I came running out and she asked me what took so long, her fingernails were scratching at the ceiling.

As we pulled out, we were delayed by something else. The wheel of a truck ran over a can of engine oil, it burst open and sprayed over the windscreen. I switched the wipers on thinking it was water but that only spread the oil right across the glass. I couldn't see. I got out and wiped the windscreen with my sleeve. I still couldn't see. It was like frosted glass. The car was a bathroom. I had to get something to clean the windscreen before I could drive on again.

It's here, she shouted, it's coming.

She was pushing the dashboard with her hands.

The oil, I said, I can't see with the oil.

I ran around looking for paper. I found a bucket of water, a sponge, I washed the windscreen but that made everything worse, it turned to paste, grease, tiny beads of oil on everything, oil on my hands, oil on my jacket, oil spreading to every car in Dublin, the city was covered in oil.

She howled the unending words – come on.

I drove through oil. Guessing what was in front of me. We didn't get anywhere near the maternity hospital. We were passing by the general hospital, it was an emergency – stop, she said, we're not going to make it.

I parked next to the ambulance and ran inside.

A baby is being born, Rosie shouted.

Helen smiled, or fought off the pain. She was taken inside on a trolley. It took no more than ten minutes, spontaneous birth, in accident and emergency, people with all kinds of injuries and acute lung disorders in the same room cheering. The nurses said it was the first in twenty years. I couldn't see a thing. I heard them say it was a boy. I was blinded with the oil in my eyes, they gave me a towel.

It was more of a homecoming than a christening. Helen's mother was over from Canada, her uncles were back from London, Birmingham, France. Gathered in the pub with the bronze goddess holding the lamps up outside the door. They had taken over the end section of the pub, handbags and coats on seats all around, the baby was asleep in a carrier basket, people leaning over making baby faces, voices like tiny hands.

Helen's mother sat in the elbow of the red velvet corner seat, straight in from the airport, her suitcase was by the door, her arms clamped around Rosie and Essie on either side, claiming them back. She wore gold-rimmed glasses, lightly tinted. Her elegant Canadian clothes gave a feeling of prosperity, made me want to pay for everything.

Helen introduced me as a person you waited all your life to meet. Her mother stood up and shook my hand. The smile, the magnetic eyes. She said I must be such a proud father, two lovely girls and a boy, her voice exposed my emotions to the entire pub, I felt so welcome.

Thank you, I said.

She looked at my shoes. My hair. My beige jacket with the copper sheen. I made a poor impression. I could understand her point of view, you come back to the country of your birth and find so many things disappointing. She was used to hearing only the best about me from Helen, condensed into a promising outlook over the phone. I had become vastly overrated. The photographs were misleading. I attempted to say something funny, but it was too late, that first impression cannot be revised, you can spend a lifetime trying.

Her mother sat down again, she was in conversation with her sister, the aunt in the bible group. I could see the resemblance only the bible aunt sat hunched a little and spoke as though she was afraid of infection. They talked about the time they were both working as nurses in Dublin, the strict rules of behaviour and hygiene.

I found a velvet stool and picked a place for myself on the fringe, listening to them all talking at once.

I could see where Helen got her laugh. Her mother had the identical shoulder movements. Matching hoops. At one point, I had to check to make sure which of them it was, both laughing together in the same voice.

We ordered sandwiches.

Everyone had the fresh salmon sandwich on brown bread. It was unique to that bar, a piece of tradition. The barman took the order, then he picked up a beige phone on the wall behind the counter and called the order upstairs to unseen people in a kitchen where they prepared the food. The sandwiches seemed to be constructed in a distant place, by people with no faces. The barman wore a white shirt and a black bow tie. Speaking on the phone made him look like the commander of a submarine, passing on the order to his crew above with an assertive voice. He was doing what he might have done as a boy, imagining he was part of a fleet of submarines moving across the floor of the North Sea. A while later, the food elevator descended with the order, the bell rang as though the bar had reached the required depth. He opened the hatch and took out the food.

Each fresh salmon sandwich was a re-enactment of the last fresh salmon sandwich, the same two slices of brown bread, the same amount of salmon, the same leaf of lettuce. There was a jar of Hellmann's mayonnaise replicated on each table. You opened the sandwich and spread the required amount of mayonnaise onto the bread with a knife, you put the leaf of lettuce back into position, then you closed it over and allowed the mayonnaise to bind the sandwich together by pressing down lightly on the bread with a flat hand. You held it pinned down while you cut it in half, making sure the leaf of lettuce was divided into two equal sections along with each part of the sandwich, a small bit of green like an undergarment on view at either end. People sometimes left the knife in the jar of mayonnaise, with the handle sticking up.

The day was full of stories.

They took up exactly where they had left off the last time they met. Even the ranking of brothers and sisters remained intact, looking up to each other, looking down on each other, interrupting each other, getting the better of each other.

I sometimes got a bit lost in the multiple strands of their stories. I admired how easily they could talk without any great agonising over the words. It didn't seem to matter where a story began. They jumped in effortlessly. The order in which the details emerged was jumbled, funny things coexisting happily alongside serious news, no great message attached. Facts were often ridiculed and defended at the same time. The plot could be diverted many times, looping away into different zones, urgent things were pushed forward for priority.

Helen's mother jumped in and told everyone about their father in the town of Borris not being able to reverse the car, he could only drive forward. This had nothing to do with the story being told about a man in one of the apartments in London who had a collection of art from all over the world, he kept a death mask from Madagascar in his living room.

The main story was never the main story. It was the revisions that counted. The contradictions. Things unfinished, to be picked up later.

I ordered more drinks.

Helen took the knife out of the mayonnaise jar and put it on my plate.

They gave ridiculous tips to the barman. They struck up conversations with people at the bar. The entire pub became part of the family, even the lawyers in suits with their fresh salmon sandwiches at the small round tables were included in the celebration. A poet sitting by the door with a book on Argentina. The doorman from the Gaiety Theatre with his newspaper laid on the bar counter, wearing a pair of glasses that were crooked on his nose, one arm over the ear missing. A tall man standing at the bar with sunken pockets in his jacket.

At that moment, I realised that all my worries disappeared. The shakiness of our future became trivial. None of that mattered. This reunion had the effect of writing off my debts. My obligations were annulled by a warm feeling that allowed me to laugh off what I owed the world. This was my turn to celebrate. Helen was breastfeeding. Her mother was teaching Rosie and Essie how to fold paper serviettes.

One of the uncles asked me a question. It was the uncle back from France, Uncle Martin. He had heard I was writing a book and wanted to know what it was about.

Everyone stopped to listen.

I was put on the spot.

Helen's mother was eagerly waiting. Her head was tilted at the same angle as Helen's. The bible aunt was tilted in the other direction. Everyone in the entire bar held their breath, even the barman seemed to have stopped, his elbow placed on the marble counter, no bell ringing.

Helen smiled encouragement.

Out of hand, I had nothing to tell them. Everything I wanted to say had to be written down first and examined forensically, all the permutations, all the misunderstandings had to be eliminated before it could be given out. My mind was so displaced, I could only reach for the first word that came up.

Prague.

Their eyes were on my mouth.

Prague?

Prague, I said again, but I had no words to continue.

My thoughts were suddenly caught up in the assassination of Reinhard Heydrich, the Nazi Gauleiter of Prague. I had no wish to talk about him. I had no intention of writing about him. He was preventing me from speaking, placing himself into the forefront, standing in his black uniform blocking my way. Nothing else came to mind but the morning of his assassination, his open-topped car driving through the streets of Prague. His killing was followed by a brutal reprisal in which the inhabitants in the town of Lidice were put to death. I felt the day of the assassination coming back again and again, followed by the day of the reprisal massacre. They would kill him many times over in books and movies.

The town where all the people were murdered was erased from the map.

Let him eat, Helen said.

I was off the hook. They finally resumed talking. I picked up my sandwich. I brought it to my mouth, but I had no bite. They quickly moved on to other stories. Uncle Damian began describing their father standing in the living room one day with the Garda sergeant, one of the boys had broken into the Vicar's house and turned on all the taps, flooding the place. Their father looked down at his own son aged six and asked – do you smoke? I was laughing, I wanted their story to be mine.

By the time they got back to the house it was dark. I was home ahead of them, preparing dinner, high with excitement. Helen was driving, her mother had the baby in the back seat, her uncle from London in the passenger seat, the rest came by taxi. I ran out to carry the baby in asleep in the carrier basket. I ran out again to take in the suitcases, brought them upstairs into the box room, then I looked out the window.

The car doors were open. The headlights were left on, they had music playing, it was the Vienna Waltz.

I watched them standing around by the car, laughing, her uncle holding onto the bonnet to steady himself, the others walking down the drive arm in arm. The music lifted the whole street. It was in the hedges, in the pink tamarisk, in the rosemary bush, the garden was Brazil at night. Helen dropped her bag. She bent down to start picking things up but was pulled away by the elbow. I saw her dancing with her uncle from France, her mother was dancing with the uncle from Birmingham, the headlights of the car shining across the concrete dance floor, their shadows enlarged along the walls up to roof level, the children had a partner each.

Greta brought my mother up to the party, but they didn't stay. She had a short conversation with Uncle Jerome. He offered her a small glass of whiskey, but she was not very well. She stayed only long enough for me to get a photograph of her with Helen's mother. Two mothers together on the couch with the new baby boy, his eyes were open, my mother's word for sweet was the same as the word Helen's mother had, no difference between the languages, they loved babies equally.

There was an altercation at the hall door at one point when the aunt with the keys arrived. Helen's mother was about to embrace her sister, but she was given a slap across the face instead. Her gold-rimmed glasses flew across the hallway. She stood holding her cheek – what was that for? The aunt with the keys said – for buggering off to Canada and leaving us all here to rot. Minutes later they were clutching each other in tears, on the sofa together, sisters reunited, inseparable, laughing, I handed Helen's mother back her glasses.

The dinner table was crowded. Rosie and Essie sat on the piano stool together. We found enough chairs, including two foldable white garden chairs, for them all to sit on. We began with celery soup, Uncle Damian said it was the most extraordinary soup he had ever tasted in his life, no soup like it had ever been served to man or woman before. Followed by roast chicken and stuffing, roast potatoes and cauliflower with a cheese sauce. Again, they praised the food – no restaurant in the whole of London, or Paris, anywhere in the western world, could match our menu.

Uncle Jerome said – this is the meal I want on the day of my execution.

I had made a side dish from an Indian recipe, a tomato-based sauce with chick peas and hard-boiled eggs, it was my mother's favourite, but she was not able to stay for the dinner. Everyone tasted a bit of the Indian dish, but it seemed out of place, a little incongruous along with the roast chicken and roast potatoes, it was full of turmeric, it made their lips green, their napkins had yellow smiles. Afterwards, we had apple crumble, they asked me how on earth I could make something so delicious, it had to be more than apples I put in, some secret ingredient, cloves, raw cane sugar, a touch of lime?

Uncle Damian started the singing early.

Holding Helen's mother by the hands, he stared into her eyes and sang a Nat King Cole song.

Unremarkable, that's what you are.

It amazed me how they could happily keep insulting each other around the table without anyone getting offended. They found the worst things to say, as though the most extreme abuse was really a way of showing the most extreme affection. Helen's mother was laughing her heart out while Uncle Damian continued singing to her with a serious gaze – that's why darling, it's incredible, that you could be so unremarkable, so unexceptional, so average …

… and so unforgettably mediocre, too.

Only then did Helen's mother finally pull her hands away and slap her younger brother across the head.

All through the meal, I kept refilling glasses. Clearing away dishes, going around to see if there was anything needed, some salt to pour over a wine stain. I brought out the bottle of whiskey, new glasses, a small jug of water. For a while they discussed political developments in Northern Ireland, then things began to degenerate a little. Uncle Jerome was asked what life would have been like if he was born without a nose, he ignored them. The bible aunt was asked what life would be like without an arse, she ignored them. One of them broke in and said – I thank the Lord every morning that I have an arse.

Helen's mother brought them all to order again. She made them focus and give her an answer – now listen to me for a minute, who wants an Irish coffee? They went back to talking and cutting across each other, voices all speaking at once, silent moments in one corner, singing a couple of lines at the other end, a burst of laughter, Helen's mother was asked if she cared for a lozenge – no, thank you.

I stood with a plate in each hand listening. The aunt with keys took the plates from me and put them back down on the table. What was this obsession with clearing up and moving on? She pulled me away and forced me to sit on the sofa with her, something she was going to tell me. She would not let go of my arm. She whispered, pulling me into a conspiracy. Helen went upstairs with the baby. Her mother went to bed. Her uncles were staying in my mother's house, it was not far to go. When everybody was gone, I sat looking around the room, the empty bottles, the glasses, the ashtrays, everything still in place. The smell of roast chicken all around the house. I memorised the order in which they sat at the table, the sequence of stories and songs and interjecting remarks, I left it until morning to clear up, recounting the entire night to myself in reverse, each plate, each napkin, each fork.

The walls were covered with photographs of houses. The desks were at various angles, a large poster of the company name with a childlike drawing of a house and a family moving in. There was a poster for mortgage companies. A large portrait of the estate agents together in a group, smiling. I spoke to the man who had sold us the house. He had a bowl with hard-boiled sweets on his desk. I told him I didn't want the sign going up outside. It was important to me that Helen's mother did not hear of our decision to sell. It was also important because the bank manager who had given us the business loan lived nearby, a little further along the same street, in a newly built row of detached houses. I didn't want him seeing the sign up – for sale – it might activate urgent proceedings. Our solicitor was delicately negotiating a settlement schedule.

That same evening, a couple came to the door. First, I was afraid they might be looking for money, I told them I had visitors. I stepped out into the porch and closed the door on the latch behind me, so they could not be heard inside. They apologised for disturbing us so late, but they had heard we might be selling the house, they wanted to get in ahead of anyone else.

Helen's mother was in the front room with her two sisters. The fire was on. They had gin and tonics. The uncles had already gone back, so it was a quiet evening of recovery. Helen looked like a schoolgirl again, wearing her black velvet jeans, a loose blue shirt open at the neck, easy for her to manage breastfeeding. Martina was there. She had come with a gift, a silver spoon and pusher. Rosie and Essie were standing over the carrier basket, José was on the floor with his soldiers.

Martina was singing a lullaby for the baby when the doorbell rang. The couple at the door heard the song and smiled. It was in the ghost language, the voice carried a remote part of the Dingle Peninsula up to the city, something about our house felt in that moment to belong to a childhood country brought back from past. It filled the hallway and spilled out onto the porch with a memory of homes and families going back in time, a kind of ancient rocking in the words that created a calmness in me, in the couple at the door, it made the transactional purpose of their visit disappear. We remained suspended in this childhood on the doorstep until the song was finished and we heard clapping from the front room.

They said there was no need for them to view the property. They offered me the full asking price. On the bonnet of the car, they made out a cheque for the deposit, subject to a surveyor's report. They handed over the cheque as though they were paying for listening to the song, they wanted to live in the house where the words would remain in the walls, in the space underneath the floors. I was disappointed because I wanted to invite them in to look around the house. Talk them through some of the things that had been done, the wiring, the plumbing, the wall knocked down between two rooms, the steel reinforcement, the underfloor speaker wires running into the kitchen, so much I had to tell them, but I couldn't bring them inside.

I folded the cheque and put it away in the Mennonite cookbook. I put the book back on the shelf in the kitchen and started clearing the counter. I began drying glasses, lightly rotating the clean towel inside, holding them up to the light to review the shine, then stacking them upside down into the shelves. I returned some items taken out earlier for dinner into the cupboard. I found half a packet of oatmeal in the press which I poured into the porridge tin, exactly enough to fill it up, that allowed me to throw out the paper bag. I stood for a while in the hallway looking up the stairs. I heard their voices in the front room, a burst of laughter, Helen was talking, but I didn't catch what she was saying. I had my hand on the newel. I saw the street light coming through the window on the landing, the shapes of trees thrown across the walls, like arms waving. I was thinking of a couple of things that still needed to be finished off, like the gutters at the back of the house, they were cast-iron, they were in danger of falling off some night in a storm, the clamps holding them were rusted to nothing, I was hoping to replace them with new PVC gutters.

Everyone was still seated in the same positions in the front room. Rosie and Essie had an aunt each for themselves, tiny faces peeking out under large wings. José was in middle of the room, he had a bunch of keys to play with. Helen looked up when I came back in, I could see how happy she was that her mother was able to stay a bit longer. I glanced around to make sure everyone had a drink. I put another briquette on the fire. The sudden sale, the snap disposal of the home from underneath us was a piece of information I carried inside myself along with so many other things that were impossible to say.

Helen's mother was talking about Canada. How heavy the rain can be in the summer, how unexpected, how much you begin to trust the weather. She said she was caught in a shower one day, not prepared for it, not like you would be in Ireland, she didn't bring an umbrella, it was not something she ever carried with her. She had just come from the hairdresser's on the square. Her car was miles away outside the Nova Scotia bank. After a hot and humid morning, the rain came from nowhere, she said. She was getting soaked, right through her clothes, her blouse was sticking to her shoulders, she had the handbag held over her head. She found cover in a doorway.

Directly in front of her, the headlights of a car began flashing through the rain, the car horn was blaring. She told herself not to respond, she was taking whatever shelter she could get with her back pinned flat up against a door. She could hardly see two feet clear in the rain, her glasses were blurred, the water was running into her eyes.

She said she heard a familiar voice.

Mary, look at you.

It was Nessa, her former friend.

Helen's mother turned away. Pretended not to hear. With expert defiance, she placed her chin on her shoulder and let on she was waiting for somebody to pick her up – when I think of who I am. She ignored the flashing headlights and the blaring car horn, it was a show of inspired mockery. The woman who had once been her closest companion in the world was now taking enormous delight at her misfortune, caught in a Canadian drowning, her hair only just done up, flattened like a field of blonde barley.

Nessa stepped out of the car. She was now getting soaked as well, blinded with the rain in her face, standing by the open car door and the seat getting wet, screaming at this point – Mary will you get in, for God's sake.

That was it. Helen's mother walked over and got into the car with Nessa. They sat for a moment without speaking a word, staring at the rain, you could not hear a thing it was so loud on the roof. The windows were steamed up like a bathroom. Two Irish women drenched to the skin, to the skull. The water was dripping from their ears, water going down their necks, water in their shoes. They shook them-selves. They sneezed. They elbowed each other. Best of friends again.

*

The letter arrived from the Canadian embassy turning down our application. The decision had been struck on medical grounds. It was my illness that let us down. They had contacted our GP to let him know my chest X-ray showed up something. The interview at the embassy had gone very well, I thought, we had spoken to a tall man at the immigration department. He had been very positive. Helen had told him about her family living in Canada. He went through the details, occupation, she put down journalist, I put down musicologist, three children, no financial resources, none of that was any problem, he let us know that Canada was open to ready-made families.

The rejection was put down to a serious pulmonary condition. My lungs full of sand. My teeth made of glass. The shadow on my voice. I was admitted to hospital that same day. The same hospital where the baby was born, we called him Donal, after Helen's father.

They did a range of tests. I sat up in a hospital bed on the first floor, by the window. A team of doctors swept in. They talked about me in the third person, a character in their novel, I had to surrender.

They put a name on my condition – sarcoidosis. It sounded like they were making it up out of their heads.

It explained everything, the silence, the shrugging, fear, fatigue, the inability to feel at home, restless nights walking around the city, retreating from society, the wish to know nothing, to remember nothing, outbursts of male aggression followed by intense spells of remorse and remaining indoors. They told me there was no known cause and no cure. For a while it was believed to be triggered by the sap of pine trees, possibly the scent of pine in detergents, floor polish, air fresheners hanging from the rear-view mirror in cars, those sachets that turn the flushing water in the loo green. That was soon ruled out as well. It remained clinically unresolved. It might be described as a fungus, but they could not identify any spores. It affected mostly the lungs and the joints, the nerve endings, patients often presented with swollen knees or swollen elbows, calcium deposits under the fingernails, the retina. The range of symptoms could be varied and elusive, some people burned it off without diagnosis, it remained latent. A progressive disease that led to death in the past, now it could be controlled by cortisone.

Nothing more was known about the condition, they told me. Did it have to do with motion, migration, people not living where they came from? Some research studies carried out among population groups around the world would indicate that it predominantly affected Irish people and African Americans and Jewish people.

Helen came in with Rosie and Essie and the baby. One of the other patients dragged over a chair for her. She took out a pineapple and some tangerines. The nurses from accident and emergency came up to have a look at the baby, a boy in a hurry, they called him. The girls wanted to draw the privacy curtain but there was no need.

It might have been the steroids, they had me on a high dose, the consultant said – we're going to hit this hard. I was bursting with happiness. I was full of gratitude. They would not allow me to go and live in Canada, but I wanted to thank the immigration authorities at the embassy for sorting out my mouth. They had solved the mystery of my silence. They had rescued me, they had freed me from my speckled condition. Now I could deal with anything. Helen said I had a big round face. Rosie and Essie were arranging the bedside locker as though I was settling down for good, they had brought me a pair of tartan slippers, I laughed – slippers?

When they were gone I stared at the small hill my feet made under the blue blanket. I could not help remembering a bar myself and Helen used to go to in Berlin. We loved the place, even though Helen found it too smoky. It was in a triangular building, on a corner site. We went to hear a harmonica player from Cuba, he had incredible lungs, he could hold a note for ages, like one of those pearl divers able to stay underwater for five minutes, longer, it took nothing out of him. When he finished a solo, he held the harmonica at the side of his mouth like a cigar while he clapped a backbeat and sang his heart out.

My lung-envy.

I didn't even hear the tea trolley coming.

Tea, love? Biscuit, love?

They left a mug of tea and two biscuits on the mobile tray and pushed it towards me – there you are love. I listened to the trolley moving on, the progress of cups ringing along the corridor going further and further away had a joy attached to it. This was a good time for me. I was going to get better. I was going to be able to speak. I was getting to know a lot of patients. Six of us in the ward, all in for pulmonary investigations, this small nation of lung casualties living under one roof.

Each one of them was me.

The man by the door on my side was silent, he lay on his bed in a dressing gown. His wife came and sat with him for an hour, they didn't speak much, then he went back to waiting for her again. He must have spent a lifetime on cortisone, the flesh under his chin was hanging, his eyes were bulging, his skin was thin as tissue paper, even a light knock against the end of the bed would give him a purple bruise. The man in the centre bed on the far side was attached to a plastic bag hanging from a steel rod on wheels – my mobile crozier, he called it. At one point, he got up and said he was going out for a smoke. In the other end bed, the man had a late visitor, maybe his brother, they were talking about fixing something together, a bathroom, moving the sink to the far side where it wouldn't be getting in the way. The man by the window opposite me had grown up by the sea. He got quite emotional and said he wanted all his life to go back to where he was brought up, he missed the blue space in front of him. Before going to sleep, he was given a glass of warm milk. He drank the milk and ate two marshmallows, sitting on the side of the bed with his legs swinging. He had done this ever since he was a boy. Then he woke up an hour later coughing with homesickness. It was impossible to sleep. The cortisone. The snoring. The light in the corridor. The man next to me was gone mad with steroids, he got up and started dragging the blue blanket off my bed, then he gathered up the blankets from the other patients already asleep and piled them on the floor, the nurses had to come and put him back into his bed, they strapped him in.

Six men, six human clocks, each breath, each cough a measurement of time.

During the night, we were all coughing at once. It might have been a toothbrush falling on the floor that set us off. We were like dogs in a small mountain village outdoing each other. Coughing and barking to show who was the best. Everyone saying – I'm a better cougher than the lot of you. One person went quiet to allow the next person a solo fit, somebody else broke in with a raucous cough from the other end, then we all came back in a combined chorus, coughing everything our lungs had to offer before the ward finally went silent again.

A pair of lungs with rooms, a hall, a staircase, a window looking out onto a flat roof. An X-ray would show the layout underneath the floorboards, the wiring, the heating pipes, layers of memory and scars from childhood. I walk in and out of these lungs, the front door is wide open, the wind blows in, the draught makes a hum, one of the inner doors slams shut. I carry boxes out, most of the stuff goes into a big yellow skip outside.

Now and then I come across things that cannot be thrown out. A box of drawings. A shoe carton full of photographs. Lumberjack coats they no longer wear but I have become attached to. All of Helen's stuff. The butterflies. The garden shears turned into antlers. Wooden bits I have carved, the ear, the mouth, the singers and the listeners, we call them. Other body parts that are not eligible for display, a nose I have started in limewood with the nostrils not hollowed out yet, a set of blind eyes open.

And the sick bowl, how can I throw out the sick bowl?

And my journal. All those notes and bits of paper with descriptions of people I had encountered. Some lengthy passages about being alone. Alongside the continuous family log, things the children said, things Helen told me, happy, uneventful stuff I could not leave behind.

Most of the things are stored in boxes and brought to the new place we're renting temporarily. A small town house, Helen likes it because it's warm and well insulated, the children like it because they can play on the street, there is a fountain and lots of trees, fallen branches they can collect. I like it because nobody can find me.

While I am clearing the house, people stop to ask where we are going. I tell them nothing, only that I'm getting rid of a couple of things, unbelievable the amount of junk you collect. One of the neighbours tells me how his dog got run over at the corner outside our house, the children on the street ran up to him saying – mister, your dog is dead, the postman still believes the dog is alive and continues to be afraid of the dog as he delivers the mail every morning. And the local grocery shop, when I go to pay off a couple of things, I tell the shopkeeper we're moving, he gives me a bar of chocolate each for the girls.

I work late.

There is an echo in the rooms, a hollow sound that seems false, there is no such thing as an empty house. I can hear myself breathing. Whistling. I go around dismantling the remaining bits of memory and find a children's book hidden behind the bath, curled up with the steam. A book in which the boy character goes on a trip at night to the country of monsters. Their faces are full of comic exaggeration, their teeth are jagged. I had started comparing the creatures in the book to Rosie and Essie, holding the wild faces up to theirs, matching monster teeth with the gaps in their smiles. At some point, they refused to open their mouths for me, they must have hidden the book.

Many of the other non-functional projects have got to be abandoned at that point. In the front garden lie some components gathered to assemble the short stretch of railway line. So far, I have only the sleepers and some of the metal fixings, along with a mound of hardcore stones ready to be laid out for the base. I have been given prices for the sections of disused rail and the buffer stop. For months, I have been on the phone to my contact at the rail company, we leave messages for each other, we talk about logistics, the transport costs. I have a reasonable estimate for the manpower needed to extract the parts from the rail yard and have them delivered to the house. The only thing left is to source one of the signal pylons, the old version I want with the flap falling to a forty-five degree angle is still widely in use, they are slowly being replaced, so it's a matter of waiting until one of them becomes available.

I spend a long time in the bedroom looking at the sea. The beam of light reaches into the bare room. The lighthouse will not allow me to move. I force myself to leave, like I need to be taken by the arm, somebody to pull me away and escort me down the stairs, out of the house.

We were all there. My three sisters, Gabriela, Greta and Lotte, gathered in the room. My brother Gerd got back from Germany, my mother held his hand for a long time. My little brother Emil was on a cycling tour in northern Spain, he was on his way, Greta asked my mother to hold on. The doctor on the corner came in to speak to Greta about the medication, he left the dosing up to her to manage. The house was full of laughing, we talked about the things that made my mother laugh, the language contradictions that she loved. We laughed about nothing. Helen was there. Rosie and Essie came. Baby Donal was in the room with my mother for a moment, then they were all looked after downstairs in the kitchen by a cousin. It was not long, just after Emil arrived, we were together around the bed and I heard my mother speaking in a low voice with her eyes open – I'm ready. I heard Greta say the words – we're all here now.

The house was full of crying and praying. Helen put her arms around me. She then went around the room to embrace each of the others.

My sisters stayed with my mother and got her ready, Gabriela placed rose petals around her, Lotte found there was still warmth under her arms, Greta closed her eyes and placed a rolled-up cloth under her chin. The doctor came back. Our uncle the Jesuit arrived. Gerd spoke to the undertaker, a group of five men came in carrying the coffin, the lid separately. To get around the return on the stairs, they had to reverse into the room on the first-floor landing before continuing up to the next landing, this had been done many times before with furniture, beds, tables, a bookcase, the wardrobes. The door of my room flew open, the coffin was pointed inside, enough to clear the landing, then it was brought forward again up the stairs into the room at the front of the house where my mother lay. We heard them moving around, their feet heavy, their deep voices. They were there for a good while. We were standing in the hall when they came back down, the lid was on the coffin.

This time, when they reached the first-floor landing, the coffin was brought all the way inside the room where they could turn the direction and continue leading with her feet first. One of the men went backwards down the stairs with his hand on the front of the coffin to guide it. The coffin descended at an angle, I could hear the men breathing, then it levelled out as they reached the hall. They rested the coffin on a pair of trestles in the hallway and my uncle the Jesuit said some prayers, we kneeled, the men stood with their hands clasped. The coffin was carried out the front door, down the two granite steps, out along the path, through the gate being held open for her by my brother Gerd. On the street they straightened out to face the back of the hearse with the door open and slid the coffin along the steel floor.

There was a small gathering of neighbours on the pavement, they were blessing themselves. When the hearse drove off, the house was silent, I thought they had taken my mother back to Germany, it was the only place I could think of her going, back to where she was from.

What came to mind at that moment was the German word – Flecken. The word my mother used to describe a stain, a smudge, a blot, a soiled spot on a shirt or a coat. But it was also the word used to describe a place, a piece of earth, a smudge on the map, a little fleck of ground you have taken to heart and want to go back to.

In English, you might call it a grand spot. Our street with the big corner house. It had one of those palm trees in the front garden. The sun shone so bright, we never noticed the tree itself, only the shadow of straight black leaves dancing on the white gable wall.

It was August. The house was full of flowers. We had no idea how to grieve. We didn't know what to say when people came around to let us know they were sorry. At the funeral, I met people I had not seen since I was a child. Their handshakes made me feel I had been away for a long time, somebody asked me was I living in Berlin now. I was overwhelmed when they remembered my name. People who knew my mother well, they felt close to her, they loved her accent, her way of dressing in European clothes, talking about Ireland with such affection, like a newcomer who had just arrived.

My little brother Emil was there shaking hands with all the mourners. I could not help thinking about the time he was electrocuted. Up in my mother and father's bedroom. He must have been only five then, inquisitive, going through the wardrobes looking for clues. My mother told him to keep singing, so she could tell where he was. He stood by the table with the bedside lamp, the song about two frogs jumping into the water together. Under the fringe of tassels, his hand went up along the smooth marble stem to find the switch. The light failed to come on. His fingers reached into the opening at the top where the bulb was meant to be. The current rushing through him was like a slap across the chest. It threw him across the room. My mother knew there was something wrong because he had stopped singing. He woke up in her arms as she ran down the stairs, shaking the dead boy out of him, kissing his forehead. His hand was burning red. At the hospital, they grafted on a piece of skin taken from his leg. The patch is still visible, a different shade, the shape of a country stuck on, it looks like Australia.

Helen's uncle came back over from London. Uncle Jerome. He went around to shake everyone's hand like a member of the family. He spoke to the other mourners. They remembered my mother on the street with my father, he was determined to keep moving, stepping from one foot to the other, while she stopped to smile and exchange a few words.

At the cemetery, I could not remember the coffin going into the ground, I was distracted by thoughts of her life, how easily she laughed at what was hard. After the burial, we came back to the house. It was just the family that evening, in the dining room around the table. My brothers and sisters, Helen, the children. And Uncle Jerome.

He made sure my mother got an Irish funeral.

He told every story he knew. Lots of jokes I never heard before. He had facts about history we never thought possible. The coal mines in Germany being discovered by an Irishman, the submarine invented by a man from Tralee in his back garden, the German philosopher who came to Ireland and was driven mad by barking dogs. Lots of facts about movies and famous actors getting married and divorced and married again. He told us about the greatest known geographical contradiction, a place in Wexford where you pedal your lungs out going down the hill, the gravity keeps pulling you back up again. He said the poem about a man travelling all the way around the world in search of the most beautiful spot only to be told it was in a place he never thought of looking, back home in Tipperary. He sang the September song. He stood up for it. When he was halfway through he began to collapse. He tried holding on to a chair, but it gave way and fell over with a slap on the floor, his fingers grabbed the table, some cutlery flew around him. We got up to help him, but he continued sinking, he came to rest under the table, singing the final words on his back.

It was the biggest wedding in history. The wedding of the world. Guests from all countries, people celebrating in every corner of the earth. Thousands gathered on both sides, crowds standing on top of the wall, cheering, helping each other up. Some of them chipping away at the cement, carving holes into the wall so they could look through. People waving, kissing, crying. November. The Berlin Wall is open. Nobody can really believe it. The news is everywhere. Repeated images of people rushing through the barriers, the smiles, the shock of disbelief in their eyes. The same images shown over and over to make sure they can be true. People storming the offices of the Stasi state security, demanding to see their files, the prison where dissidents were held is abandoned, a newspaper left behind on the desk like a moment in history standing still while the world lurches forward into a new time. A man walks into a library to bring back a book he borrowed before the wall went up.

I was free to go on a journey to find the places where my mother had been during the war. Salzburg, the train station where she had been arrested. Prague, the castle overlooking the city where she was held captive in the basement. On the streets of Prague, the silent revolution had just begun to break out, people were gathering on the main square, a quiet confidence was growing. It felt to me that the world had been placed in the freezer all these years, since the end of the war, now it had been brought out to warm up in the sun.

I found the place where my mother spent the last days of the war, the garrison she was transferred to on the edge of a small town in Bohemia. Nothing had changed much in the intervening years, only that the garrison was now occupied by the Russian military, a large red star over the gates. I took some photographs from the outside, remembering how my mother described the last days of the war, trapped

273

in the garrison, with the Russians advancing by the minute. The commanding officer has got to wait for the phone call from Berlin to say the war is over. They finally get on the trucks, they bring the Czech prisoners with them. The Czech resistance fighters have agreed to escort the Germans back to the border at Eger, where the handover will take place.

I took photographs of the roads.

The trucks merge into the stream of people on the move. They pass by an ambulance overturned, some bodies lying around. The trucks lurch forward. The roads are slow. Behind them, the Russian armoured cars are catching up, no more than a few hundred metres away. The Russians doing their best to reach the fleeing German trucks, crossing through the fields to cut them off. The ground is holding everyone in place, everything is delayed by the suction of the earth. The fields are full of mud. It has been raining heavily in the past month. Mud on wheels, mud on boots, mud splashed up in faces. Everyone travelling at the speed of mud. They seem to be stuck in this ratio, unable to move forward, the German trucks only slightly ahead, the Russian vehicles within sight, within shouting distance.

I took photographs of the place on the border where the Germans surrendered their weapons to the Czech soldiers in return for the freed hostages. The place where my mother saw a huge mound of helmets and discarded uniforms nobody wanted any more.

When I got to Berlin, it was hard to grasp all that change. The whole century seemed to have shrunk into a few short months – the war comes to an end, Berlin is divided into four zones, the Russians cut off their zone, they blockade the city, the Americans rescue the people of Berlin by flying in food relief, the Berlin Wall goes up, the world stands still, an artist sweeps the street, a revolutionary figure is shot down on the main shopping street riding his bike, the Lord Mayor of Berlin is kidnapped, David Bowie comes to live in the city and writes a song about a couple kissing by the wall, a film is made about a man flying over Berlin in the form of an angel, crowds gather to say they are the people, the Berlin Wall comes down, the earth begins to rotate again, everyone on the streets, the wedding of the world was in full swing.

The confetti, the bottles, people embracing, lovers on every street. Multiple spontaneous weddings breaking out all over the city. It was hard to get a place to stay. I found a room where people kept coming and going all night, celebrating without end, a couple mistook me for an empty bed. I found the café where Helen stole the spoon. I found the place on the grass where she sat eating a tub of quark. I went back to the place where we stood looking across the wall. Everything was already being dismantled like a stage set, ready for the next production. The city was being spray-painted, grand architecture covered in graffiti, history being brought up to date. I kept hearing the song about standing by the wall, the song about us being us. This was our wedding, our wall wedding.

★

It has become part of us now, that condition of arriving and not arriving. Going away. Returning home. Waving. Embracing. Looking back. Not looking back. That feeling of elsewhere inside us, the places we miss, the people we love, simultaneously close and far away on the other side of the world.

The Canadian immigration authorities granted our visa. The consultants at the hospital had given me the all clear, they wrote to the embassy on my behalf to assure them my condition was under control. All we needed to obtain our landed immigrant status was to set foot on Canadian soil. We had six months grace to complete the transfer. We didn't tell people we were going. We didn't want them to think we were running away. The plan was to slip out quietly, as though we were going on holidays, the way my mother came to Ireland on holidays and stayed for the rest of her life.

We had a small bit of money left from the sale of the house to get us started in Toronto. But then we decided to stay in Dublin. I was no good at leaving. I started writing a book. My silence began to dissolve. I found a language to be heard in.

The book is about a woman making her way home at the end of the war. The roads are filled with refugees. The sun has come out and things quickly begin to dry. The chestnut trees are in full bloom. It's spring. The war is over. Celebrations have broken out all over the world. Time has begun to move forward again. Cracked chunks of mud are falling from the wheel rims. Large sections of mud imprinted with the design of tyres, tracks left behind in endless directions. People brushing mud off their coats, rounded crusts of mud from shoes stamped on the ground. There is a cloud of dust over the crowded roads, a human stream, moving slowly, families, children walking, carts piled with possessions, vehicles being repaired and pushed to start again. Everybody is on the move. The woman has a long way to go, many things preventing her getting home. At one point, she stands on the roadside watching American army vehicles going by. The exhaust fumes make her cough and turn away. One of the trucks comes to a stop. The soldiers ask her where she is going. They help her into the back of the truck. They give her chocolate. She smiles and agrees to sing a song for them.

We can face what we lost. What we left behind. We can start again, make up a new story for ourselves. We can invent new ways of telling who we are and where we come from. We can speak our way home.

The author would like to thank the following people for their generous support and encouragement. Nicholas Pearson, Peter Straus, Petra Eggers, Cathy King, Christine Popp, Grusche Juncker, Karsten Roesel, Jordan Mulligan, Iain Hunt, Michelle Kane, Mary Byrne, Hans Christian Oeser, Joe Joyce, Kate MacDonagh, Terence Herron. Special thanks also to *An Chomhairle Ealaíon* and *Aosdána* for their ongoing support.